I0677417

STATION FOSAAN

DEE GARRETSON

Month9Books

This book is a work of fiction. Names, characters, places, and incidents are either products of the author's imagination or are used fictitiously. Any resemblance to actual persons, living or dead, business establishments, events, or locales is entirely coincidental. The author makes no claims to, but instead acknowledges the trademarked status and trademark owners of the word marks mentioned in this work of fiction.

Copyright © 2017 by Dee Garretson

STATION FOSAAN by Dee Garretson
All rights reserved. Published in the United States of America by Month9Books, LLC.
No part of this book may be used or reproduced in any manner whatsoever without written permission of the publisher, except in the case of brief quotations embodied in critical articles and reviews.

EPub ISBN: 978-1-945107-43-6 Mobi ISBN: 978-1-945107-45-0
Paperback ISBN: 978-1-944816-51-3

Published by Month9Books, Raleigh, NC 27609
Cover design by Monika MacFarlane

Month9Books

For Hope and Garret

STATION FOSAAN

Chapter 1

When a civilization comes close to extinction, what emerges out of the ashes? On Fosaan, music did not, and art has turned to survival craft. Perhaps if I record what I know, some in the future will understand us better. The coming of the Earthers may be the end of us, and I do not want our memories to fade to ash. I may be giving myself too lofty a title, but for now I shall sign my musings,—
Erimik, historian of the Family

A flash in Fosaan's sky distracted me from my work for a moment. If I hadn't known better, I'd have thought a large ship just entered the atmosphere, but none were scheduled to land.

The flex wall rustled behind me. "Piper?" I said, not looking up from the display slip. One more minute and I would have the depiction of the snake-like creature completed, right down to the exact interlocking star pattern on the skin and the red speckling on the forelegs. Duplicating the vivid greenish yellow color would be trickier, but I had imaged it so there'd be a reference when I got down to mixing colors.

It was pure luck I had found a dead one on the walkway to study. I didn't know what happened to the other deceased animals on Fosaan, but if the shrieks and howls that came from shore were any hint, I could guess. I'd just have to make sure I got rid of the thing before Piper got home. My younger sister hated seeing anything dead.

"Piper?" I turned around, but no one was in the unit. The rustling sound had moved into the kitchen.

Magellan squawked and flapped her wings from the window ledge, "Intruder Alert! Intruder Alert!"

Since the parrot said the same thing at every sound she didn't recognize, I wasn't too worried. "Mags, relax. It's probably just an olon." I got up and grabbed the stick I always used to shoo away the tiny nuisances. If I let one in, a whole flock of them would follow, perching on every available surface, chittering and staring as if expecting me to put on a show for them. Me, Quinn Neen, whose talents, such as they were, did not include entertaining anyone or anything. It was even worse when they brought in their latest catches from the sea, treating the floating living units like their own picnic area, dropping bones all over the floor.

Now that Mags felt like she had done her guard job, she lost interest. Balancing on one leg, she examined a talon on the other. "Beautiful toe," she declared.

"Yes, you've told me before," I said, knowing I'd never be able to convince the parrot a talon was not the same thing as a toe. I wasn't sure she grasped the concept of "beautiful," but she applied it more frequently to herself than anyone else. Leaving the bird to her talon inspection, I pushed aside the divider to get into the kitchen.

No olons. No more rustling noise either, just the faint splash of the waves rocking the walkways that connected the individual living quarters. A gust of wind brought in the briny scent of the water, sharper smelling than the oceans of Earth. It overpowered the pine scent I had set on the room control, which I liked to use as a reminder of the pine forest reserve my grandmother managed on Earth. Another gust rattled the beads Piper had attached to her favorite house bot, but there were no other sounds. Maybe an olon had come and gone.

I turned to go back when a flash of white caught my eye. Startled, I dropped the stick and then tripped over it. A girl, a Fosaanian girl, stood clutching a wafer loaf to her chest, a cloud of long shimmery white hair quivering. In fact, all of her was shivering. She was soaked, water dripping off her. I could see her wet footprints all over the kitchen. Her silvery eyes held mine and I couldn't think of a thing to say. I wasn't usually so speechless around girls with incredible eyes, but I'd never encountered one I didn't know in my own quarters.

"What are you doing?" I finally managed to croak, even though it was obvious she was taking the loaf, or more accurately, stealing the loaf. Fosaanians never came out onto the Earthers' floating compound.

"I'm sorry," the girl said, putting the loaf back on counter and edging to the door.

"No, wait!" I didn't mean to shout, but my words came out too loud. The girl froze like I had issued an order, though I could tell she was ready to bolt. "It's okay," I said. "I mean, if you're hungry, take it." Picking the loaf up, I held it out to her, hoping it would convince her to stay for a little while. She would be the first Fosaanian I had talked to, if I could get her to talk. The small population of Fosaanians, the descendants of the few who had survived the planetary apocalypse, kept away from all of us Earthers, except for the ones who worked at the supply depot or who delivered the iridium sulfide. None of those could be called the least bit friendly.

She didn't take the loaf, but she didn't run either. Instead, she stood there looking around the room, clearly curious.

"I have an even better idea," I said, trying to come up with one. "How about I fix us both something to eat? I'm hungry too." The girl was too thin, but then all the Fosaanians I had seen were skinny. I assumed it was a Fosaanian physical trait that went along with their long fingers and thin necks, but now it occurred to me that if she was here to steal food maybe they weren't getting enough to eat.

"The food, it is not for me," the girl said. "My little sister, she had an accident and some of her teeth were damaged. It's easier for her to eat soft food … " Her voice trailed off, and she clutched her hands together.

"You can take it. We have plenty. I'll find some other stuff too." I grabbed a carryall and opened the storage cabinet, looking for soft food. "Why doesn't your sister just get replacement teeth?"

Her eyes widened. "You can replace teeth?"

"Sure, people do it all the time." I had two replacements already, from running into a low bulkhead when I was trying to get some exercise during the long dull journey to Fosaan from Earth.

"How much do teeth cost?"

"I don't know." I found some milk bars and added them to the carryall. "Not much, probably." I'd never even thought about it.

"If it costs as much as wafer bread, then it would be too much." She sounded angry.

"Maybe not. I have a friend up on the space station in charge of inventory," I told her. "I can ask him if they have some extra teeth. They probably do."

Her eyes narrowed and she took a step back. "What would I have to do for them?"

"Nothing," I said. I was struck by how suspicious she sounded. "My friend, Gregor, he isn't too strict about things. Giving you some teeth for your sister isn't going to break the budget of the station." I knew Gregor would actually be pleased to do something that was outside the rules. He took so much pleasure in breaking military protocol, I sometimes wondered why he had signed up for more service after the mandatory enlistment was up.

An olon flew in and perched on a stool, folding its wings into small pleats and settling down like it intended to stay. I recognized it from its abnormal markings. Most olons had a bright green streak under each eye, but this one was missing the streak on the left. It was also the one who seemed to have an uncanny knack for knowing when food was out. "You're not getting any of this," I said to it. "Don't be lazy. Go find your own food." It hooted at me.

At the noise, Mags hopped into the room and then flew up and landed on the counter, flapping her wings and screeching, "Intruder Alert! Intruder Alert! Dog! Dog!" She hated the olons and "dog" was her word for anything she hated.

The olon just gazed at the parrot, not moving. "Easy, Mags," I said, "It's 'olon'. 'Olon.'"

"Dog!" Mags flapped her wings threateningly. "Man the weapons!" My father had taught Mags the weapons line, and he and I thought it hilarious, though my mother wasn't crazy about the parrot threatening any guest the bird didn't like. When the olon didn't move, Mags added in some incoming missile sound effects to indicate she was extremely displeased.

"Calm down, Mags." The olon didn't appear perturbed at all by the parrot. It sidled to the edge of the stool, its attention totally focused on the wafer loaf.

"Your creature talks? You communicate with them?" the girl asked, her amazing eyes widening.

It took me a moment to answer; I was so caught up in looking at her. "Uh, no, I sort of communicate with Mags, but I just talk to the olons. They don't understand me. It's a habit when I'm by myself." Now she would think I was strange. I'd only started talking to myself once we'd arrived. There were fifteen other younger Earthers onplanet and an assortment of scientists who came and went to the orbiting space station for their shifts, but we often got tired of each other. I spent most of the time working on my own projects.

The girl eyed the olon. "I've never seen one without two markings on the face," she said. "I did see one once with double markings, but never just one."

"I'd like to see one like that." I was intrigued that she had noticed. Most people didn't pay much attention to them. When I had first observed the marking and pointed it out to my friend Lainie, she had pretended to be interested, but the way she smiled made it clear she was just humoring me.

The olon hooted once more and then flew back out the window, like it had given up on the possibility of a handout.

"All clear!" Mags announced, using another of the military phrases my father favored. She began to preen herself. "Beautiful feathers."

"Quinn!" Piper shouted from the walkway. The bells my little sister wore in her hair jangled crazily as she ran into the room. "Quinn, guess what? The shuttle landed but nobody was on it. Not mom, not anybody. Nobody knows why." Piper skidded to a stop, noticing the girl. "Why is a Fosaanian here?" she demanded, her eyes wide.

"Um ... She was out swimming," I said, not wanting to explain the conversation about the bread. There were never simple explanations for Piper. Everything always led to another why. "I invited her in," I added.

"Hello," Piper said, moving closer to the girl and sniffing the air. "You don't smell. My friend Lia says Fosaanians smell."

"That's rude, Piper. I'm sorry," I said to the girl. I had heard the same rumor, that Fosaanians smelled like the sulfur permeating the atmosphere.

"I said she DIDN'T smell." Piper glared at me. "It would be rude if I said she DID. What's your name?"

"My name is Mira," The girl answered almost in a whisper.

Piper reached out and patted Mira on the arm as if she was some shy creature. "Mira is a pretty name. Mine's Piper. How old are you? I'm seven. Why do you have that funny mark on your face?"

The girl jerked back like the question shocked her. I didn't understand her reaction, and after she didn't respond, I said to Piper, "It's a tattoo." I didn't think much about it because the small three-sided red mark on her cheek matched the ones on the two Fosaanians who worked at the station.

Mira's lack of response didn't stop Piper. "Why do all the Fosaanians have white hair? It makes everyone look old." Piper moved closer like she was going to touch Mira's hair.

"Piper!" Time to distract my sister before she did anything embarrassing. "What about the shuttle?" I asked.

"It landed without anybody on it, and nobody at the supply depot can talk to the space station. Is it true Fosaanian babies are born with black hair and then it turns white?"

Piper's jumps in topics were hard to follow, and it took Mira some time to answer. "We all have white hair all along," the girl said.

"That's strange." I was puzzled, not about the hair, but about the shuttle. There were always communication problems between the depot and the station because of the weird atmospheric components on Fosaan, and because of the frequent volcanic ash that spewed into the air from a nearby island, but I couldn't think of a reason why the shuttle wouldn't have anyone on it. "Maybe everyone decided to stay for a double shift. Mom said they were having problems with the newest version of the MIbots."

Piper shrugged. "Mick didn't say anything."

"What's Mick doing about it?" I asked. Mick ran the depot, with the help of a few Fosaanians and some ancient bots he refused to replace. He was good with supplies and machines and bots, not so good with other people.

"He sent the second shift up. They're supposed to report back." Piper twisted her finger through her own hair, and the bells jingled softly. I knew the hair-twisting meant Piper was nervous.

"I'm sure they will," I said to reassure her. I was about to go back to talking to Mira when I realized there was something odd about Piper's last statement. "How are they going to report back if the link isn't working?"

"I don't know. Do all Fosaanians have such curly hair? I wish I did."

"Piper, stop with the questions. You're being nosy. Why don't you see if you can get Mom on the comm here?" I suggested.

"Okay." Piper darted out of the kitchen, and too late, I remembered what I had left on the work table.

Piper's shriek came a second later. "Quinn! Disgusting! It's dead! Get it away!"

"Sorry, Piper," I said. The Fosaanian girl was edging for the door again. "Wait, don't go yet. Maybe you could help me with something. It's in here." I didn't want to let her go so I gestured towards the other room and walked out of the kitchen hoping she would follow me. She did, stopping in the doorway. I heard a sharp intake of breath.

When I turned around, the girl was staring wide-eyed around the room. "How is this possible?" she said, reaching out her hand to touch one of the holographic pine trees.

"Oh, I forgot," I pointed at the scene setter on the table. "I had the scene set to be a pine forest. I really miss one I used to go to on Earth, so I like to set that surrounding when I work."

"I didn't know such things existed," Mira said, kneeling down to touch the stream that ran around the chairs. I turned the sound up so the faint murmur of water came from it. The girl's hand went into it and touched the floor. "This is amazing! It looks so real. I smell something strange too."

"I've got it set to pine forest scent. I can switch it to something else if you like, flowers, or a camp fire. Do you want to see it snow?" I changed the scene to snowfall and immediately drifts appeared, covering most of the furniture. Holographic snowflakes fell from the ceiling, which had changed to the gray of a winter sky.

Mira lifted her hands out and smiled. "It's cold! I have heard of snow, but I didn't know it was cold."

"Excuse me," Piper said, standing by the work table with her hands on her hips, her face screwed up in disgust. "Does anyone besides me care that there is a dead thing here?"

"It's okay, Piper." I said. "It can't hurt you. I meant to get rid of it before you got home." I switched the snowfall back to the forest. The falling flakes were too distracting most of the time.

Piper stomped her foot. "Why do you have to drag stuff inside to depict it? Why can't you just image things like normal people?"

"There's no challenge to imaging it. Anybody can do that. Depicting objects sharpens a person's power of observation." I'd heard one of the tests to get into the reconnaissance corps training program measured how well the applicant could observe tiny details. "Besides, I needed to scan its measurements so I could record them." We'd had this argument many times and I didn't get why Piper couldn't understand. It wasn't like I kept the specimens around forever, though sometimes to tease her I pretended I'd accidentally lost one in her room. She fell for it every time.

The Fosaanian girl got up and walked over to the table, stepping around a moss-covered boulder that wasn't really there. She looked down at the creature. "You didn't kill this, did you?" she asked.

If I had been the type to lie, I would have told her I caught it barehanded as it ran past me. I was a terrible at lying though. "No, it was already dead when I found it." I switched the room back to normal.

"I thought so. Most beings don't survive getting close to an anguist."

"I didn't know," I said, somewhat pleased I had managed to study something so lethal. "It's called an anguist?"

"I don't care what it's called!" Piper wailed. "Just get it away!"

Since I was done with it anyway, and it was already starting to smell in the heat, I reached over to pick it up, intending to drop it out the window into the water.

"Wait!" The Fosaanian girl said. "How did you get it in here? Did you touch it?" She sounded horrified.

My hand froze. "Uh, yeah, I picked it up and brought it in. Why?" I asked, not sure I wanted to know the answer.

"How did you pick it up?"

I pictured how I had found the creature. "I picked it up behind the forelegs. Why?"

"They exude poison when they're threatened, particularly from their tails." Mira's face showed the same alarm that her voice held. "It's so lethal, it paralyzes you almost immediately."

I couldn't remember exactly where I had touched it. I'd moved it around a lot as I was measuring it. Was my hand feeling a little numb? I flexed my fingers. They still worked. "I feel fine. I guess I didn't touch the poison part." Good to know I hadn't managed to paralyze myself. It had been idiotic of me not to think of that possibility. I knew there were dangerous life forms on Fosaan, and the Earthers were forbidden to go anywhere except the depot and the beach, but I hadn't even imagined a small dead creature could hurt me.

"You shouldn't just pick up what you find," Mira said, putting her hands on hips just like Piper did. "There are many deadly animals and plants on Fosaan."

At first I didn't hear what she said. The amazing color of her eyes distracted me again. I had thought all Fosaanians had dull gray eyes.

"Quinn, didn't you hear her? Deadly animals are a BAD thing," Piper said.

"Um ... I heard. Do you know how to identify them?" I asked the girl. She had just given me an idea.

"Of course I know," she said, as if I were slightly dense. "I wouldn't be alive if I didn't."

I tried to pick my words carefully so I could get her to go along with my idea. "Could you show me which ones are dangerous? I really want to know, because I'm making a guide." Her expression grew more puzzled and I realized she didn't understand, so I kept talking. "The life forms that survived the Apocalypse haven't been completely logged, I mean logged by our people. If you helped me, I could make a real guide. We could work on it together. I've got some great recording equipment my friend on the space station lent me and I've made this capture device to get some of the smaller flying creatures, so I can observe them and then release them. I'll show it to you ... that is ... if you want to see it ... " Her face was expressionless, and I realized she might think it was all too boring.

Finally she said, "No ... I don't think my uncle would allow me to help you ... I don't know."

Since it wasn't a flat-out no, I persisted, "It wouldn't take much time."

"It's not a good idea," she said, sounding certain.

I slumped back against the table. At this rate, I'd never get the guide done before the deadline to submit my application to the reconnaissance corps. Without something unique like a guide to add to my application, I didn't stand much of a chance of acceptance. My examination scores fell right in the middle of average. And if I didn't get in, my grandfather would make sure I was assigned to one of the officer academies. I knew that would only lead to a spectacular failure. I'd make an even worse officer than my father.

Piper's voice caught my attention. "Quinn, I thought we were going to talk to Mom."

"You can speak to someone on the space station from your own home?" Mira drew close to the comm unit and put out her hand like she wanted to touch it.

"Yes, everyone has one of these," I said.

"Haven't you seen the ones inside the depot?" Piper asked.

"Fosaanians aren't allowed inside unless they work there," Mira said.

I hadn't realized that. I just assumed the Fosaanians preferred to keep to themselves. "Why not? It's nothing special."

"It's a rule. Are these hard to work?" Mira's hand still hovered over the touchpad. "My uncle and my cousin operate the one at the depot, and they say you can get information from everywhere in the galaxy, and pictures of other places. My cousin told me he's seen images of other planets, and they have giant buildings on them." She said it like she didn't really believe it.

"Sure, tall buildings are everywhere." I wasn't interested in ordinary buildings, but if she was and it got her to stay, I'd show her as many as she wanted. "We'll look at some once I talk to my mother."

I was about to speak the code to call up the Comm Center at the station when a voice said, "Incoming message. Secure channel. Turing Seven. Response."

"That's Grandfather!" Piper squealed.

I restrained myself from groaning. My grandfather was the last person in the galaxy I wanted to speak to. "Not good timing," I said, turning to Mira. "I'm sorry, but it would be good if you go in the kitchen while we're talking to my grandfather. I don't want to have to explain to him what you're doing here."

She didn't question me, which surprised me, though at the same time I was happy I didn't have to go into more detail. My grandfather did not like to be kept waiting. I spoke the response. "Turing Five."

My grandfather's attaché appeared on the slip, a woman who Piper called Lieutenant Bark because every word the woman spoke came out short and abrupt. "Hold a moment for Admiral Neen," the woman said.

It didn't take a moment. Almost instantly the grim, lined face of my grandfather filled the display. I knew everyone remarked on how much I looked like the man, down to the dark brown eyes that were nearly black, the sharp lines of our faces, and the set of our jaws, but I hoped I never grew to look so rigid. In a dress uniform, the dark green sheen of it rippling in the sterile light of his office, the man would have projected authority even if you didn't know he was head of the Konsilan.

"Good day, Quinn."

"Good day, Sir." I instinctively sat up straighter. I'd learned long ago not to slouch in view of my grandfather.

"Hi Grandpa!" Piper pushed in besides me on the chair.

"Hello, Miss Piper." A smile appeared on the stone face, something rarely seen. "How's my girl?"

"Good! When are you coming to visit?"

I hoped he'd say "Never." The last argument between my father and grandfather had been so terrible, I couldn't imagine them meeting again.

"I'm not sure." The admiral turned and said something to the attaché and then turned back. "I'm sorry, Piper, but I don't have much time and I need to talk to your brother."

"Okay," she said, sliding off the chair. I heard her move to the kitchen and begin chattering again to Mira. "That's a pretty necklace! Can you show me how to make one like it?" I didn't hear Mira's reply and I tried to block out their voices so my grandfather wouldn't comment on my lack of focus, an almost criminal offense to him.

The frown had reappeared on his face. "Quinn, I understand you haven't yet submitted your application for any of the officer academies. The deadline is coming up."

"I know, Sir. I ... uh ... wanted to speak with you about that."

I felt sweat running down my back and wondered why the room had suddenly gotten so hot. I tried to think of how I had practiced my speech to my grandfather, but instead all I could see in my head was the sweep of wall in the man's office that contained image after image of Neen ancestors in all their military glory.

My grandfather raised an eyebrow. "Go ahead."

I reminded myself that it was my future at stake, not my grandfather's. "I ... " Before I could say anything else, the slip went blank. "That's weird," I said.

"What's weird?" Piper came back in the room.

"We lost contact with Grandfather."

I spoke the code to call up the Comm Center. The display flickered, then the familiar logo of the station came up, the words *Advanced Artificial Intelligence Research Center* emblazoned across a rotating triple torus. I waited for the next slip. Someone on first or second shift communications should appear.

Instead, a voice said, "Due to technical difficulties, AAIRC is not available at this time." The slip went clear.

Chapter 2

I do not know how well the northern continents have recovered from the Apocalypse. Here in the south, so far from the worst of the devastation, much of the plant and creature life was lost, but enough remained to keep the survivors alive, though there were many years of starvation. Only the strong lived. It has never been in our nature to coddle the weak, yet I do believe we may now go too far in demanding perfection.—Erimik, historian of the Family

"That's very odd." I sat back. I couldn't decide if I should be worried. "Piper, is Becca home? What did she say about the shuttle?"

"Doctor Becca brought me to the walkway and then she went right back to the depot. Did you forget you were supposed to help her with the children's science lesson? She's really mad at you right now."

I groaned. I had forgotten, even though I had the samples for the classification lesson all ready to go. "I'll apologize."

"You'll have to do it later. She's going up with the second shift because somebody got hurt on the station and they don't want to move them."

"Who got hurt?" Now I *was* slightly concerned. It couldn't have been my mother, because designing bots wasn't a dangerous job, but everyone up there played a vital role.

"I can't remember. Somebody who's staying on the station. Lia got to go with her. I wanted to go, but Dr. Becca said I had to stay here."

"We should go to the depot," I said. I couldn't believe Becca would go up on the shuttle with second shift, leaving Mick as the only Earther adult on the planet. There were too many younger ones under twelve around, and Mick wasn't good babysitter material. The man loathed most anything living, especially living things who talked back to him. I got up and went into the kitchen. "Mira, we need to leave. If you come back when the link is working again, I'll show you how to use the comm unit."

"I don't know if I'll be able to return," she said.

I thought I could tell from her voice she actually did want to come back. "Sure you can," I urged. "And you don't have to swim to get here next time. Just take the walkway." Mira appeared so startled by that idea that I added, "At least think about it. You live in Hadestown, right?" As far as I knew, all the Fosaanians lived in one place, close to the base of the volcano where they worked. "We'll walk with you as far as the depot."

She looked shocked at my suggestion. "What if someone sees us?"

"Who cares?" I didn't understand.

"My uncle wouldn't like it. I'm not supposed to be here," Mira said.

The uncle again. "But you came anyway," I said. "So you don't always do what you're supposed to do, right?" Mira didn't answer. She did smile, so I took that as a promising sign. "Wait." I picked up the carryall and handed it to her. "Don't forget the food for your sister. Let's go. Mags, don't get into trouble."

The parrot stopped her preening long enough to say, "Send word when you find work."

"What does that mean?" Mira asked. "Does the creature actually think you are going to look for work?"

I laughed. "No, it's just something my father taught her. She thinks she's saying something like goodbye. It's a joke. My father jokes a lot."

Mira looked at me like I was gibbering in some unknown language, so I tried to explain as I pushed open the door flap. Before I could get very far, I ran right into an outstretched fist.

"Watch what you're doing!" I said to the person attached to the fist, Decker Rigan. I had no idea why Decker had shown up at our door, but I could bet it wasn't for any reason I'd like. At seventeen, Decker was only a year older than me, but he considered himself self-appointed overlord of anyone younger, and never stopped reminding everyone his father was the station commander.

"You should look where you're going once in a while." Decker said, rubbing his knuckles. "I was just getting ready to knock. Why aren't you on the nets? You were supposed to be there at thirteen hundred." As usual, Decker was so tense, his skin practically rippled like a sun storm was about to erupt. Whatever furies were inside him made him boil about as hot as a sun most of the time. He touched the 'on' section of the datapatch he wore on his arm and a small holographic slip appeared. "Show Quinn's work schedule," he ordered it. My name appeared, along with a list of times.

"You don't have to remind me," I said. Actually, I had forgotten. Everyone over eight years old had some sort of daily chore and mine was to haul in the nets, collecting the solger, the semi-edible plants that floated just underneath the surface of the water. "I was busy. I'll do it later. They aren't going anywhere."

"You mean you forgot. I bet you were busy working on your little nature pictures, weren't you? Well, since it's my job to make sure you get yours done, I'm reminding you. So do it now." Decker jabbed a finger at my face.

I pushed away Decker's hand. I'd learned long ago never to back down. Decker could always smell weakness. It was unfortunate he was a couple of inches taller than me and quite a bit wider. If I let him get in my face, he would add his size to his intimidation techniques. "I don't like it when you get in my face, and I'm still busy," I said. I had no intention of doing something just because Decker told me to. So I had forgotten the nets. It wasn't the end of the world. "And why are my nature pictures any more of a waste of time than you practicing your music?" I motioned to the black carine Decker wore around his neck. It frustrated me that Decker thought his music important, but everyone else's interests were just time-wasters.

Decker opened his mouth as if to argue some more.

"Hi Decker," Piper interrupted. "Look, we have a new friend. Her name is Mira." Piper grabbed the Fosaanian girl's hand and pulled her forward. Mira pulled back but it was too late. Decker had already seen her.

"What's she doing here?" Decker looked back and forth between me and Mira, frowning. "Fosaanians aren't supposed to just wander around the living quarters."

"Since when was there was a rule?" I asked. "Why can't she go where she wants?"

"My father gave the order. There have been some inconsistencies with the supply manifests. He thinks the Fosaanians are stealing supplies and either using them themselves or somehow selling them to space raiders."

Mira flushed, her face very red against the white of her hair. She shifted the bundle of food closer to her.

"That's a stupid rule," I said. "Anyway, she's with me. I'll check the nets later, but right now we're on our way to the depot."

"That would be a no. You'll check them now." Decker jabbed his finger at me again. "I'm getting really tired of your attitude."

I could swear Decker got more obnoxious by the day. "My attitude isn't any of your concern."

Decker paused and then said, "I don't think the Fosaanians would be too happy to see the girl with you. What would the one who works at the depot, the one named Ansun, say if I told him you two were together? He doesn't let the boy who helps him even speak to Earthers." Decker smiled, and I didn't like the malice I saw in it.

Before I could answer, I felt Mira's hand on me arm. Her fingers trembled but when she spoke, her voice was steady. "I don't like to be threatened, Earth boy. Go ahead and tell Ansun. I don't care. Just remember he already hates Earthers, especially ones who take it upon themselves to cause him displeasure. Most of my people do everything they can to avoid displeasing my uncle."

"So he's your uncle, is he?" Decker looked like he had been given a present and I knew that could be a problem. He had quite a talent at turning anything into an advantage for himself. "I'm not worried about upsetting him," Decker added. "What's he going to do to me?"

"Some who have asked that find their tongues missing." Mira's voice was almost taunting now. "Go ahead and see what happens." I was amazed at how quickly the girl had gone from terrified to angry, though Decker could manage to irritate almost everyone to fury.

"Whoa, missing tongues are extreme," I said. I'd never heard anything like that about the Fosaanians.

"How did they lose their tongues?" Piper asked. "Can he do magic? Does he give them back?"

"Never mind, Piper," I said, shooting a warning glance at Decker who was about to say something. If it was true, the uncle sounded brutal and Piper didn't need to hear it. "Let's forget about it. Piper, go on to the depot if you want. I'll be there soon." I didn't want to let Mira go until I could convince her to come back again.

"I want to get Teeny first." Piper grabbed the house bot she pretended was either a pet, another child, or a doll, depending on the day. "We're going to have a bot race later. Decker, do you know why the shuttle came back empty?"

The expression on Decker's face made it clear he didn't. "That's the first I've heard of it." When Piper explained, Decker lost interest in Mira. "I'll go to the depot with you," he said to Piper.

"Good!" Piper dashed around us and down the walkway connecting our unit to the center hub of the compound. "Decker, I bet you can't catch me!" she yelled, as she reached the security gate to the ramp leading to the shore. For some reason Piper liked Decker, and didn't mind him ordering her around.

"Yes I can!" Decker yelled. "Don't forget those nets," he barked to me before he took off after Piper. Their running made the walkway bounce up and down, and Mira reached out a hand for the railing. "Are these buildings common where you come from? Buildings floating on the water? I like them, except the rocking is strange."

"The first day we got here, I noticed the motion, but now I don't think about it. Lots of people do live out over the water on Earth, if they have the currency. It's nicer and less crowded. We couldn't afford it when we lived there, but the planners decided it would be best for the scientists because of all the unknowns on Fosaan."

"It's a good design," Mira said, "putting all the living quarters in a circle and attaching them to each other. Our quarters are just in rows. These would be easier to defend."

I was struck by her last comment. "What do you have to defend against? Do creatures actually attack your village?" The Earthers had a security field around the depot, but I hadn't thought about how the Fosaanians protected themselves.

Her gaze shifted away from mine. "Not usually," she said. "And anyway, it's better to be prepared." She looked away from me and motioned toward Piper who was dancing in a circle around at the end of the walkway. As soon as Decker drew close, Piper darted off in the direction of the depot, laughing. She was a speedy little thing and I didn't think Decker would be able to catch her.

"Is your sister always so happy?" Mira asked. "I've never seen a child who smiles so much."

I shrugged. "She's happy most of the time except when she's worried about something. Sorry there were so many questions from her."

"I don't mind." She fell silent, and I struggled to find something to say. I wanted to ask her if she had snuck out to the living units before, but that was probably something she didn't want to talk about. As we got closer to the beach, I could feel the air get heavier and I could taste the sulfur in my mouth. The breeze from the ocean kept the air clean out on the pavilions, but the windbines weren't finished on the shore.

The sea turned purple on either side of the walkway. "Do you know what those are called?" I pointed into the water at a school of miniscule crustaceans, millions of them moving like a purple cloud. "Piper likes to watch them."

"They're called squilla," Mira said. "They taste terrible, but you can eat them if you are hungry enough."

"Then I don't think I'll tell anyone they're edible. Someone will get the brilliant idea that I need to catch them. I could really use your help, you know, learning about the life on this planet. You said your uncle wouldn't allow it. What about your parents?"

"No!" Mira exclaimed. "I can't explain. We don't ... we aren't supposed to mix with Earthers."

"Why not? You work for us. I mean, not you, but the Fosaanians work for the Earthers. It isn't because of Decker's father is it? Commander Rigan? We're not all like him." She didn't answer and I tried to think of another way to convince her.

"Would you pay me with food?" she blurted out suddenly. "If I helped you, would you give me food for my sister?"

"Sure, I mean, I'd give you food anyway if your sister needs it." I felt terrible to hear the desperation in her voice. "Look, if she's still not recovered from her accident, we have a doctor who could probably help."

"It wouldn't be allowed," Mira said angrily.

"It would only not be allowed if someone knew about it to forbid it," I couldn't believe someone would forbid a doctor to see a person. "Can you bring your sister to the depot?"

Mira stopped and I was amazed to see the change on her face. It was lit up with excitement. "The doctor would really see her? I don't have any currency to pay."

"Becca wouldn't charge you! She's paid by the military."

"I'd have to get my cousin to help me," Mira said, almost to herself as if she were planning it out. "Cadia can't walk far. She's always been frail and the accident only made it worse. When can we bring her?"

"As soon as Dr. Becca gets back down from the station," I said, "but I don't know when that will be."

"Thank you." She gave me a dazzling smile. I felt like life had suddenly improved.

When we reached the end of the walkway, Mira pointed to the sky. "I think you have a follower." The olon was above us, gliding silently.

"I don't know why that one hangs around so much." I said.

"Maybe it likes to be talked to. They seem to be intelligent creatures. They nest in communities and work together to care for their young. What type of creature is your animal?"

"It's a parrot, a species of bird." There weren't any true birds on Fosaan, only the olons, which flew but didn't have any feathers. When I had first seen them, I couldn't get over their bizarre appearance. It was almost as if someone had taken hairless flying squirrels, added beaks and painted them in bright colors.

"Do all birds speak?" Mira asked. "I never imagined such a thing."

"No, there are thousands of species of birds on Earth but only a few can mimic human speech. And only some parrots can actually understand the meanings of words."

"I'd like one of these parrots someday. It would make Cadia laugh." Mira smiled again.

"Will you come with me to the beach?" I asked, taking advantage of the way Mira's mood had lightened. "I want to show you something." If she liked buildings, I knew of something that might interest her.

She looked toward the depot. Piper and Decker were already there, talking to some of the other Earthers. The Fosaanian, Ansun, was standing outside with Mick. It appeared the two were arguing, or at least Mick was, his voice loud as he pounded one hand into another. Ansun stood with his arms crossed over his chest. I couldn't make out his face. "Yes," Mira said, "for a moment." I wondered if she didn't want to go past the depot to the beach path with her uncle outside. The only other way back to the Fosaanian village, as far as I knew, was through the jungle and that was supposedly too dangerous.

We headed away from the depot, crunching over the black lava rock that was the "sand" on the beach. It shimmered with so much heat, I could feel it through my shoes. When my mother had tried to sell us on coming to Fosaan, she had really played up the part about the untouched beaches for us to enjoy. She hadn't told us the sand was made of volcanic slivers so sharp you couldn't sit down on them, and so quick to heat to unbearable levels, you didn't want to stand around too long. It wasn't her fault, really. Whoever had written the briefing papers about the planet probably wasn't the type to have ever actually been to a real beach.

"Before we came, we heard about all these incredible places on Fosaan, but I haven't seen many of them," I said. "I'd really like to.

There are supposed to be waterfalls longer than any on Earth and caves full of crystals of all different colors."

"I know some of those places. I didn't know Earthers would find them interesting. What is this other place you want to show me?"

"It's over here." I climbed up on some boulders piled in a jumble where the beach met the dense jungle and pulled away some of the wirevines, yanking at one that seemed to have grown several meters since Lainie and I had been there last. I'd heard the Fosaanians called the jungle "the snare" and I could understand why.

Behind the growth of vines stood a wall, almost hidden by the patches of vivid green and blue plants that covered it, each individual plant the size of a tiny dot. I reached out my hand and cleared off a section of it. "My friend Lainie and I found this. When you rub off the lichen-like plants you can see it was built of some sort of rock that's almost clear." Mira held back like she wasn't sure she should get close to it. I had hoped she'd be more excited about the find. "There's a lot more," I told her. "We can get inside over there."

The wall was only a few meters taller than me, but because it was so smooth, there was no way to climb it except through a broken section. "Right here," I said.

Mira frowned. "I'm not climbing into something when I can't see what's inside."

"There's nothing dangerous in there. It's just a big room attached to two other rooms. I've been in it several times." Technically, none of the Earthers were supposed to venture off the beach, but I thought that rule was ridiculous. I'd never learn anything about the planet if I just stuck within the allowed areas.

"Just because there was nothing in there the last time doesn't mean it's empty now." Mira picked up a small stone and pitched it over the wall. It thudded down. No other sound came from inside.

"See?" I said. "Empty." I climbed over the wall hoping she'd follow. Inside I waited a few seconds until Mira climbed in too. The overhead plant canopy made the light dim, but I could see she still looked wary.

"It's okay, really." I tried to ignore how still and hot the air was. Away from the beach, the ocean breeze was blocked by the wall and the vegetation and the temperature inside always made me break out in a sweat. "It's almost like being underwater in here, with the way the light comes through the walls. Lainie and I call it a ruin, but it's not really one. It's in good shape except for that one spot."

"What is this place?" Mira asked, running her hand along a section of wall.

I was surprised she didn't know. "It's an old Fosaanian building. One of your people's buildings, from before the Apocalypse. Where do you get this kind of building material? Are your houses made of this?"

Mira walked up and down, "I've never seen anything like this before. I don't think it was a building people lived in. The curving walls don't make sense. What would people do in this room? And where's the roof?"

"I guess it collapsed," I said.

"Where? There's no rubble."

I hadn't thought of that. The floor was made of some dark material in a triangular pattern. There was no broken stone on it, nothing except fallen leaves. "Maybe they used something that has decayed over time, so there's no sign of it now." She was right about the room though. A narrow three-sided room with curving walls that met in a sharp point was about as impractical as you could get. "Is it some sort of religious shrine?" I asked. I'd read a little about Fosaanian religion which mentioned shrines, but there were no images and I'd seen nothing that was an obvious religious building."

"No, it's nothing like a torey." She began to turn around very slowly, like she was memorizing each wall.

When she stopped, she went back over to one wall and touched it again. I said, "There are two more rooms like this and something in the center we think is a room but we can't get in. If you pull back the vines you can see the doorways into the other two, but they're all empty."

Mira's hand drew back. "There are three rooms? Are they all shaped like this?"

"They're exactly like this." I traced the shape on the wall, rubbing off some of the plants in the process. "Now that I think about it, each room is kind of in the shape of a bird talon or an animal claw. See how it curves and comes to a point." Mira didn't say anything; she just stared at the drawing as if I had sketched something that shocked her. It hit me that the shape I had just outlined was exactly the same shape as the tattoo on her cheek. She had to realize it as well, but she didn't mention it.

"It isn't familiar to you?" I asked.

"No," she said, taking a few steps back to the broken spot in the wall. "I should go."

"Don't go yet!" I decided to back off the shape issue if that was upsetting her, though I couldn't figure out why it would. I flicked on the flashmark on my sleeve to give us some better light. "We did find something that might be words on the inner wall. It could be instructions on how to get in or find a door. I'll show you."

I was relieved that she did follow me to the shortest wall. I pointed to red markings glowing in the light. "Someone embedded these on the wall with bits of iridium sulfide, just like the compound the scientists are using to coat the new holobots. Is it really writing?"

Mira knelt down, setting the carryall of food beside her so she could touch the marks.

"What does it say?" I asked.

She frowned, leaned closer and then jerked her hand away. "I have to leave," she said, jumping to her feet.

Chapter 3

I would have liked to have seen and heard the glories of the Old World, the art and the music. My grandfather spoke to me of the wonders of the Palace and the capital. There were scholars then as well, though their freedom was not as great as it should have been. Even my grandfather admitted this when he grew old and it no longer mattered who heard him speak. The dark began long before the Apocalypse.—Erimik, historian of the Family

"Why? What's wrong?" I scrambled to catch up to her. "It is writing, right?" The thought came to me that maybe Mira couldn't read. I didn't know if the Fosaanians even had a school. "Maybe the writing of your people was different a long time ago," I said, not knowing the right way to ask her. "Or this is a different language. I don't know how many languages there were on Fosaan."

"I don't know either." She whirled around. Her voice and her face were furious. "If you are so interested, you should ask the Earthers if they kept any records when they destroyed our civilization." She grabbed the carryall and climbed up and over the broken place in the wall.

"Wait!" I yelled, chasing after her. "We didn't ... Wait!" I climbed up after her and nearly fell over it in my haste. "You have it wrong. We didn't destroy your civilization. The supervolcano did. It caused the Apocalypse from the ash and the poison rain." I'd read about the dense layer of ash that covered everything, smothering most of the plants, and about the black rain so acidic it burned the skin of any living creature. It wasn't until very recently that reconnaissance ships had even ventured to the planet, to find it recovering far more quickly than predicted.

She stopped and spun back toward me, shouting, "Earthers started the war with us before the volcano. If you had left us alone, to live our own way, our ships wouldn't have been off fighting and more people might have escaped."

"Oh," I said. I'd never thought about it in that context. "But the war started because the emperor here was brutal and oppressive. I can't believe the Fosaanians at the time would have wanted Earth to let things stay the same. It was just a fluke that the volcano erupted when it did. And all the Fosaanians who were already on the ships escaped. They surrendered and ... " I realized I didn't know what had happened to them. "I'm sorry for what happened, but that was a long time ago. I didn't start the war. You can't be angry at me."

"You know nothing. The war was all about power, about Earth wanting power over the planet. But you'll never believe that, will you? All Earthers think they are right about everything. I have to go." She turned away from me.

I was stunned by her vehemence, but couldn't let her go just like that. "Wait. I'm not like all Earthers," I called to her. I'd never even questioned the history I'd read of Fosaan. Maybe I should have. Mira didn't stop, but before I followed her, I pulled the vines back down to cover the wall. Lainie had convinced me we needed to keep it hidden for the moment. If others found out about it, it would be declared off limits until a scientist could examine it, and that could take far too long.

"Wait!" I called again when I was finished. Mira was already halfway down the beach and I sprinted to catch up.

"I don't know much about the history of the war," I said. "We were taught the royal family never allowed any dissent. They killed anyone who questioned their rule, or at least that's what the histories say."

"Who wrote those histories?" Mira practically spit out the words. "No one portrays themselves as in the wrong. They cloak their actions in higher purposes when all they want is power, always more power."

She sounded so angry, I had a feeling she was talking about more than ancient history. "You're right," I said. "Earthers wrote the histories I read. Tell me the Fosaanian version."

"It would take hours," she said. "And you wouldn't believe me anyway."

I was glad her voice sounded a little more calm, and since it did, I decided not to push her on the topic of the war. "I'd really like to hear what happened, whenever you want to tell me."

She shrugged. "Maybe some day. It will be a waste of time

though. Aren't you supposed to check your nets?"

"I'll check the nets later." The thought of cool ocean water was appealing, but I didn't want to stand around in it trying to free the solger from the nets. "It's not like we even really need the plants. Have you ever tasted them? They taste like salty slimy rags."

"Why do you have to collect them then? I thought supply ships brought all your food, and they say you never run out." The bitterness came through in her voice, and I realized I had to talk to someone about the food issue. Clearly it was a bigger problem than any of the Earthers knew. If someone in charge had known, they wouldn't let it go on. It was odd no one had observed the problem before now.

"Supply ships bring most of it," I said. "My father pilots one of them. But we still collect food because the scientists voted to try to become as self-reliant as possible." It irritated me that the ones who voted were actually too busy with their work to carry out the jobs. None of them seemed bothered by the fact that they weren't the ones doing the work to be self-reliant.

"That Decker will be angry if you do not do your job." She didn't add in the threat Decker had made to tell her uncle.

"If you're worried about Decker telling your uncle you were here, I have an idea. I'll introduce you to my friend Lainie. Decker listens to her because he's crazy about her, and she'll stop him. I don't think he'd really do what he said anyway. He's all bluff."

"I'm not worried," she said scornfully, but I detected a faint tremor in her voice. I didn't blame her, especially if she hadn't been bluffing about the man cutting out people's tongues. I feared she had been telling the truth, just by the man's appearance. He wore a fierce expression all the time, the fierceness heightened by his long angular face and the scar that marred it. The scar cut across the corner of his mouth, and looked as if it had come either from a knife slash or an animal claw.

"So you'll stay around for a while?" I was afraid if she left now, she wouldn't come back, and I really wanting to see her again. She gave me what might have been a faint smile and I took that as encouragement. "Let's see what's happening at the depot," I said. She nodded and fell into step beside me.

We were almost at the end of the beach when Mira stopped so suddenly, I walked a few feet beyond her before I realized she wasn't keeping up. She pointed to the path along the cliff to Hadestown. Ansun was walking toward it, followed by the boy who worked with him. I was shocked to see an MI holobot in its basic icosahedron form hovering behind them.

"What is that strange red ball floating after Ansun?" Mira asked.

I held up my hand to shade my eyes, still not believing what I was seeing. "It's the whole reason we are here. That's what the scientists are working on up on the station, but it's not supposed to be down here. They only have a few prototypes so far and those are too valuable." I didn't voice the thought, but after what Decker had said, I wondered if the Fosaanians stealing it.

The holobot came to a halt and let out a high-pitched "stop" command that could be heard even from the beach. A hologram of a woman in field gear formed around the icosahedron and Mira gasped. I nearly did too. My mother had told me the holobot could generate thousands of different forms, but I hadn't imagined it would produce such a solid-looking image. The holowoman gestured toward a spot in front of Ansun. It must have spoken again, though we couldn't hear it, because Ansun picked up a nearby rock and slammed it down on the ground near a clump of seathread.

"What is he doing?" I asked.

"How did that woman appear out of the machine?" Mira sounded interested rather than frightened.

"It's just an image the MI projects. It's not real. Why did Ansun throw that rock?" I asked again.

"I think he just killed an anguist," Mira said. "It's best to kill them with a large enough rock so the poison doesn't spatter, but I don't understand how the machine knew it was there. It was behind Ansun."

"It really does work!" After so many setbacks, I never believed the MI project would meet all its goals. "The MIs are the first robots that have something like all the five senses of humans, but even more powerful. The sensors can detect odors and can analyze what something would feel like as if it could touch it. It maps the surface of everything with spectroscopy. There must have been something about the anguist the robot sensed. I wish I had one of those to take with me when I get out into the jungle."

"I thought Earthers had many machines like that."

"Not like the MIs. They can make decisions like humans, not just decisions based on the specific data from limited sensor input. That's why they are MIs-multiple intelligences. But I still can't figure out why it is down here."

Mira shrugged. "My uncle is very good with operises. Perhaps your mother is having him test it."

"No, she wouldn't do that. She says there's something not quite right yet but she knew how to fix it." I hadn't been paying much attention when my mother had left for her shift, but I did remember her talking about a glitch in the design of the bots. I tried to remember what she had said. She'd mentioned Gregor. That was it. *"Your friend Gregor may seem like he spends all his time trying to get out of his work, but he's actually a mechanical genius. He adapted and recalibrated the plasma nanoslicer for me to cut the iridium in a new way. I don't know exactly how he did it, but that piece of equipment may solve all our problems."*

I had been happy Gregor had done something right for once, though even if the problem was solved I couldn't imagine my mother letting one of the bots out onto the planet without her right there to watch over it. "She's been worried about what would happen to them once they are exposed to the atmosphere here. It's so different than the clean air on the space station and she thinks it's too hot here. Wait, what's an operise? You mean bots?"

Mira hesitated and then said, "We called intelligent machines operises before the Earthers came."

"I thought Fosaanians didn't have technology like bots." I knew from the briefings we'd had to attend before we arrived that the Fosaanians had been extremely advanced before the Apocalypse, but now the only remaining village just had mechanical devices that ran on wind, water or human power. There was no way they could have real bots. "Did the Fosaanians buy some?" I couldn't see how they could. Even Mick's ancient ones were too expensive. The Fosaanians didn't have anything of value to earn currency to buy bots, because the Earthers didn't pay them much for collecting the sulfur iridium compound.

"I meant when we first learned about them from the Earthers. Is that your friend?" she asked, pointing to the group of Earthers.

I couldn't see Lainie, but everyone else had their backs to us, cheering at something. "From the sounds of it, they're playing splitball," I said, "And Lainie's probably winning."

"Splitball? I don't know that word."

"It's a game." I was still puzzling over the bot. There had to be a good reason my mother allowed it to be brought down to the planet surface.

"It must be an exciting game from the way everyone is yelling." Mira sounded interested. That was good. Anything to keep her around was good.

"Come on, it's interesting to watch." When we reached the group, I saw there were two left playing, Lainie, and her brother Saunder. I wasn't surprised. The two were determined competitors, never wanting to let the other win. I had to admit splitball was one of Decker's better ideas. "We get the pods off those plants with the giant fronds." I pointed to one growing on the edge of the depot platform. "The trick is to get a pod to one of the four goals as many times as possible before it split opens. Do you know that plant? When it splits, it explodes and in the game if you get any of the fruit pulp on you, you're out." It was easy to tell who was out in this round. The sticky yellow stuff spattered all over, staining clothes and skin.

Mick, the depot manager, was nowhere in sight. He usually tried to chase everyone as far to the edge of the grounds as possible, claiming the fruit goo made such a mess. Everyone always came back anyway, because the depot had the only flat cleared area.

"Quinn!" Lainie yelled. "I need you on my team. I'm down to just me."

She stopped, noticing Mira, but when I yelled, "Later!" Lainie whirled around, back at the game. Her foot shot out and caught an incoming pod, blasting it right back at Saunder. It hit him on the arm, bursting open and showering him with pulp, scenting the air with the odor reminiscent of wet dog, not the sweet fruity smell you'd expect.

"Yes!" Lainie was yelling and running around. She launched into a couple of back flips and then danced around, pumping her hands in the air. Saunder came up behind her and shook off some of the goo on her head. Both of them chased each other around in circles laughing until Saunder noticed Mira too. He said something to Lainie and his attention drew the attention of all the other Earthers. Some came closer, including Piper, who dragged one of her friends up to them.

"This is Mira," I said, hoping all the interest wouldn't faze the girl. I should have realized she would attract a lot of attention.

"Hi," Saunder held out his hand and then drew it back, grinning. "Sorry, I'm kind of sticky right now." He introduced everyone else so fast I knew Mira would never keep them all straight, but the Fosaanian girl nodded her head like she was taking it all in.

"We need some new people for our games," Lainie said, examining Mira. "You look quick on your feet. I call Mira for my team!"

"Wait a minute!" Saunder held up his hands in protest. "Give the rest of us a chance. Mira, you should be on my team. My sister is very uncoordinated and doesn't often win. That last game was just a fluke."

"Hah!" Lainie said, doing a series of handsprings in a circle, her long legs flashing through the air. Her black hair, which she wore in a crazy curly ponytail on top of her head, flew around in swirls, like it had a life of its own. "Top that, brother. Who's uncoordinated?"

"You know I can't resist a challenge," Saunder said, and took off on his own exhibition of handsprings. He didn't manage quite as many handsprings as his sister, but when he was finished, he gave a bow anyway. I was always struck by how Saunder and Lainie moved in exactly the same way, though the twins didn't look alike at all. Saunder's skin was much darker than Lainie's, and he was stocky compared to Lainie's wiry build. They had very different personalities too, though they always seemed to know what the other was thinking. Lainie's brain worked with incredible efficiency when it came to anything technical, while Saunder did much better with people. He wanted to be a doctor, and we all knew he'd make a good one.

Mira hadn't said a word. She seemed bemused by all of them. We were kind of a motley group, with everyone adopting their own versions of an offEarth look. None of the younger ones wore anything that matched, and most had taken up Piper's idea of bells tied into their hair. Lainie had introduced a new fad of cutting geometric holes in clothes, because the cooling fibers wouldn't work in the Fosaanian atmosphere, but while hers looked good, the rest hadn't been as precise, so their clothes just looked holey.

"Lainie, you promised you'd referee the bot race," Piper held up Teeny in front of Lainie to get her attention.

"I did, didn't I," Lainie said. "But you'll be on my team later, right?" she asked Mira.

"If I can," Mira said. I was astounded. I thought Mira would try to get out of it. Even in the short time since we met, it was hard to imagine her playing a game.

"Terrific!" Lainie punched Saunder in the arm. "Don't try to change her mind. Come on, bot racers! Who's playing?" There was a babble of voices.

"I'll help too." Decker said, not even acknowledging Mira's presence. At least with Lainie around, Decker tended to tone down his obnoxiousness. She was the only one he didn't try to boss around.

"Saunder, wait," I said, as most of the rest of the group gathered around Lainie. "What's happening? Piper said the shuttle came back without anyone one it. Our comm link won't work. Do you know if the one at the depot is up?"

"It's still down," Saunder said. "Mick came outside a while ago and said not to worry."

I didn't trust Mick's assessment of the situation. The dangers of Fosaan had been drummed into all of us, and while I wasn't intending on doing something stupid, I didn't like the idea of being out of contact with the station. "I guess we just wait awhile and see what happens," I said. "Mira, do you want to watch the bot race?"

"Do you play games all day?" Mira asked. She motioned toward the Earthers setting up the obstacle course for the race.

"No," I said. "Well, some of the younger ones do except when one of the scientists gives them a lesson. The rest of us study on our own and with each other, and I help Piper with her reading and math. The teacher who came with us hated the place and left right after she saw the first ash cloud and that latest volcanic eruption. She was sure another supervolcano was going to wipe us all out. There's a new teacher coming with the next supply ship, my father's ship." I felt defensive all the sudden. I didn't just hang around wasting time all day. "And we have our jobs we're supposed to do," I added, and then realized that part didn't sound very impressive, considering I'd blown off doing my own job.

The race started and the racket drowned out my last sentence.

"Is this really a game?" Mira asked. "Everyone is just running in circles and yelling."

"Racing isn't in the house bots' programming, but they do listen to commands, so each participant is trying to give theirs the right command to avoid an obstacle or to go through the hoops. The bots end up bumping into each other a lot, and that throws them way off. Most never make it to the finish line, but nobody seems to really care." Piper had added bells and fastened ribbons to the little bot and the ribbons streamed out behind it as it zipped along. I guessed all of the bots would soon have ribbons the way Teeny was drawing admiring glances from the younger ones.

"What is that one doing?" Mira asked, pointed at one which was leaning over and trying to pick up another bot that had tipped over.

Lainie joined us. "It's been programmed to clean so it's trying to get hold of the one that fell over to put it away somewhere. Only problem is that once it gets it, it won't know where to put it. It will just try to carry it around." I was gratified to hear a small laugh from Mira.

I noticed one of the bots had become more colorful since the last bot race. "When did the duster acquire Liger fighter stripes?" I asked Lainie. The Ligers were Earth's most advanced two-person fighter ships, known for their distinctive orange stripes on either side.

"Decker did that for Pauli," Lainie said, motioning to the small boy who ran alongside the bot shouting encouragement. "Pauli was embarrassed his bot is so old compared to the rest."

Teeny had almost reached the finish line when a larger bot moved in front of it. Piper yelled, "Now!" A small door opened in Teeny's main compartment and a ball flew out, hitting the bigger bot, which stopped and turned around. I was surprised. I didn't know who had adapted Teeny to do that.

"No fair!" one of Piper's friends shouted.

"You parasites are making too much noise!" Mick came out of one of the supply buildings with his main helper, an old Labor5 model. Another one of the new MIs hovered after it. I couldn't believe another prototype was down onplanet, especially since it was with Mick, who didn't need such a specialized bot.

"Mick looks sick or something," Saunder said as he walked over to us.

I thought the depot manager did look pale, and he was rubbing the back of his head as if it hurt. Mick was a big man who liked jewelry, lots of jewelry, especially the silvery Argite stones he wore strung on big chunky necklaces and bracelets, but today he didn't seem to notice the stones clunking against his face as he rubbed his head.

The MI opened one of its faces. Mick took a program helico from it, then placed it into a slot in the Labor5. He rubbed his head again and started walking into the main building.

"Mick, wait!" Decker yelled.

"Can't talk now," Mick said as he went into the depot. The door slid shut after him and I heard it lock down. All the windows darkened as their coverings activated.

The Labor5 went behind the building but the MI stayed in place. No matter how pleased my mother was with the MIs, I thought the bots were ugly in their basic mode, like giant red insect eyes which gleamed with the indium sulfide coating.

"Take form," I ordered as I walked over to it. Each bot was programmed with its own standard hologram form, and this one took the shape of a blond young woman in a lab suit. The hologram smiled at me, but then the shape flickered, becoming an old man dressed in a bizarre collection of clothes. As the gram solidified, I instinctively took a step back at the thing in front of me. The man didn't have any eyes and the white ovals where they should have been were unnerving. An instant later, the thing switched back to the smiling woman.

Definitely a programming glitch. "What's wrong with the station?" I asked it. If Mick wouldn't answer, I'd get the information another way.

It took the hologram several seconds to respond. "Technical difficulties," it responded.

"What kind of difficulties?"

"It is too difficult to explain to humans such as yourself." The bot was supposed to be programmed with a variety of voices to match whatever hologram image it projected, but something was off in this one. It was a woman's voice but the words were too raspy, the pitch going up and down as if there was a malfunction in the speech programming too. It also wasn't an answer I had ever heard from a bot before.

"It can't be that difficult," I told it. "There's either something wrong with the station itself or with the communications link. It can't be the shuttle, because the shuttle took off again."

"Is that a question?" the bot asked.

I had been around bots long enough to figure out how to avoid frustration when talking to them. The original artificially intelligent bots, the AIs, were usually fairly good at understanding humanoid speech patterns, and I assumed the MIs would be too, but I decided to make my question as clear as possible. "What part of the station is malfunctioning?"

"Technical difficulties." The hologram disappeared as the bot stopped projected so that the red floating icosahedron was again visible. It propelled itself backward to where Mick's Labor5 stood. A small light on one face appeared, and I could tell it was sending signals to the older machine.

"That's abnormal," I said to Mira. "The MIbots should be programmed to answer questions."

"I can't believe it can talk to you," Mira said.

"Most bots can communicate, though it takes some practice to talk to them so they understand what you want."

"There's probably a fault in it," Decker said. "My father said he didn't think it was ever really going to work the way your mother claims."

I bristled at this. "She knows what she's doing."

"Quinn is right," Lainie said. "My father told me that Quinn's mom has made a tremendous breakthrough. Maybe it just needs to run a diagnostics."

"Good idea." I walked over to it and ordered it to run through its maintenance diagnostics. Instead of responding, it came closer to me, too close. Without thinking, I reached a hand up to stop it. When my fingers were just a few centimeters away, a stream of blue light shot out, running through my hand into my body. For an instant my arm felt like it was on fire and then the jolt hit my chest. I fell to the ground, unable to breathe.

Chapter 4

These Earthers are puzzling. Their societal structure seems quite chaotic. I cannot understand the hierarchy. The Earther called Mick appears to have power, but I see no reason why he is deserving of respect. I do not understand how such a society became so powerful.—Erimik, historian of the Family

"Quinn!" I heard Piper scream, the sound dim and far away, even though when I opened my eyes I could see her right in front of me.

A heavy weight pressed on my chest and I couldn't draw any air into my lungs. I wanted to yell at someone to do something, anything. But my voice wouldn't work, and everyone just stood there looking at me, their mouths open. I thought my heart was going to explode. Then my chest heaved, and I drew in one breath and another, trying to suck in as much air as I could.

"Quinn!" Piper was crying now.

"I'm okay," I gasped, trying to decide if I was going to live. "It's okay."

I wanted to roll on my side, thinking I'd be able to breathe better. My body wouldn't obey and someone put a hand on my shoulder.

"Don't try to get up too fast," Saunder's voice said. I lay back, wondering if I was going to throw up.

Mira knelt down beside me and started to speak. Her necklace, a green stone surrounded by some knotted cords, swung back and forth in front of my face and the motion made me sick. I looked away in time to catch sight of the MIbot behind her as it started to float towards us. Flickers of light like small lightning bolts flashed across the sensors.

"Get out of the way, Mira!" I tried to shove her aside and scramble backwards at the same time, but my arms and legs still weren't working quite right.

The MIbot stopped and the holowoman reappeared. Its voice sounded even more raspy. "If you approach this model again, the beam will be increased substantially. It could cause a member of your species to cease functioning." We didn't move as the bot rolled backward to where Mick's helpbot still stood. The MI's sensor flashed signals at the other's intake tap, and then the two bots moved toward the depot. The door opened as they approached, and closed right after they went inside.

"Quinn, are you okay? I think I actually saw sparks coming from your eyes," Lainie asked.

"I don't know. I feel strange, shaky." My heart was jumping and my fingers were tingling. The images in front of me wavered like underwater ripples.

"Try to breathe slowly," Saunder said. "That was a really bad shock."

"No one told us those machines were so dangerous," Decker said.

"They're not supposed to be dangerous." I stood up, but my legs were so wobbly I leaned over and put my hands on my knees, trying to brace myself. "They aren't programmed for weaponizing."

"It looks like their programming has changed," Lainie said. "Somebody should have told us."

"What did your mom do to them?" Decker grabbed my arm and swung me around.

"Decker!" Saunder yelled. "What are you doing?"

I nearly went down. "Let go of me," I said. "I'm about ready to throw up and I'll be happy to do it all over you." Decker backed off and I tried to quell the tremors running through my body. It was as if something was shaking me from inside. Mira came closer to me, which would have been nice in normal circumstances, but I didn't want to throw up on her either. That wouldn't have been a good start to anything.

"My mom didn't do anything!" Piper yelled. Tears ran down her face and she began to tremble. I put my arm around her, trying to get in some more breaths. "Piper's right. She would never program a bot to do something like that."

"Somebody did," Decker said, moving over to the door. "Something isn't right. Mick, what's going on?" He pounded on it with his fist.

Mick's face appeared on the slip next to the door. "Fiss it! Stop that pounding. You're making my headache worse." He was so pale now he looked like one of the albino cockroaches that were the bane of every spaceship. "Go away!" He made a snarling sound like he was trying to chase us off.

"Mick, get out here! That MIbot is malfunctioning. It sent out an electric shock on purpose," Decker said.

"Leave it alone then." Mick added a few more curses. There was a faint whirring sound from inside. Mick turned his head away from the slip.

"Don't you understand?" I said. "It threatened to kill me if I touched it again."

"So don't touch it, genius." Mick stood up, glancing over his shoulder. "Just go home for now."

"Mick, open this door." Decker pounded even harder. "We need some answers! When my father finds out what's happened, you'll be out of a job."

A smirk appeared on Mick's face. "I don't think so, kid. Things are changing around here. Now this is the last time I'm going to say this. Go home."

"We're not doing that," I said.

"Your choice, but right now, I'm controlling things down here. Let's just say the situation is in flux. Things are happening, and you'll be notified of any news when the time is right." The man moved away from the slip. We were left looking at the corner of his grubby office full of old drink mixers and empty food envelopes.

"Mick?" I called. There was no answer. I waited, and then called again. "Mick, at least tell us what's wrong up at the station. Who got hurt?"

Still silence.

"Why won't he come out?" Piper asked.

A faint sound came from inside the depot, barely perceptible at first, then growing steadily louder. It sounded like almost like someone was humming, humming a tuneless song without a melody, except it wasn't quite human.

"What's that?" Mira whispered.

"That doesn't sound like Mick or a bot either. Is somebody else in there?" I turned to Lainie and Saunder. "You two were here earlier. Did somebody go in?"

"We were too busy to notice," Lainie said. "That doesn't exactly sound like a person to me."

The sound cut off and the slip changed to clear.

"Mick didn't make that ... that sound, did he?" Piper asked. She twisted a strand of her hair around her finger, knocking one of the bells out.

It rolled toward me and I bent down to pick it up for her. The dizziness struck me and I had to stand back up before I could get the bell. I looked down at my hand and saw it was quivering. "No, it didn't sound anything like him," I said, grabbing hold of the shaking hand with my other one, hoping no one noticed. I didn't know what had made the noise, and I wasn't sure I wanted to find out. Mira gave me a worried look, and then reached down for Piper's bell.

One of the other youngest boys, a quiet kid named Arne, started to cry.

"I don't like being alone," another one said, and then several voices chimed in.

"I want my mom!"

"I'm hungry!"

More tears came down Piper's face.

"I think Mick is right," Saunder said. "We should go home and wait for the communication link to work again, or the shuttle to come back down."

"What if it doesn't come back?" Piper asked. I wished Piper hadn't spoken that thought aloud. I could tell by the stricken looks on several faces that a group panic was in the works.

"Of course it will come back," Saunder said. "Everything will be fine. It's getting late and I'm getting hungry too. Why don't we all go to Lainie and my quarters and get together a picnic we can share?" Saunder sounded so unconcerned, his voice had an immediate calming effect on the younger ones.

They immediately started to chatter about the idea of a picnic and I was relieved they could be distracted. "Would you mind taking Piper with you?" I asked Lainie. "I want to see if I can get Mick to open the door."

"He didn't sound like he was in any mood to open it," Lainie said. "I wouldn't make him any angrier."

"What's he going to do to us?" I said. "You know he is just all talk." While Mick had no problem yelling at us, I couldn't imagine the man taking any action beyond that.

"Go ahead," Decker said. "I'm staying with Quinn. We'll be there soon."

"I think you should come with us," Lainie said, keeping her eyes on Decker.

"No." Decker kicked at the door, and it reverberated with a dull thudding noise. It was too solid to dent. "Mick is coming out of there, one way or the other."

"Hang on, Decker, let's figure this out once everyone is out of here." I didn't want Piper or the other younger ones to see Decker get too worked up. No matter what was wrong, it wouldn't do any good if people starting crying about it. I wiped the sweat from my forehead. Even though the sun was already going down, the heat radiating off the ground wasn't helping with the dizziness.

"Let's go then," Lainie said. "You will come over soon, right? The little ones will like it if you play some music for them. It will calm them down."

"Yes," Decker said. "Go on without us."

"Good. Who else is hungry?" Lainie took Piper by the hand and pulled her along, the others falling into place behind her.

As soon as they were gone, I noticed how quiet the depot area became. The only sound was a distant thundering from far off in the jungle. Mira heard it too, because I saw her look in that direction as if she was trying to judge the distance. I rubbed my face. Even though almost everyone had left, I felt like I could still see them with one part of my brain, and I could hear the conversation that had just happened. My brain felt too overloaded, like the shock had made everything inside my head scream for attention.

"You do look like you are going to be sick," Mira said. "Maybe you should go back to your living quarters."

"Soon." I wasn't sure I could walk that far yet.

Decker kicked the door again. "What does Mick mean he controls things down here? It's like he's staging some sort of coup, trying to take over. My father is going to kill him."

I had never heard Decker quite so furious. "But that's crazy," I said. "Think about it. Mick can't control the whole space station, not from down here. Even if he went up there, no one would let him take over. And why would he even want to do that?"

"My father has been worried about raiders with all the valuable bots up there," Decker replied. "The raiders could get in and get out so quickly there's no time to fight them. That's why they've increased the defense capabilities on the station." Decker tried the door control again and ended up pounding on that too. "Maybe Mick is working with some raiders. My father's been suspicious of him for a long time. He says they never should have hired Mick and he's planning to order an investigation."

"But it's a government facility," I argued. "I can't imagine raiders stealing bots, knowing the government would come after them. Besides, how would they even know about it? It's all supposed to be top secret." None of my relatives, except for my grandfather, knew what planet we were on, so I didn't know how raiders could have found out about the station. It all sounded too improbable to me. I knew raiders operated throughout the galaxy, but they usually just went after supply ships. I'd never heard of any bold enough to raid official stations.

"Mick could have sold the information about the location to them," Decker said.

Knowing Mick, I could almost believe that. Maybe Decker was on to something. The man didn't seem to like anyone, or act like he cared about the work going on, as long as it didn't interfere with his little domain. "Mira, does your uncle ever talk about Mick? Has he noticed anything odd?"

"He wouldn't speak of such things to me," Mira said. She added, "The dark is coming and the mists are rising. We shouldn't stay out in the open much longer."

"We don't know what's going on up at the station," Decker said. "Maybe there are people up there on Mick's side. If he does it fast enough, how can anyone stop him? The nearest base is fifteen standard days away."

"You're getting way ahead of yourself," I said. "Can you imagine the researchers agreeing to work with raiders?"

Decker snorted. "They probably wouldn't even notice what they were agreeing to do. Sometimes people who are really smart about one thing are really dumb about everything else, like most of the technos up there."

"That's ridiculous. Don't you think they'd notice raiders strolling around the station?

"Well, then you explain it."

"I can't," I admitted.

"I'm getting into this depot one way or the other. I bet the Fosaanian can get in." Decker turned to Mira. "Why don't you go get your uncle? He can help us."

"No, no!" Mira backed away from us, looking frightened. "Not my uncle."

"Fine," Decker said. "If you won't help us, Quinn and I'll go to Hadestown and get him ourselves."

"You can't just walk into the camp without warning!" Mira darted forward and clutched at my arm. "It's not allowed!"

More allowing and not allowing. And why was she calling her village a camp? What was it with the Fosaanians?

"It's allowed by us," Decker gave one more half-hearted pound on the door.

"It will be all right," I said, "once we explain what's happening."

"It's too dark," Mira protested. "You can't take the path at night. There are too many dangers for an Earther who doesn't know Fosaan. It will be dangerous even for me. I should have gone home long ago." Already the sounds from the jungle were starting, the nightly hoots and bizarre screaming noises. "Wait until morning."

"We have lights." I pointed the flashmarks on my shirt.

"You can't use those. You'll make yourself a target for anything that wants a meal!" Mira spoke as if she was talking to a child.

"I'm sure Mick has some small wrist lights in the supply pod," Decker said. "We'll use just enough to see our way. That's not going to stop us. Right, Quinn?"

I couldn't imagine waiting around for hours, hearing the humming noise playing over and over in my head. "Right," I said. "We can take Mick's ricquin. We'll fly it along the beach and keep it high enough off the ground that nothing could get us."

"Good idea," Decker said, "as long as Mick hasn't been taking it apart again."

This wasn't exactly the way I had planned to get to see the Fosaanian village, but now that the opportunity was there, I wasn't going to let it go. "Mira, you should come with us," I said. "If it's too dangerous for us to take the path at night, it's too dangerous for you too." Another shriek sounded and then cut off.

"No it isn't. I know what to look out for in the jungle." Even though she spoke the words confidently, I didn't think she looked very eager to go. She hesitated and then added, "But I can't let you go alone, if you are determined to do this. You'll get hurt if you tried to pass the sentries without me."

"Why do you even need sentries?" Decker asked. "There isn't anyone else on the planet besides us, right?"

"It is just our way. Now if we are going, let's not stand here." Mira shifted her gaze away from us back to the jungle.

I could tell she was being evasive about the sentries, but I didn't want to waste time finding out why. Her uneasiness made me uneasy.

"I'm in the pilot's seat then," Decker said flatly.

"Fine, as long as you don't ditch us in the ocean," I said. Considering how shaky I felt, I wasn't going to waste time arguing over who got to pilot even though I was far better at it than Decker, who thought the thing would fall to the ground if he didn't keep it at full speed. No subtlety in Decker's flying, just as there was no subtlety in anything else he did.

The riquin was just a two-seater, so Mira and I crammed into one seat. The design was considered old-fashioned, based very loosely on an old Earth vehicle called a rickshaw, but I knew Mick liked them for how easy they were to keep running. Mick would joke that in a pinch they could always add wheels, remove the power bot and replace it with a young Earther to pull them around, just like a real antique rickshaw. I didn't think it was funny until I had looked up a picture of a rickshaw. Mick wasn't too far off.

As soon as we were away from the lights that surrounded the depot, it was almost completely dark, except for a band of orange to the west. Because of the atmosphere, Fosaan's sun appeared far more orange than Earth's, and it always led to a spectacular glow on the horizon at the end of the day. Without any moons, everything turned to black as soon as the sun set, except for the faint light from the stars. Decker ordered the running lights on and a small circle illuminated around us.

"Don't get too close to the cliffs," Mira warned.

"I'm not going to fly us into them," Decker snapped. "I know what I'm doing. I've got the distance sensors set."

"I'm not worried about your capabilities. The caves in the cliff face hold some creatures who might be hungry," Mira said. "You need to move further away."

Decker spoke the command, and the ricquin shifted out further from the dark shapes. The night mists were thick along the cliff and I couldn't make out any caves in the stone faces, but I didn't doubt Mira's word. What did live in the cliffs? I'd need to know before I did much exploring, but I didn't want to quiz Mira with Decker listening. Decker didn't need to know about my plans. I was fairly confident I was going to be able to convince Mira to go along with me. It was a good sign she seemed to want to be around Earthers, maybe even around me in particular, though it was tough to tell.

I wouldn't admit it to Decker, but it was partly true what Decker had said about the researchers. They only concentrated on their work. When my mother was involved in solving a problem, she didn't even notice where she was half the time. I had gotten used to reminding her she should eat and sleep once in a while.

The ocean glowed faintly like someone had sprinkled yellow glow paint all over it. I had seen the glow from the microscopic phosphorescent plankton before, but now, this far away from the lights of the compound, I realized the entire ocean was full of them, billions of them. As I watched, the water beneath us darkened and I wondered why the ricquin was suddenly casting a shadow. I looked down and saw a huge dark shape in the water running right beneath us. At first I thought it was the shadow of the vehicle, but I couldn't figure out why it didn't have the right shape. Then the shadow changed shape, extending wing-like flippers and I could see it was a body, a massive body with a narrow head, so out of proportion, it was grotesque. The thing moved in tandem with the ricquin, easily matching its own speed to the vehicle's movement.

"Um, Mira, what is that thing down there? Is it dangerous?"

Mira leaned over the edge, and then a second later flung herself back, screaming, "Go higher! Go higher!"

Chapter 5

I have become aware that many things were kept secret from me. I am apparently considered an old fool who has no counsel worth giving. Since the Apocalypse, we have lived by the decree that to survive, we should not go beyond the known. Now I learn we have not been abiding by that for a long time.—Erimik, historian of the Family

Mira's movements made the riquin tip to Decker's side. I grabbed hold of the edge as I felt myself slam into Decker.

"Manual switch!" Decker yelled to the control. "Quinn, move, so I can drive!" He jabbed me in the side so I tried to give him room. "What's happening?" he shouted.

I leaned back over the edge. At first I didn't see anything. A geyser of water gushed up from the surface, drenching the riquin. I shut my eyes, but the blast was so strong I could still feel the salt water sting them. When I opened my eyes I was staring right into long needle-sharp fangs coming out of the impossibly narrow mouth.

The fangs gnashed at the edge of the riquin, making a screeching sound as they scraped on the door panel. They caught on the latch and the weight of the creature made the riquin tip almost completely on its side. I felt myself sliding toward the water so I grabbed hold of the edge with one hand, bracing my feet. With the other, I hit at the creature's ugly snout. I was hardly thinking at that point. I felt Mira next to me, and then saw a flash of silver light. She had a blade in her hand and she stabbed at the creature's bulging eyes. The blade connected with one, and the thing gave a squeal so loud and high-pitched I thought my eardrums were going to burst. Finally, the mouth opened, and the creature fell back into the ocean, the huge splash nearly engulfing the riquin.

I held on, knowing there was nothing else I could do. If Decker couldn't keep control of the riquin, we'd all go into the ocean, and that thing would be waiting for us.

The riquin leveled off. "Do you still see it?" Decker shouted.

I looked over the side. The water below was calm again, except for the receding ripples from the creature's impact. No shadow, no nothing. "I think it's gone." I sat back and took a deep breath, waiting for the hammering of my heart to stop. "What was that?" I asked Mira, feeling her trembling beside me.

"It's a rheisious," she said. "They are usually only out in the deep ocean. I've never even seen a live one, only drawings of them."

I wiped my face, tasting the salt on my mouth. "Those definitely weren't listed on the planetary inventory. I wonder how high they can get out of the water?"

"I don't want to find out," Decker said, directing the riquin up another few meters.

I watched as Mira cleaned her blade on her tunic. Her hand was still shaking. "Where did you get that knife?" I asked. It was like it had appeared out of nowhere. I couldn't see any place where she could conceal a weapon in her clothes, which consisted of leggings and a sleeveless tunic belted at the waist. The only place to conceal it would be a tiny pouch attached to the belt, but the knife wouldn't fit there.

She didn't answer. The knife handle looked more like jewelry than a weapon. I looked more closely at the belt and then I understood. "The handle is part of the design on your belt." Rows of cylindrical beads in black and silver studded the belt, all in the same design as the knife handle.

She snapped the blade closed, folding it into a slot in the handle and snapping it back onto a spot on the back of her belt. "It's necessary to carry weapons on Fosaan. You both should carry something."

"I didn't think," I said. "I have a small impak back in my room, but I didn't think to bring it. It probably wouldn't have done much good on that thing. It's only rated to stop something less than a hundred kilos."

"Where'd you get an impak?" Decker snapped at me. "You aren't supposed to have any weapons at all. It's not in the protocol for Fosaan. Only authorized military personnel can have them here."

This didn't seem like a time to complain about my possession of a weapon. "My father left it with me," I said, wishing I hadn't brought it up. Decker could make trouble about it. "When he's doing a supply run, he doesn't like it that we have so little protection. He's not one to rely on other people."

"He's breaking the rules," Decker snarled. "That's why he's just a runner hack these days. Everybody knows he got discharged for refusing to follow orders."

I tried to keep my anger in check. "Just leave it. You don't know the whole story, and I'm not going to bother to enlighten you now." I didn't know the whole story myself. My parents wouldn't talk about why my father went from defense commander of an entire planet to just a contract supply runner pilot, or why my grandfather now only contacted us when he wanted to talk about my future training.

Deciding I was done talking to Decker, I focused on Mira. "All the Fosaanians I've seen wear the same belts," I said to her. "So they've all been loaded down with knives?"

"Didn't you understand me?" she replied. "It's necessary. We're almost at a site where we can land. Look for a small sandy area between two boulders. There, do you see it?"

"How do you know that thing won't attack again when we come down?" Decker asked, keeping the riquin in a hover mode.

"Good question." I didn't want to imagine what those fangs would do to an arm dangling over the edge.

"I think the water is too shallow for it," Mira said, "but I don't know for sure. Can you go in steeply?"

"If it's the best way to avoid that thing, we'll go as steep as we can." Without warning us, Decker practically dived into the landing spot, and I held on to keep from falling out the front. Once we were down, I had to admit the landing was perfect. The beach wasn't much larger than the riquin, and Decker had set it down right in the center.

We all looked back at the ocean, but it was perfectly quiet. "Rheisious aren't able to go on land, right?" I asked.

"No, not as far as I know." Mira got out and opened the pouch on her belt. She pulled out some pieces of gray leathery cord which had some small flat round stones attached to them. At first I couldn't tell what they were, until she put them on. They were bracelets, but instead of putting them on her wrists, she put them around her hand so that they encircled her palms.

"Do you mind if I ask why you are putting on jewelry right now?" The stones were too small to have knives concealed in them, but I suspected this wasn't ordinary jewelry.

"Walking through the jungle at night sometimes requires more than just knives as weapons." She didn't explain in any more detail, instead saying, "We must approach the sentries carefully. They will be very alert now that it's dark." She pointed at a spot between clumps of gigantic grasses, nearly hidden by the mists. "There's the path."

"Exactly what are the sentries guarding against?" I asked. "It can't be us, Earthers I mean. There's no one else on the planet."

She didn't answer my question. "Stop here and wait," she cautioned. "Don't speak." Moving away from us, she disappeared around a corner before I could ask why. Decker and I just stood there. Clicking bug noises filled the air. There weren't any true insects on the planet, but there wasn't another good word for the smaller arthropods, some of which flew and some of which scuttled along on the ground. I could hear the sounds of other creatures that sounded a little like tree frogs.

The sulfur scent was overlaid with a whole array of other scents, odd mixes of odors that were hard to pin down or describe. It seemed everything on Fosaan, plants and creatures, had their own scent to try to stand out from the oppressive sulfur smell. The closest I could come to identifying the scent around us in this place was something similar to orange peel.

"You like the girl, don't you?" Decker said, breaking the silence. "I'll admit she's not bad, but you know fraternizing with the locals isn't allowed on any military outpost."

"I'm not 'fraternizing' with her." I said. "I just met her. And that rule is only for government employees and the military anyway." Even though I'd just met her, there was some sort of connection happening. At least I thought there was. There had been another girl I'd been missing, who was supposed to be here on Fosaan, but things had gone wrong and she'd never made it. I hadn't heard from her in so long, I suspected she no longer missed me.

Decker was quiet for a moment and then said, "I guess that's true about the rule. So is she interested in you?"

I knew why Decker was asking. My friendship with Lainie made Decker angry and jealous most of the time, as if the friendship was what kept Lainie from falling into Decker's arms. Actually, I didn't know what kept Lainie from falling into Decker's arms. I didn't want to know. Deciding I wasn't going to make life easy for him, I said, "She might be interested. She *is* good-looking, almost as pretty as Lainie."

I could hear Decker's intake of breath, but Mira's voice sounded in the distance before Decker could respond. "The password is 'Remember'," she called. "May I approach?"

A man's voice barked, "Mira, is that you? Show yourself!"

"This is more than a little weird," I said softly. "Why do they need passwords?"

"I don't know," Decker shifted beside me, brushing at his arm as if something was crawling on it. "I don't like this. I don't like going in blind into the jungle either."

"Quinn, Decker, come forward." Mira ordered.

"I don't know," Decker said again.

"Look, we're here." I didn't want the trip wasted. "Let's go ahead. The worst thing that can happen is Ansun sends us away." At least I hoped that was the case. The more I learned of Ansun, the more I realized I didn't know.

Decker slapped at his leg like a bug was biting him, but I couldn't see anything. "Okay," he said. "I don't want to stay here. Let's get this over with. I'll go first. You keep an eye on the rear."

When I got a look at the sentries, I was glad Decker and I hadn't tried to come alone. The Fosaanian sentries were big, and managed to tower over us, even though both Decker and I were as tall or taller than most of the Earth adults. None of the Fosaanians who came to the depot matched the size of these two. One in particular was as tall as my father and had arms that bulged with muscles. The man didn't look underfed as did the other Fosaanians I had seen. Both wore clothing that resembled uniforms. All Fosaanian clothing was made of some roughly woven greenish fiber, but over their tunics these men had sashes of a lizard-like skin across one shoulder. I saw they had belts that resembled Mira's, and they also carried weapons strapped to the belts. Not knives or the spears I had imagined they might have, but old-fashioned Earth walthasers by the look of them. I didn't think anyone used those anymore.

"These Earthers need help," Mira said. "There is a problem at the depot."

"You know it is not allowed." The sentry who spoke looked very angry. "I've never seen a more foolish female, roaming in the jungle at this time of night with Earthers! You need to get in and stay where you belong. These two may not pass."

"I've never been foolish, Sato," Mira shot back. "Not *ever*," she said.

The sentry made a strangled noise like a growl. He and Mira stared each other down, and I could feel the tension between them. It was clear the two didn't like each other.

"My uncle will want to see them," Mira insisted, speaking to the other sentry. "He will be displeased if he learns they were kept away. They have important information."

I tried to look as if I knew some important information. I didn't think Mick's locking himself in the depot counted as such, but I'd go along with Mira's efforts if it got us past the sentries.

The other sentry, who acted interested rather than angry, said something I didn't quite catch and motioned for the bigger one to move away from us. The two moved a couple of meters down the path and spoke to each other in voices too low for me to hear. Finally, the muscled one gave a slight nod of his head and the other said, "We've decided you should take them to Ansun."

Mira gestured to Decker and me to follow her. As I passed between the two men, I could feel their tenseness, and as I moved away from them, I knew they were watching, hands no doubt still on their weapons. I hoped they didn't have a change of heart. The muscled one said again, "Foolish girl!" but neither followed us.

"Is your uncle in charge here?" Decker asked Mira. "They acted like he was important."

Once again, Mira didn't answer the question. "When we get there, it would be best if you let me do the talking," she said instead. "And you should quit talking now and pay attention to the ground when you walk. Sometimes the night worms crawl onto the path. If you step on them, their insides will burn through your foot coverings into your skin."

I stopped dead, one foot still in the air. "*Now* you tell us. I don't know what a night worm looks like. How easy are they to see?"

"You'll see them. They glow slightly." She walked off, and I hurried to catch up, trying to stay close without stepping on her heels. I assumed the worms wouldn't speed crawl onto the path in between Mira's steps and my own. The area around us was quiet, except for the occasional slap Decker gave himself. I was glad my blood wasn't as tasty as Decker's to whatever was munching on him.

The path continued on through dense plant growth, barely wide enough for one person. Foliage brushed against us as we went along. I could see flickering lights in the distance and hear the sounds of voices. Just before we reached the edge of the village, I heard a rustle in the foliage.

"What's that?" I tried to grab at Mira to pull her to a stop, but before I could, a dark shape jumped in front of us, the shadow of a knife in an upraised hand. I was amazed when Mira sprang at the shape.

"No, Tasim!" she hissed. I trained my light on the figure. It was the younger Fosaanian from the station, Mira's cousin.

"Move, Mira." The boy kept his knife raised and tried to shove her out of the way with his other hand, but she grabbed hold of his arm. I saw he wore the same type of bracelets around his hands as Mira did.

"Get out of my way Quinn," Decker ordered. "I've got this."

"I don't think so." I stayed put between the boy and Decker. I could see Mira's fingers digging into her cousin's arm. She seemed like she had no intention of letting go, but if she did, I didn't think Decker stood much of a chance. Fists against a knife didn't make for great odds, and Tasim looked as if he knew what he was doing with the weapon.

"Did they force you to bring them here?" the cousin asked, never taking his eyes off Decker.

"No, I offered to bring them," she said.

Tasim dropped his attention from Decker and turned to Mira. "That was foolish! You know it's not allowed."

"There's trouble at the depot." Mira let go of his arm. "Will you two stand down so I can talk and you can listen? Please, Tasim." I could see the reluctance in the boy's expression, though he did lower the knife.

Mira stayed close to her cousin, but turned so she could speak to all of us. "Tasim, the Earthers need help. I wanted to talk to Uncle about it."

"No, Mira, you can't disturb him. He's in a staff meeting and something important is happening. In fact, it's the only reason you're not in trouble. Nobody but Cadia and me has noticed you've been missing. She's been asking for you. It hasn't been one of her good days." Tasim said in a louder voice to Decker and me, "Ansun won't see you."

"We'll wait until Ansun is done and ask him ourselves," Decker said.

"It could be all night. You can't stay in the camp that long and you don't want to wait in the jungle," Tasim said.

I became aware of a hissing noise off to my right. I didn't like the sound of it.

"It doesn't matter. We'll wait." Decker crossed his arms like he was settling in to wait right there.

The hissing noise grew louder. Mira shifted, her face uneasy. "Let's get into the camp at least," she said. "We shouldn't stay out here any longer."

It sounded like a good plan to me. I was more than ready to get to some place of relative safety. Whatever the source of the sound, I could guess it wasn't something I wanted to come face to face with in the dark in the middle of the jungle. I didn't envy the sentries having to listen to that noise all night.

"Tasim, let's get to the camp and talk about this more," Mira urged. Tasim seemed to decide the hissing noise was more of a problem than we were, because he finally gave in to Mira's pleading, and hastened down the path in front of us.

The path grew easier to see the closer we drew to the village, and I realized the light from the village was spilling out into the jungle. We reached two sentries in front of a stone archway. While Mira talked to them, I examined the entrance, wondering why the Fosaanians had bothered to build an entrance to their village when there were no walls surrounding it. I looked more closely at a thick line of plants came right up to either side of the archway. I recognized the leaves of the santovi, the plant with the thorns as long as my hand. It was clear no one could sneak into the village undetected through those.

Once again Mira had to use the threat of her uncle's displeasure to get us past the sentries. This time it took less argument, perhaps because Tasim went along with her request. The girl led us into the village while the sentries muttered. Tasim waited until we were through and then followed close behind us like he was our guard. As we entered, I tried to keep from staring, but I wanted to take in as much as I could. If the Fosaanians were so unfriendly to visitors, I knew I might not have an opportunity to come back.

There were torches set in the ground burning with enough light to illuminate the whole place, what there was of it. The more I studied the place, the more disappointed I became. It was completely quiet. The village was small and stark and barely appeared lived in. All the houses were exactly the same size, located in a precise pattern in a square around a larger building in the center. Each house had a lower sections made of stone, with woven panels for the walls and the roofs. They all had a strip of bright yellow color applied to the base of them.

"That's the same color as the anguist," I said.

"Yes, we paint them because it deters other creatures from coming into the houses. Nothing on the planet wants to be near an anguist, not even the tachesums. That's why most of the creatures on Fosaan won't eat the fruit of the splitpod, as you call it. It's the same color."

"What's a tachesum?" I asked, struck by the unfamiliar word.

"Something you never want to encounter," Mira said. "This way."

A few elderly people and one younger woman sat on three-legged stools outside the buildings, all of them occupied with some sort of work. One old woman was sewing, the others either sharpening knives or polishing bits of metal. Everyone stared at us as we passed.

I didn't know the total population of the Fosaanians, but I couldn't imagine they were all crammed inside the houses, asleep or silent at this hour. No light or sound came from the center building either. Mira led us all the way through the village until it seemed like she was leading us back into the jungle. As we passed the last house, I could just make out tiny flicks of light from behind the almost solid screen of plants that ringed the village.

I could also smell something cooking in the distance, something spicy and unfamiliar. Whatever it was, it smelled good enough to set my stomach rumbling. Mira lifted a panel made of vines and led us through a tunnel of plants. This time we emerged into a whole other village, one full of people and activity. The buildings behind the screen were larger, and made of stone. A large building guarded by two sentries stood in the center.

I couldn't believe it. "Why is your village divided like this?" I asked. "It's like two different places."

"Among our people we believe it is useful to conceal your strengths."

"Mira, stop! You should hold your words." Tasim sounded angry.

"Concealing from whom?" Decker asked. "Us? The Earthers? Has my father seen this?"

"The Earthers are not very curious about us," Mira said, "As long as we collect the sulfur crystals without complaint, they don't notice or care that we have a whole life of our own."

"Mira!" Tasim was almost shouting.

"Oh, what does it matter?" Mira said. "I hate this. Why does everyone want to live in the past? I want to live in the now. Tasim, you should see what the Earthers have in their living quarters! There is no reason our people can't live well too."

Before I could ask more questions, cheering broke out on the other side of the main building where a group of young Fosaanians stood in a circle. I could see a glimpse of a girl in the middle of the crowd, a girl about my age, who took a flying kick at someone, leaping so high in the air it looked like she could fly. I heard an "umph" and knew the kick made contact.

As we drew closer, I could make out a boy on the ground holding his side. The boy motioned to two others in the crowd and they came forward and helped him up. "She must have quite a kick," I remarked.

Mira shrugged. "Lieta is good. Very few of us like to train against her."

"That was just training?" Decker asked.

The boy spoke to the girl, taunting her with sharp words in a language I hadn't heard before. I should have realized the Fosaanians had another language besides Standard. Whatever the boy said made her so angry she rushed at him. Just as she reached him, he took his foot and hooked it around her leg, knocking her down. She wasn't down for long. In seconds they were facing off against each other again. I thought the kid was an idiot for going back for more punishment. The girl, Lieta, wasn't even breathing hard. Both were wearing the bracelets that Mira and Tasim had. Mira took hers off and put them back in the pouch on her belt as we watched. I still couldn't figure out how they were considered weapons.

"Didn't she just win?" Decker asked.

"No," Tasim said, "You only win when your opponent can't come after you. Lieta made an error. She took the victory of the body and forgot about the mind and the clan."

It looked like Lieta was going to correct her error. She came in close and lightning fast to the boy, backhanding him across the face. The boy stopped in mid-attack for a moment like he'd been frozen. It was enough. She knocked him to the ground and put her foot on his chest.

"That's intense," Decker said. I thought I caught an admiring tone in Decker's voice.

"What happened there?" I asked. "Why did he stand still?"

"It's the sian," Mira pointed to the stone on the back of her bracelet. "It's a last chance weapon, because you have to be close enough to hit the attacker on uncovered skin. If you hit hard enough, the stone makes them unable to move for long enough to take them down, if you are lucky."

"That's bizarre," I said. "How could a stone do that?" There was far more to Fosaan and the Fosaanians than I had ever realized. I couldn't think of any reason a stone would have that kind of effect, unless it was highly magnetic or something.

"We heat them and soak them in ... " Mira began.

"Enough!" Tasim shouted, cutting her off.

Tasim's shouts made everyone turn their attention to us. There was silence and then a murmur of voices grew. Several adults came out of the houses, as if the change in the sound of the voices outside had alerted them to trouble. A group of younger Fosaanians started toward us, but Mira called, "Not now. We're waiting for my uncle. We'll wait in here." She pointed to one of the houses, and I was glad to go in. It was too strange being the center of so much attention.

Once we were inside, I couldn't contain my interest at the chance to see the contents of a Fosaanian house. It was very dim, but from what I could tell, the furniture was minimal, made of plant material, and all of it looked uncomfortable, like no one spent much time just hanging around inside. There was no clutter, nothing like the stuff I had strewn all over our unit, except for a collection of crystals and rocks lined up on large chest. A second room behind a divider of woven fibers revealed some narrow beds, but that was it.

A movement from the corner caught my eye. A white feline, bigger than an Earth house cat, jumped off one of the beds and stretched, fixing its gaze on us as it did. It padded over to Mira and jumped up on the table next to her, butting its head against her arm. I couldn't believe what I was seeing. There were no mammals of Fosaan and there never had been, not even before the Apocalypse. I'd read the entire list of known species. Where had this creature come from?

"It's a cat," I said.

"Wow, brilliant observation." Decker rolled his eyes.

"I don't know this word, 'cat'." Mira said. "Narween is a felal."

"Do you mean felis?" I asked.

She shook her head. "No, I don't know that word."

"Felis is the Standard scientific name for cats, for felines, but I don't know this species." I moved over to the cat and held out my hand to pet it. "You don't understand, Decker. There aren't supposed to be any cats on Fosaan. There are no indigenous mammals here at all and never have been. Mira, where did you get it?"

The cat's tail whipped toward me and wrapped around my arm, squeezing it so tightly it was painful. "Hey, stop!" I tried to back away but the cat dug in its claws. I thought if I didn't find a way free from it, my fingers would explode from the pressure.

Mira tapped the cat on the head. "Stop, Narween! Be good." The cat's tail gave one last squeeze and then went slack. It threw a baleful look at me and then jumped off the table.

"Sorry," she said. "Narween doesn't like strangers."

"That's no ordinary cat." I rubbed my arm, trying to remember if I'd ever read about a cat species with a death grip tail. I knew I hadn't, because I'd remember something like that. "Where did it come from?" I asked again.

"We've always had felal." Mira sounded puzzled.

"A few survived the Apocalypse," Tasim said.

I wished there were more Fosaanian records. How had a creature like this been overlooked by zoologists? And surely if there had been one type of mammal, there would be others. The felal looked at Decker, who backed up and stood by the door.

"How much longer do you think it will be?" Decker asked. I

could tell the animal made him nervous.

"I told you it could be all night," Tasim said. "Why don't you just leave?"

"Are you hungry?" Mira asked. "I am." She didn't open up the carryall, but instead went over to a small cupboard and pulled out some pieces of flat hard bread and a clay crock. "Here, you dip the bread in the mashed fruit." She held out both to me.

I took a piece of bread and dipped it into some sweet-smelling pulp, then tried to take a bite. My teeth nearly broke off. No wonder her sister couldn't eat it.

"You must wait for the fruit to soften it," Mira said, smiling.

Mira and I were the only ones who ate. Decker and Tasim stood staring at each other like they were just waiting for one to make the wrong move.

An awkward silence fell on the group until I heard children's voices. "Those sound like children cheering. Do they train too?"

"The younger children are listening to the storytellers," Mira said. "They are doing a retelling with mankins ... I think you call them puppets."

"I'd like to watch," I said.

"You won't understand what they are saying," Tasim said. "They tell the story in an ancient language of ours."

"Let's see it anyway," Decker said, striding out the building, ignoring Tasim's protests.

I followed Decker to the other end of the village, Tasim and Mira trailing after us. We passed a huge stone fireplace blazing with flames. One man added wood to the fire while the other held some sort of metal rod in it. "That's a forge, right?" I said to Mira. "I read about those in a history about Earth." It all clicked together. "That's where the blades came from, right?"

She just looked at me, frowning, and then Decker asked, "Is your uncle the leader?"

Mira glanced at Tasim and then said, "No, he is the vice commander. The commander is my grandmother."

"Why don't you just invite them to become one of us?" Tasim started to storm off, but then stopped and came back, refocusing on Decker like he had to keep watch on him. Mira led us to a spot in the rear of a crowd of children seated on the ground in front of a large wooden frame with a woven cloth as a backdrop. The puppets were large and made of painted fabric mounted on sticks.

Tasim was right about the show. I couldn't tell what was going on beyond some big creature attacking Fosaanians, who fought back. Even in small scale, the thing was kind of horrifying. It walked upright and was sort of like a big lizard, dull orange in color, but it had a lower jaw that stuck out with lots of teeth. The worst were the eyes. There were two protrusions on either side of its head, each with a large yellow and black eye. The creature could also use its forelegs like a human, or like a bear, swiping at things and scoping up one tiny sacrificial Fosaanian and then tossing him aside.

There was also a large three-sided puppet thing, not a person or an animal, that wasn't doing anything. It was remarkably similar to the shape I had drawn on the wall at the ruin and to the tattoo on Mira's cheek.

"Are those lizards, or whatever they are, really that big and that ugly?" I whispered. Without mammals as predators, some extremely large lizard creatures were reported to have developed on Fosaan. I really wanted to see one, but hadn't been able to find much information about where they lived.

"The tachesums are much bigger in real life," Mira said. "They made the figure of it too small."

I thought maybe I didn't want to see one so badly after all.

"What's the story about?" Decker asked.

"Not much," Tasim said. "It's very dull."

The lizard puppet made some loud hissing and clicking noises and then killed or wounded one of the Fosaanian puppets. The rest of the puppets fell back, then surged forward to pick up the now prone injured one. One remaining puppet launched a furious attack on the creature, leaping on its back and stabbing it in its throat. The children must have been waiting for this, because they erupted in a loud cheer. The victorious puppet climbed on top of the dead lizard puppet and acted as if he was giving a speech. The other puppets did a celebration dance. Red sparks exploded in the air behind the figures like miniature fireworks.

"Whoa! How are they doing that?" I had never seen a puppet show with fireworks before.

"One mankinner is heating up the sulfi crystals and then throwing them. The crystals break down when they get too hot."

"Is the sulfi the same as the iridium sulfide the researchers need?" Decker asked. "Isn't it too valuable to waste on a puppet show?"

"It's only value to us is for torches and things like the story." Tasim shrugged. "We have much of it. If the Earthers think it is valuable, that is nothing to us."

"I thought you said this was a dull story. It looks exciting to me," I said.

"It's just something that happened in the past," Tasim said.

"What did the hero puppet climb on? That three-sided thing?"

"Mira!" A harsh voice sounded behind us. I had time to see a look of fear flicker across Mira's face before I turned to locate the voice.

Chapter 6

Our youth train to be strong, so that they are worthy of the clan, and it makes one proud to see them. We have so little else now, that I do not question the rightness of the training for most of them. I do wonder if we should give more weight to the importance of the mind, especially to the youth with the intelligence to use it. Are those who lack in strength, yet strong in mind, so worthless?—Erimik, historian of the Family

Mira's uncle strode toward us, a fierce scowl on his face. He was accompanied by two younger men on either side of him, their hands resting on the weapons strapped to their sides. As the three came forward, all the other Fosaanians except Mira and Tasim fell back, forming a circle. I had never paid much attention to Mira's uncle when the man worked for Mick at the station. It was almost as if this man were another person. He walked differently here, quickly and confidently, like he was used to people getting out of his way.

The man stopped inches from me, the sulfur smell radiating strongly off him. I instinctively took a step back. "What are the Earthers doing here?" the man said, his mouth drawn in an angry line. I resisted the impulse to move even farther away, not wanting to look afraid. The man's eyes were so pale they were almost white. I shifted my gaze to the scar on the man's forehead, red and jagged puckered skin red over an indented spot. There was a matching scar on the side of his head, as if something with a very large mouth had tried to bite down on his skull. Even though I could feel the sweat running down my back, I felt cold.

Mira slipped between her uncle and me, in a space so small the curls of her hair touched my face. "Uncle, the person who runs the depot has locked himself in," she said. "And all the other Earther adults are on the space station and no one can communicate with them from Fosaan." I could see Mira's whole body trembling, like she was terrified to speak up, but her voice didn't waver.

"You didn't tell us that." an elderly man from the crowd said.

"The Earther at the depot is unimportant." Ansun said, taking Mira by her shoulders and moving her to the side without even looking at her. Once she was out of the way, the man just stood there looking at me. I noticed Ansun's sash didn't match the rest of them. It had the same three-sided shape of the object from the puppet show worked into it. I realized Ansun, Mira and Tasim were the only ones with tattoos on their faces, but I didn't suppose this was a good time to ask why or what the shape meant.

"Grandfather, some of the Earther children are afraid." Mira addressed the older man now like she was appealing to him to do something. "The younger children." The man frowned and turned to the crowd like he was looking for someone.

"Mira, be silent!" her uncle barked. "There are matters which you do not understand. We'll talk later about why you were even at the station." He motioned to the two younger men accompanying him and then at Decker and me. "Detain these two."

The men moved forward and I took another step back. Mira's grandfather said, "Let them go, Ansun. They're just children."

The two stopped on either side of Decker and me. I wondered if we could make a run for it. It took me only an instant to decide we couldn't. There were too many people pressed too close together.

"This one is more than a child, or at least he thinks he is," Ansun pointed at Decker and then spat on the ground. "He likes to give orders, not take them." I hoped Decker was smart enough not to respond. I had a feeling Ansun was just waiting for a reason to take Decker down.

"Wait." The order came from an older woman with close-cropped grey hair who appeared next to Mira's grandfather. She walked up to Decker, her eyes narrowing as she examined him. The woman wasn't tall, but she looked strong and athletic, and moved like she was much younger. I saw that she had the three-sided symbol tattooed on her cheek. The crowd fell silent. A toddler started to speak, but the mother shushed him, and carried the boy away.

The woman turned her attention to me, but only for a few seconds. "We don't need to be encumbered with them," she said, like she was making a pronouncement. "It's too much of a bother to detain them, and we have more important matters to think of. Send them away. They probably won't survive the trip back to the station anyway." Without waiting for anyone to reply, she left the circle, the crowd parting for her.

"Great," I muttered. No one appeared at all shocked at the woman's words, or acted as if they cared Decker and I might be eaten in the jungle. I wished the Earthers would have worked a little harder at befriending the Fosaanians.

Mira's uncle looked as if he wanted to disagree with the woman, but after a moment he spat again and turned away. "Go then and don't return," he said, moving over to the older man and speaking in a voice too low for me to hear.

I wasn't going to wait for Ansun to change his mind. No matter what we might face in the jungle, I wanted to get away. This whole place and the people in it made me uneasy. "Okay, we're gone," I said to no one in particular, taking a few steps in the direction of the other village. If we were lucky, the crowd would part for us too so Decker and I could just walk away like the woman had done.

"Uncle, what about the young Earthers?" Mira asked.

"In the morning, I will open up the depot," Ansun said. "Someone will deal with the children then." I stopped. I didn't like the sound of that. What did he mean by deal with?

"I need to take Quinn and Decker back," Mira said. "They don't know the dangers."

"NO!" Ansun's face turned red as he yelled at Mira. "You stay. Their lives are not your responsibility. Tasim, take these two to the sentries and tell them the Earthers are not allowed to pass again."

Tasim scowled and motioned for Decker and me to follow him. The crowd did part for the Fosaanian boy. I had one last look at

Mira. Her uncle was lecturing her, but she had a stubborn expression on her face like she didn't care what he was saying. For a girl who seemed terrified of the man, it was impressive she stood up to him.

I followed behind Decker and Tasim, keeping my eyes on the people watching us pass. Most of them didn't look as hostile as Ansun. They seemed more curious than anything else. A few of the younger ones even smiled at me.

When we pushed through the vine screen, the outer village appeared either completely asleep or completely empty. I couldn't tell which. Tasim walked faster and I had to jog to catch up, going around Decker to get close enough to speak to the Fosaanian boy. "So that older woman, the one with the tattoo on her face," I said, "that's Mira's grandmother, right? I guess that makes her your grandmother too. Mira said she was in charge."

Tasim didn't answer, but I knew he was right. When the woman had spoken, everyone had listened to her. I tried another question. "If Mira is your cousin, does that make Ansun your father?"

Tasim stopped and whirled around to face me. "You don't need to know any of this," he said. "I'm warning you. Don't speak to Mira again. You'll only bring harm down on her."

"How could that harm her?" I asked, but Tasim was already moving again, calling out to the sentries by the archway.

The two were slouched over, as if they were bored out of their minds. They straightened up when Tasim spoke to them. "I'll return in moment," he said. "These two are not to reenter." The sentries stared at Decker and me like they were trying to memorize out features, as if so many Earthers tried to come to the village, they couldn't keep us all straight. Tasim took off so fast down the path that he didn't appear the least bit concerned about the worms Mira had warned us about. I went slowly enough to see what was in front of my feet before I put them down. Decker pushed around me, acting impatient at my pace. I saw that he was pale and drenched in sweat, his shirt soaking. It was still hot, but not enough for that. Seeing Decker shaken up was a new experience.

It didn't take long to reach the outer sentry post, and once there, Tasim practically pushed Decker and me down the path, then stood between the sentries with his arms crossed as if daring us to try to come back.

Decker started to jog and I sped up to keep up, trying to listen to sounds from the jungle and keep my eyes on the path at the same time. I didn't hear the hissing noise anymore. A rustling in the protoferns next to the path made Decker leap backward, knocking me off balance. "What are you doing?" I asked.

"Didn't you hear that noise?"

"I hear lots of sounds. Are you going to jump at every one?"

"It's hard not to jump."

That was true. All I could think of was Ansun's scar and the creature that could have caused such an injury. The night mists were coming up thickly, obscuring everything more than a meter away. For some reason, I found I could remember all the details of the path, knowing where it narrowed and where it turned. I noticed my hands were quivering again, and the dizziness was back, though not nearly as intense as it had been. I hoped I didn't have some sort of weird nerve damage from the shock the bot had given me.

"I don't get it," Decker said. "There is more going on here than anyone guessed, but I don't know what they are hiding or why. My father never knew they had weapons. He'll be furious when he finds out the Fosaanians have been trading with raiders for arms."

"But their weapons are old," I said. "If they were trading with raiders, wouldn't they get better ones?"

"Depends on what they have to trade. There's nothing on the planet raiders would want, unless the Fosaanians are stealing some of our supplies to trade."

I knew we were missing something. I just couldn't figure out what. "It doesn't make sense. Why would they hide their real village behind another one? And why did it seem more like a military camp than a village? The ones who were fighting weren't just playing around. They were serious." I thought back to what else I had read about Fosaan and their culture before the Apocalypse, but there hadn't been much information, except something about a weird secretive trial of strength.

"Having your planet nearly destroyed might make anyone a little less peaceful," Decker said. "Let's just get back and see if Mick is still barricaded inside."

I spent the trip back in the riquin leaning over the side, hoping I wouldn't see a dark shape in the water again. I didn't see or hear anything. Even the sounds coming from shore were muted, as if all the creatures there were just crouched in the jungle, motionless, waiting until daylight came.

The depot stood in silence; the one lightglobe illuminated the emptiness in front of the buildings. The only signs of life came from the remains of the pulp from the splitball game. Thousands of tiny black creatures covered the splatters, making it look as if they were pulsating. Usually Mick made whoever was playing wash down the ground after a game of splitball, but no one had thought of that today. Decker pounded on the door again. As I feared, there was no answering yell from Mick. It would have been good to get Mick's take on the Fosaanians. For all his faults, he wasn't a stupid man.

Finally, I said, "Leave it, Decker. We can't do anything else tonight. If Ansun can get in, we'll just wait until morning."

Decker muttered some curses about Mick's level of intelligence, but ended up following me to the living quarters. When we reached Lainie and Saunder's unit, there was silence there too. I pushed open the door panel. In the main living area, sleeping children were sprawled all over the floor, coverlets and pillows everywhere. Piper was uncovered, curled up in a ball in one corner, like a small animal trying to keep warm. Lainie stirred and lifted her head up to look at us, pushing back her hair that lay like a black shiny curtain across her face. She yawned and got up, stepping over and between children to get to us.

"I saved you some food," she whispered. "It's not much, because everyone was famished, but it's better than nothing. Let's take it outside. I don't want anyone to wake up and start crying for their parents."

We went back out to sit on the walkway and Lainie gave us some packets of mixed nuts and fruit. I ripped mine open and ate it quickly while Decker told Lainie a little about our trip to the village. He left out far more than he told, and I suspected he didn't want to worry her.

"So we just wait until tomorrow," Lainie said, yawning.

She was right. There wasn't anything else to do. I could feel a yawn coming on myself.

We sat there for a while looking at the water until Lainie said, "I'm tired but I'm awake now. Decker, would you play me a song? I like your music now that you are better at it."

I was surprised at Lainie's request. I didn't remember anyone ever asking Decker to play, though the few times I had come upon Decker practicing, the music hadn't been half bad. Acting embarrassed, Decker took the carine from around his neck and began to play very softly. The peculiar notes of the instrument floated out across the water. I had always thought it strange for someone like Decker to choose to play such an unusual instrument.

Decker finished one song and Lainie complimented him on it, moving a little closer to him and asking for another. Suddenly, I felt out of place. It was an established fact that Decker had a thing for Lainie, but it had also been an established fact that she wasn't interested. Now it felt like she was.

I got up. "I'm going back to my place too." Nobody protested, so I decided it was a good time to leave. When I reached home, Mags as waiting for me.

"Hallelujah," she said, her way of saying hello. "The bird is hungry," she added, hopping up and down indignantly.

"Sorry, Mags," I said, getting out some food and filling a tray for her. She settled onto her perch and cracked seeds with a relish. I watched her.

"Nighttime," she said.

"You're right about that." Flopping down on a chair, I laid my head back and closed my eyes. It was too quiet. Besides the sound coming from Mags, the only other noise was the sound of the waves lapping on the living quarter supports. Usually I didn't notice the noises around me when I was alone, because I had too many projects to work on, but now there was too much silence. I turned the sound on the scene setter to rain. Mags liked that one, except sometimes it inspired her to make thunder noises which were a bit too realistic.

As I was about to check the comm unit again, I heard another rustling sound from the kitchen. Even though I knew it couldn't be Mira, I found my breath speeding up at the thought she might have come back. A louder noise, like something falling, made me jump up. I went into the kitchen and found the olon sitting on an empty container in the middle of the floor.

"I'm too tired to chase you away," I said. "But you can't stay if you're going to make a racket." The olon stared at me unblinking. I didn't know why I kept talking to the little creature, except it actually acted like it was listening to me. Being in the kitchen made me realize just how hungry I was. I found some fruit packs in another container and filled a bowl with it. We were getting low on food. With any luck a supply ship would arrive soon, I thought, and then caught myself. What was I doing thinking about food when we had much bigger problems to worry about? The olon hopped closer, its attention focused on the bowl in my hand. It gave one little squawk.

"Okay," I sighed. "I get the message." I tossed a bit of fruit in the air and the olon caught it neatly in its beak. "You'd better get out of here before Mags notices you." Taking the rest of the food back into the living area, I sat down at the comm unit. When I activated it, the slip stayed clear, no error message, nothing. I couldn't think of what to do, and I was so tired it was tough to stay upright. Not wanting to leave the comm unit, I stretched out on some cushions on the floor, looking out at the night sky and the stars. The light of the space station, bright and steady, stood out, glowing strongly. I got up and reset the room to mimic the night, surrounding myself with stars all over the room. I lay back down, staring at them, wondering if Mira had worried about us in the jungle, wondering if she had thought of me at all after we left the village.

Right before I fell asleep, I turned over and thought I saw some random light flickers on the comm unit. I stared at it, but the slip stayed off. Deciding I must be imagining it, I let my eyes close.

A soft ping from the comm unit woke me some time later. I could tell it was very early in the morning by the dim light filtering in through the window. Mags was in her cage, her head tucked under her wing. The comm pinged again and the slip came on. To my surprise, the message light was flashing.

"Play," I said.

No image appeared, but after a few seconds lights began to flash on it in different spots on the slip. It was like watching a light show, the kind young children learned how to make in school in art class. Whatever it was, it wasn't a message. Probably just another glitch. I was about to turn it off when one of the patterns caught my attention. It went on and off so fast I almost thought I imagined it. Some of the lights looked like they were making the letter "n." I sat back down, concentrating hard on the slip. Not all the lights making the "n" were on at the same time, but if I stared at one spot on the slip, the lights flashed in sequence quickly enough so that it looked like a letter for an instant.

It *was* a letter. I focused my attention on the left, trying to see if there was another letter. I wrote down each letter, until I had a message. I sat back, stunned. It read "N dont get on the … " That's all there was. I watched again, hoping more of the message would show up, but after nearly ten minutes I sat back. There was nothing more.

I knew the message was from my mother. She was the only one who still occasionally called me Nin, from back when I was learning to talk and couldn't say my own name.

I sat back, watching the message flash over and over. Now that I knew what to look for, I could see it clearly. Why would she send a message like that?

"Info," I ordered the unit, and then waited to see the data behind the message. Nothing came up, no time stamp, no sender, nothing.

Chapter 7

We have always been taught to hide our strengths. It is one of the earliest lessons for the young, but by hiding strengths, are we also blinding ourselves to the nature of them? In our congratulations of our own cleverness, does that give us a false sense of superiority? I suspect every people think themselves superior to all others.—Erimik, historian of the Family

I didn't know it was possible to block the source of incoming files. I'd never spent much time delving into how the comm units worked. I needed Lainie. She had incredible skill with the comm units and was always after her father to teach her more, though she'd be considered a security risk if he taught her too much. Lainie's father was the techno manager of the space station, and he could outwit and outcarve any carver who tried to break in.

When I went out the door, I glanced toward the shore, hoping to see some activity at the station. The night mists hadn't burned off completely, still cloaking the whole area in light fog. There was no movement except for one small creature scuttling across the flat area. I couldn't make out what it was.

Inside Lainie and Saunder's quarters I had to pick my way through the sleeping bodies to where Lainie lay. Kneeling down beside her, I whispered, "Lainie, wake up."

Her eyes flicked open and then closed again. "Go away," she said. "I'm really sleepy."

"I know, but this will only take a minute. There was something on my comm unit, something strange." That at least made her open her eyes. "Is your unit locked down?" I asked. "I want to see if you have the same image on your slip."

She sat up and held up her arm like she was waving at the slip, and then folded her hand like she was making a rabbit shadow puppet with her fingers, hopping it up and down.

"What are you doing?" I asked.

She grinned. "It's my new security system, coded only to my hand size and specific motion. The comm unit won't recognize the image of any other hand unless it exactly matches mine doing a bunny hop."

"Good one," I said. I went over to the comm unit and tried to connect to the one at my place. Nothing happened. "I can't get it to work here." Lainie groaned softly and got up, rubbing her eyes "It was there," I said. "I think I had a message from my mother, but I can't retrieve it here. It must be set just to display on our unit."

"Let's go then," Lainie said, making her way around people. Saunder opened his eyes and Lainie just waved at him. "Go back to sleep," she said. He closed his eyes and rolled over.

As we walked over to my quarters, she asked, "So what do you mean strange?"

"I'd rather you see it than have me tell you."

Lainie shrugged, "Okay, but you'll have to approve me so I can access it. Your mom has yours voice-printed, right?"

"Right," I said. I hadn't thought about that.

When we went in, Mags was awake. "Lainie person!" she called. "Hallelujah!"

"Hallelujah, Mags," Lainie said, sitting down at the comm unit. "Give it the okay for my voice."

I gave the commands and then Lainie ordered the unit to start up. Nothing happened for a few seconds. Another giant yawn racked her. She sat back and stretched, but when the slip flickered, she straightened up, watching the lights appear and disappear. "Why are you showing me this? It's just a light show."

"Just watch for a minute, and then tell me if you see something." She stared at it, and when she leaned in, I could tell she was starting to see it.

"I see letters," she said. "The lights are making the image of letters. That's it, right?"

"Right. They say … "

"Don't tell me," she cut me off. "I want to figure it out myself." It only took her a few seconds. "It looks like 'N dont get on.' Is that what you are seeing?"

"Yes! I think it's a message to me from my mother. She calls me Nin sometimes. Could she send that from the Station without any tracking information on it? It doesn't look like it's coming through as a normal message."

"I don't know. I never thought about that." Lainie ran her fingers over the slip like she was trying to get information from it. "I can't think how someone could do it right now, but if I worked on it, I might. It's not through a normal path, that's for sure. I could probably only send it to my father's unit though, because that's the only interior spec address I know. He might think it was an attempt by someone else to gain illegal access and block it, because I'm not supposed to know it."

"That means your father would have to see it and realize it's a message from you before he blocked it," I said. "Something isn't right, more than just the bad communication link and no shuttle. The Fosaanians aren't acting like ... like we think they act." I explained as well as I could, trying to make her understand my uneasiness. I finished by saying, "So this Ansun is more like the head of a military group than some leader of a peaceful village."

"It could just be a part of their culture we don't know about," she said, getting up to look out at the station. "No one really knows anything about them."

"It just didn't feel right. I think Ansun knows why the communications are cut off. And the message. It said 'don't get on'." The only thing we would be getting on would be the shuttle."

"So what do we do?"

"I'm not sure, but I'm not getting on the shuttle if it comes back."

"I want to tell Saunder and see what he thinks." Lainie yawned again. "I'm really having trouble waking up." She frowned. "Do you realize your hand is shaking?"

I looked down to see my hand trembling. I put my other hand over it. "It's a side effect from the shock, I think. I can't really feel it."

"That's not good," Lainie said.

Just then Piper burst in. "Lainie, there you are! We're eating teinbread at your place. Come on, Saunder's making the bread cook in funny shapes for everyone. He made me a moustache. I was going to save it to show you, but I got too hungry and ate it. Do we have any juice tablets? We're all sharing what we have."

I was hungry. The snacks from the night before hadn't been enough. "We're out of tablets, and we don't have much else." I'd given a lot to Mira.

"That's okay," Lainie said. "I'm sure there is plenty of food around in other units. Let's go. We'll send people to go collect what they can find."

When we went into Lainie's and Saunder's place, Lainie asked, "Anybody seen Decker?"

"He stopped in few minutes ago and said he was going to the depot," Saunder said. He lowered his voice, "I didn't want him to stay because he's scaring the younger ones. He won't stop talking about Mick and the station and the Fosaanians." He turned away from us and in a louder voice called, "Who wants a star shape?"

I felt a flash of irritation. Why hadn't Decker asked me to come along? I grabbed a fruit pack. "I'm heading to the station too."

"We'll be there soon," Piper said. "Saunder said he'd make up a new game for us."

"Great," I said, glad Saunder had the patience to deal with all the younger ones. I knew I didn't. When I reached the station, I found Decker pounding on the door, his face red with rage. "Decker, stop. I have to tell you something."

After I finished explaining, Decker just shook his head. "Are you sure you just didn't imagine it? Maybe whatever is wrong is causing a malfunction, and you were just seeing random flashing lights."

"I'm telling you it was a message from my mother. What if she is trying to tell us something wrong is happening on the station … like … like what if the oxygen generators aren't working right? There has to be something going on for her to warn us off." I didn't think it was oxygen generators, but I couldn't come up with a better idea.

"None of this makes any sense." Decker gave one more pound on the door and the sound echoed in the building. There was no sound after that. I didn't like the silence. The building felt abandoned, as if no one had been in it for a long time. Decker turned around and then groaned. "Here comes everyone else. We really don't need a bunch of little kids around."

"Lainie and Saunder seem to be handling it okay."

Saunder jogged ahead of the group, joining us at the door. "Look, Decker," he said, "will you at least try to act like nothing is wrong? The younger ones are scared and seeing you kick and hit at the door doesn't help."

Decker didn't answer. He turned and strode off toward the shore, ignoring calls from Piper to join their game.

"At least he's not pounding on anything," I said. I thought Saunder would laugh, but instead Saunder frowned, his eyes focused on something over my shoulder.

I turned to see Ansun with Tasim beside him coming down the cliff path followed by a large group of Fosaanians. The men and women behind them were marching like a troop of soldiers, kicking up little puffs of black sand as they crossed the beach. They all had weapons strapped to their chests. I didn't see Mira. When they reached the station platform, Ansun gave a sharp one-word command I couldn't understand. The Fosaanians fanned out until they surrounded the station. Tasim scowled when he saw us.

"It won't work," I heard Tasim say to Ansun. The MIbot floated out from behind Ansun. I wondered where it had been last night when we were at the village.

"It's already in motion," Ansun said to Tasim. He headed for the station door, ignoring us. The bot followed him. "Open it," he ordered it. "You two, you know what to do," he motioned to a couple of the Fosaanians. The bot hovered in front of the door panel and when it opened, the bot went inside, the two men trailing after it. I tried to follow too, but the old man I recognized from the night before moved in front of me.

"No, you don't want to see," the man said.

"Why not?" I asked.

"The Earther is dead," Ansun said. "He was too weak and stupid to follow orders."

It took a few seconds for me to process Ansun's words. "Mick is dead? How do you know?" I bolted around the old man into the station. I didn't see anything at first, but I smelled something, a sour smell. The two Fosaanians stood halfway down the passageway and I went toward them. They were staring at the floor, at a mound of dust, like volcanic ash. On top of it lay Mick's necklace, the one with the big silver stones, except they weren't silvery anymore. They were black.

The air closed around me, the sour smell more pronounced. I stumbled back outside. Once I was out in the open, I took a deep breath and tried to act normal, though it made me angry to see the expression on Ansun's face, like the man was amused by my reaction. I straightened up, not wanting him to know I was shaken. The younger ones had been too far away to hear Ansun's words, and I didn't want any of them seeing what little was left of Mick.

Lainie came up to me, followed by the whole crowd of younger children. "What happened? Where's Mick?"

I just shook my head, hoping Lainie understood she shouldn't ask too many questions with all the younger ones listening. I took a couple of deep breaths. Lainie started to speak, but when I shook my head again, she stopped, her eyes questioning. "Later," I mouthed.

The elderly man motioned to us. "Bring the younger ones close," he ordered. When we had all gathered, the man said, "The shuttle is coming back for you. You are all to go up to the station to be with your parents. They will explain the situation."

A murmur rose from the children and then Piper cried out, pointing to the shore path. I turned to see Mira's grandmother nearing the station, a tall woman next to her. I was stunned. The tall woman was a raider, no doubt about it. I had never come face to face with a raider before, but the images I had seen matched this one perfectly. She had her head shaved, as most of them apparently did, and her face was covered with the web of fine wrinkles that developed on people who spend years in the dryness of deep space. Her silver-coated teeth shone in the sunlight. I had read the silver coating was more for show than practicality, a symbol of the most successful raiders, the ones who weren't afraid to advertise their profession. This woman didn't look afraid of anything.

Ansun walked over to meet her, and the way he spoke made it clear he knew her. That was a bad sign. If this woman was here, Decker's fears about raiders on the station were probably true. My mother must have been frantic to get us to stay away. That's why she had sent a message. The raiders had a ruthless reputation.

I motioned to Lainie and Decker and Saunder to move to the side of the group so I could talk to them. The older man's attention was on the raider now and he wasn't watching us. "My mother sent the message because of them," I said in a low voice. "Raiders must have taken over the station. We can't go up."

"I don't want to, if there are more like Bald Woman there." Lainie shuddered. "What happened to Mick?"

"He's dead," I said. I didn't want to describe what I had seen.

"Dead? How?" Decker asked.

"I don't know, but Ansun knew about it before anyone went in the station. Something just vaporized him."

"Mick is really dead?" Lainie acted like she hadn't heard anything I had just said.

Before I could tell her again, a whooshing noise drowned out my words. I looked up to see the shuttle descending. It landed precisely on the 'X' marked for it, no pilot visible in the cockpit. Even though I knew the shuttle was programmed to land by itself, it was procedure to have a pilot, just in case something went wrong. The lack of one made my uneasiness grow.

The ramp came down and an AIbot rolled out, one of the standard ones, not the enhanced models. It stopped right at the bottom. "All children are instructed to board the shuttle," it announced.

"What are we going to do?" Saunder asked.

Some of the younger children moved toward the ramp into the shuttle. The bot repeated itself. "All children are instructed to board,"

"What can we do?" Lainie said. "What will the Fosaanians do if we refuse to get on?"

I didn't like to think about that. The Fosaanians could easily force us to do whatever they wanted. Ansun's voice rose over the crowd. I flinched, hoping the man didn't have some sort of super hearing to listen in on what we were debating. Luckily, it looked like Ansun and the raider woman were arguing. The two stood facing each other, speaking in angry voices. All the Fosaanians were listening.

"We can't get on," I said, trying to ignore Ansun and concentrate on figuring out what to do.

"But if we say we won't go," Saunder said, "I have a feeling the Fosaanians would carry us on board if they wanted to."

"What if the whole station has been taken over by raiders?" I asked. "Do you think raiders would keep anyone alive? We might be walking right into a trap. We've all heard the stories about them." When raiders took a supply ship, they didn't leave anyone alive.

"We have to send the younger ones up," Decker said. "Then we stay here and figure out something to do. If we go up there and there's something really wrong, we're stuck. Besides I don't think they would do anything to children."

I didn't like the thought of knowingly sending Piper up to the station if it was full of raiders. "I think we should ask to communicate with someone on the station. We need to hear it's safe to send anyone." I walked over to the bot, glancing back at the Fosaanians. They still weren't paying attention. Ansun was jabbing his finger at the raider woman. She looked about ready to hit him. "AI 72," I said, reading the id on the bot. "Establish a link with the station commander. We have a message."

The AI complied, sending a small hologram in front of it. The slip was nearly transparent for a moment and then a man appeared, not Decker's father. I was surprised to see it was my friend, Gregor Skrim. Gregor didn't usually spend any time in the comm center. Besides inventory control, he did station maintenance and was more likely to be found floating around outside the station patching leaks than sitting in front of a slip.

"Gregor, what's going on?" I noticed the man was sweating, and his skin had an odd mottled cast to it. Gregor's wavy hair usually went in all sorts of crazy directions, but was now flattened down to his head like it was wet. His one earlobe was bloody, and I saw that the earring he usually wore against regulations, a Sondian ruby, was missing.

"Busy times up here," Gregor mumbled, looking up and to the side as if watching something near him. "I'm in charge of communications now, but there are problems, you know. I can only stay on a few seconds. What do you want?"

"We want to know if we should come up to the station," I said. "Is my mother there? Dr. Neen?"

Gregor didn't answer right away. Finally, he said, "She's not available right now." The words came out one by one as if he was having difficulty putting a whole sentence together.

Decker came close. "Where is my father, Commander Rigan?"

"He's not available either." Gregor wiped some sweat from his forehead. "Quinn, you know how it works here. It would be good times if you came up. Everybody listening to music like they always do. Never a dull moment. See you soon." The man turned his head away from the slip and then nodded. "I'm signing off now," he said, and without waiting for us to respond, he ended the connection.

"That answers it," I said, "Everybody listening to music? Nobody listens to music up there. It drives Gregor crazy how the scientists don't want music distracting them. He's trying to alert us there's a problem. And no one would put Gregor in charge of communications or anything else. He's always getting written up for not doing his regular jobs, and he's the lowest level worker there." I knew Gregor was only a few years older than myself, and spent most of his time regretting that he signed on for such an isolated job. He liked fixing things that were broken on the station, but not much else he was assigned to do.

"I think you're right, Quinn. Something is really wrong," Lainie said. "Gregor looked terrible."

"We can't all stay here. You know they aren't going to let us. You all get on board and I'll stay," Decker said. "If I go now they won't even notice me." He started around the side of the shuttle, but the AIbot blocked his way.

"All children are to board the shuttle," it said.

"Not me, botwit," Decker said, trying to go around it.

"I believe you are mistaken," the bot replied, moving to block him. "I do not have a wit. Wit has several meanings, all of which apply to humans only. The first definition … "

"Stop," Decker said. "We aren't getting on the shuttle."

"You are a child and therefore not excluded from the order." The bot rolled a few centimeters closer to Decker as if trying to encourage him to move.

I hated not knowing what to do. My mother had told us not to get on the shuttle, but I knew Decker was right about the younger ones. There was no way we could all stay on planet if Ansun wanted us off. "I'll stay too," I said. Maybe I could figure out a way to contact my father. There had to be a way to use the comm units, especially if Lainie stayed and helped.

"Quinn, are you coming?" Piper said, her foot on the bottom of the ramp.

"Wait, Piper. Don't get on yet." I changed my mind. Maybe I should keep Piper with me and let the rest go up.

"Why not?" she asked.

I went over to her and drew her aside, "I think it's better if you stay with me."

"I want to see Mom. And that raider woman is scary." Piper's lower lip trembled. "I don't want to stay here. I'm going. You stay if you want."

I could tell from her face if I made her stay, she'd get too panicky. "Okay, calm down. It's okay. Once you are up there, I need you to tell Mom something. It's a secret though. You need to tell her when no one else can hear you."

She nodded, smiling. I knew she liked secrets. "Good. Tell Mom I got her message and to send me more the same way. She'll understand."

"You got a message from Mom and you didn't tell me!" Her smile disappeared as fast as it had appeared.

"There wasn't a good time, and it wasn't really much of a message. It's important you tell her though."

"Okay." Piper looked doubtful. "I wish I had Teeny with me. You'll take care of her, right?"

"Piper, get on!" One of Piper's friends called. All the other younger children were already inside.

"I'll take good care of Teeny," I promised, feeling ridiculous saying it.

The bot announced yet again, "All children are to board."

Piper walked up the ramp, looking back at me. I tried to act as if everything was fine.

The bot moved over to where Decker stood with Lainie and Saunder. "What happens if we don't get on?" Decker asked, crossing his arms. The bot didn't respond.

"Wait Decker," Lainie said. "I have a better idea. A72, what is your primary definition of 'child?'"

"A child is defined as an immature human in the preadolescent stage of their lifespan. It cannot be defined as an exact age, because of the variability in the species."

"The rest of us here are all adolescents, not preadolescents," she told it. "You already have all the children on board."

The AIbot didn't respond. It wasn't a question anyway, so I didn't expect it to answer. I waited, hoping Lainie's argument would work. It did, because the AIbot wheeled up the ramp, apparently convinced it had carried out its job.

"I wanted to see what it would try to do if we didn't get on," Decker said.

"I didn't," Lainie said. "Besides, if there are raiders up on the station, do you really want the AIbot to report that we're still down here? This way, it thinks it's done its job. It won't even bother with us. That's the way they work."

"Good thinking, Lainie." I motioned to the shuttle. "We should move around to the other side so no one notices we're still here. We can get into the jungle where the shuttle blocks the view." I glanced over at the Fosaanians. Most were still looking at Ansun.

"Look casual," I said, sidling around the back of the shuttle as if I was just interested in examining the outer markings on it.

There were a few Fosaanians looking in our direction, as if Ansun's debate with the raider woman was either losing their interest or nearly done. I feared we wouldn't be able to leave without someone noticing. Lainie gestured to me to come back.

"Okay, Saunder and I have a plan," she said. "I'm staying, but we've decided Saunder needs to go so he can explain what's happening. He'll tell Gregor that I'm going to try to send a message via my father's comm unit only. I don't want to send up a general message that will flash on all the slips. He's also going to provide us a distraction. Act like you are about to board the shuttle, and then when he moves, get into the jungle."

Before I had time to tell Lainie there was no way Ansun would fall for something like that, Saunder bolted away from us toward the shore, yelling and pointing, "Look! Did you see that? It's gigantic!" Everyone turned to the ocean. "I can't believe it!" Saunder continued to yell as he ran, skidding to a stop at the edge of the water, still gesturing at something out to sea.

I was so startled I almost ran after him, but Lainie grabbed my arm and said, "Now!" It took a few seconds for me to realize this was the diversion Lainie and Saunder had concocted. The Fosaanians and the raider all moved closer to the water, straining to see what Saunder was yelling about. Some of the Fosaanians raised their weapons as if they expected something to rise out of the water.

"Come on!" Lainie said, pulling me along with her. The three of us ran around the side of the shuttle to the edge of the jungle. Decker stopped short and I nearly plowed into him.

"We can't just run into the jungle," Decker said. "Who knows what's there?"

"We can't stay here." I said. "They're going to realize there is nothing out there soon enough. And once the shuttle takes off, they'll see us. Just go far enough in so the plants hide us." I moved ahead and the others followed.

We made our way in only a few meters, and then Lainie stopped. "I have to make sure Saunder is okay," she said. "I want to see him get on the shuttle."

"Don't let yourself be seen." I didn't even want to imagine what Ansun would do to us if we were caught trying to make a break for it.

"I won't." Lainie edged closer to the clearing, peering around a big tree fern. I followed her back. Saunder was still gesturing, but one of the Fosaanians had him by the arm and was leading him to the shuttle.

"What if they notice we aren't on board?" Decker whispered from behind me.

"They won't notice, I hope." I said. "I didn't think it was going to work, but it looks like it did. Ansun just wants to get rid of us all and he's too busy talking."

As if Ansun had heard me, the Fosaanian leader suddenly turned toward the shuttle, staring at it. He said something to the raider woman and then began to walk in our direction.

Chapter 8

It is not our way to mourn the dead. I do anyway. I wish we had more who could give counsel. Ansun is so sure of himself, he will listen to no one. In his own mind, he is doing what is best for the clan. I cannot be so certain.—
Erimik, historian of the Family

"What do we do?" Lainie whispered frantically. "If they figure out we are gone, what will they do to Saunder? They'll know he was trying to help us."

Saunder was almost at the shuttle, talking away to the Fosaanian with him, who wasn't responding. I knew Saunder didn't realize Ansun was behind him.

"We have to get Saunder away!" Lainie said.

"No!" I took hold of her arm. "He has to get on the shuttle. Otherwise people up on the station won't know what's happening down here. The more they know, the more likely they are to figure something out. Let's wait and see what happens."

Ansun quickened his pace and caught up with Saunder and the Fosaanian.

"I want to check who's on board," Ansun said, focusing on Saunder. I saw a look of fear cross Saunder's face. "See if the older Earther youth are inside," Ansun ordered the soldier, and the man walked up the ramp. He seemed to be inside forever. I could feel Lainie trembling. The man came back down, shaking his head.

"A worthy trick," Ansun said, staring at Saunder. He came within inches of Saunder and even from a distance, I could see the beads of sweat that appeared on Saunder's forehead. Saunder hated any kind of conflict, and I just hoped he wouldn't fall apart. Ansun stood for a moment and then very slowly reached down to one of the cylindrical shapes on his belt. I knew the Fosaanian was going to draw a knife. I glanced at Decker. Decker met my eyes. He knew it too.

"We have to do something!" Lainie said.

Ansun's arm whipped forward, the knife ending right at Saunder's throat. Lainie gave a tiny cry, but Decker already had his hand over her mouth and one arm around her waist. Ansun's blade was larger than Mira's had been and looked even more lethal. Saunder took a step back and then turned as if he were going to run. The Fosaanian soldier grabbed him and dragged him back to Ansun. Ansun grabbed hold of Saunder's hair with one hand and yanked back his head, exposing his neck. He brought the knife back up to it.

Decker spoke softly, his hand still clamped over Lainie's mouth. She was struggling furiously, but he had such a tight hold on her, she couldn't get away. "So do we give ourselves up or do we try to take out Ansun and the soldier?" he said.

I knew there was no way we'd stand a chance against Ansun and the soldier with a whole group of armed Fosaanians behind them. We'd have to surrender for Saunder's sake. I held up my hands and jerked my head toward Ansun to indicate we should give up. Decker nodded, but just as I was about to step out of the jungle, Ansun lowered his knife.

"Now that I think about it," the man said, "this is to our advantage. The Earthers are foolishly sentimental about their children." He let go of Saunder's hair. "Boy, make sure you tell the others' parents about the three that have run off into the jungle. Tell them we'll try to find them and send them up to the station, as long as everyone there cooperates. We already have enough of the children to make sure some key personnel do what we want."

"What if you don't find them?" Saunder said, his voice wavering.

Ansun laughed. "Then the tachesums will have new prey." He motioned to the soldier to take Saunder on board. I realized we were too close to the edge of jungle. Any moment Ansun might spot us. I motioned to Decker and Lainie to move away, but Lainie shook her head angrily, trying to free herself from Decker's grip. The soldier came back down and the shuttle ramp retracted. As the shuttle lifted off, Piper's face appeared in one of the viewports, looking very small and scared. I knew she couldn't see me but I waved anyway.

Ansun gave one last look toward the jungle and then went back to the beach. Once he was talking to the raider woman again, I felt myself take a deep breath and then heard Decker give a muffled "Ouch! Did you have to bite me?" he said, releasing Lainie and examining his finger.

"Don't ever do that again!" Lainie pushed him away. "Who do you think you are?"

"You would have rushed out and been caught if I hadn't," Decker said. "I was trying to save you!"

"It would have been my choice! I decide what to do about me and my brother, not you! Stay away from me." She pushed him again.

"I'm sorry." Decker said, sounding like he really meant it. "I couldn't let you go."

"You two are talking too loudly, and we need to do something," I said. "We can't just stand here. You heard Ansun. He said they were going to come looking for us." I took a few steps deeper into the jungle.

Decker didn't move. "We can't just run into that. Who knows what's in there?"

"Better than what's out there." I didn't want to wait around for someone to discover us.

"Let's go to the ruin, until we figure out what to do." Lainie said.

"What ruin?" Decker asked.

"It's something Quinn and I found. It's a perfect place to hide. Right, Quinn?"

It was tough to think of anything as perfect right at the moment, but I couldn't come up with anywhere else to go. We couldn't stay in the jungle. "Good idea. Let me go first," I said. "Without a path, we'll have to be careful of the plants with spines. I know what some of them look like. Don't touch anything you don't have to."

The going was slow, pushing aside the foliage, trying to watch for danger, which felt like it could come from anywhere. Even a few feet in, the light was dim, filtered through the huge leaves. When I wasn't trying to avoid certain plants, I watched the ground, not wanting to accidentally step on something. We saw nothing and heard nothing, except the large bugs that looked like a cross between a dragonfly and a cricket and made odd little baaing noises like sheep, giving off an odor of cleaning compound.

It took us at least twice as long to get to the ruin through the jungle as it would have going by the beach, and by the time we reached it, we were all drenched in sweat. Once we were inside, Decker circled around examining the place. "You knew this was here and you didn't tell anyone?"

"We would have eventually," I said.

"Not good," he barked. "It might be important. I can't believe this didn't show up on any of the planetary scans they did before we came."

I hadn't thought of that. "Maybe it has something to do with the type of building material. I haven't seen anything like this except here."

"Are you sure the Fosaanians don't know about this?"

"No," I said. I was about to add, "except for Mira," when Lainie spoke.

"It really doesn't matter right at this moment." She flopped down and leaned her head back. "I forgot how hot it was in here. Are you sure Mick is really dead? Maybe he just went into hiding like us."

"I saw him." I couldn't meet her gaze, "what was left of him."

"Oh," she whispered.

To try to get that image out of my head, I said, "Mick had to have something to do with the communications cutoff at the station, because a Fosaanian wouldn't have had the access. But I don't think it was Mick's idea. Ansun must have convinced him to do it, probably for currency. I still don't understand how either Ansun or Mick got those MIbots down here. My mother would have to authorize them being taken off the station."

"Even though Mick acted dumb, he was a lot smarter than he looked, especially with bots," Lainie said. "He's really good with the regular AIs. We worked on one of them together one time. Since the bots communicate with each other, maybe he went through an AI to get at them. Somehow. What did Ansun mean about having enough of the children?"

I thought the Fosaanian's meaning was obvious until I realized Lainie hadn't seen Ansun's behavior the night before. "He means he's going to threaten to do something to the children if their parents don't cooperate. It's smart in a twisted way, because he knows it will work. My mom will do anything he wants to avoid having Piper hurt."

"He wouldn't really hurt them though, right? That's just wrong."

"I don't know what he would do." I doubted if Ansun's concept of right and wrong matched Lainie's. "We need to figure out what *we're* going to do."

"We just wait it out down here for help." Decker was still pacing around as if he were measuring the place. He flicked on the flashmark on his sleeve and turned the light up to its brightest setting. "And while we're here, we should make sure there's nothing dangerous hiding in this place."

"There isn't," I said, realizing every time I'd been to the ruin there had never been a single bug or creature in it. They all seemed to avoid it.

Decker didn't believe me, of course, and examined every section carefully. When he was apparently satisfied the place was safe, he sat down next to Lainie and said, "Somebody out there has to realize there's already a problem, if no message traffic is getting through. They'll send someone to investigate. Quinn, when is your father scheduled to come back?"

There had been so much happening it took me awhile to even figure out what day it was. "About two standard days," I said, a sinking feeling in my stomach. "What happens if he comes back and tries to dock at the station? What if they turn some of the defensive weapons on him?"

"They'll probably want his supplies," Decker said, "so I don't think they'll try to attack him. It's more likely they'll let him dock, but not let him leave."

If that was supposed to make me feel better, it didn't. "We have to find a way to warn him."

"The raiders can't get away with it," Decker made a punching motion like he was envisioning a raider in front of him. "Even if the raiders are in control of the station, once someone from outside finds out, they'll send a brigade and the station's not equipped to fight off something like that. The military will overpower them right away."

"I don't understand why raiders wouldn't just take what they want and leave." Lainie picked up brown leaf the size of a plate from the floor and fanned herself with it. "Load the bots on a ship and go. Isn't that what raiders do? Steal valuable stuff?"

"But there are only a few MIbots right now. They need to make more." A terrible thought came to me. "It's not just the bots that are valuable. It's the researchers. They're the only ones who can develop more bots at this point." I began to get a horrible feeling that there was far more to the situation than we understood.

"That's true," Decker said, "but there's still no way the military is going to let the raiders have the space station, and the researchers can't just do their work anywhere, not with all the specialized equipment and the iridium sulfide they need. The raiders aren't going to take them away and expect them to work on a raider ship. And the space station can't move far on its own."

"What if they are holding the researchers hostage, to get currency?" I asked.

"I don't know," Lainie got up and picked up another leaf, fanning herself with both of them. "They could be. Who knows how raiders think?"

"The Fosaanians are in this somehow. As soon as my father figures it out, he'll do something," Decker said, "He's going to squash Ansun so fast, he won't know what hit him."

"Ansun may be hard to squash," Lainie said. "He's frightening. And that bald raider woman. If I had nightmares, Baldy would be in them."

I didn't say anything, but I agreed with Lainie. Still worrying about my father, I asked, "Lainie, if we can get to a comm unit, do you think you can send a message out so that they wouldn't notice it going through the station?"

"I don't know how to do that," she said.

"We have to think of something." Decker went back to examining the place, like he feared something had crept in while he was sitting down. "And if we're stuck down here we need to get to a living unit and get some supplies."

Between Decker moving around and Lainie waving the leaves around, the motion was making me feel worse. I closed my eyes, but then for some reason the images of us walking through the jungle came back to me, so vivid it was almost as if I was doing it again. I wished my brain would just calm down. I didn't like having multiple streams of memory playing through my head.

"I do have a couple of ideas," Lainie said. "I did figure out how your mom sent that message. If I could get to a comm unit, and if Saunder gives her the message, we could at least communicate."

"If we tried to get to the living quarters, they'd see us from the station." Decker said. "The walkway is in plain view. We can keep watch and see when they leave."

"We can swim," I suggested. If Mira had done it, so could we.

"Are you crazy?" Decker shook his head. "No way. We're not supposed to go into that depth of water. The safety field still isn't working all that well."

"We'll swim to our place. It's not that far offshore but it's farthest from the depot and the least visible." I realized that was probably why Mira had chosen my quarters when she wanted to look for food. "We'll swim so that the lava columns hide us as much as possible." In the shallow water by the beach, tall narrow mounds of black lava rock rose from the ocean floor, some of them sticking several meters about the surface of the water.

"Quinn and I can go without you," Lainie said to Decker. "I'm so hot I want to get in the water anyway."

"No, I'll go too." Decker didn't look eager, but I knew he wouldn't want to appear afraid.

The three of us couldn't be seen from the station because of the curve of the shoreline, but I worried about being seen from the living quarters. If Fosaanians had come out to them and were looking out some of the openings, our position on the beach would be clearly visible. I watched for a moment and when I saw no signs of life out over the water, I motioned for the others to follow.

Lainie dived right in, while Decker held back, and I knew he was thinking about the creature from the night before, the rheisious. I was too, but the clarity of the water between the beach and the living units convinced me to go in.

Without a word, Decker plunged in, swimming so fast he caught up and passed Lainie. I went in too. The ocean of Fosaan was so much saltier than Earth, the crystals coated my skin instantly. I concentrated on keeping my mouth closed, because taking a drink would only make me much thirstier later.

By the time I reached the side of the living quarters, Lainie and Decker had already pulled themselves up on the framework supports underneath the window in Piper's room. They balanced there letting the water drip off them. "I'll go in first," I said. "Mags isn't going to be happy to see Decker."

"Decker, it's pathetic a parrot doesn't like you. What did you do to her?" Lainie asked.

"I have no idea. Besides, I don't think a bird can actually like or dislike people." Decker snapped. "Can we just get this over with? Quinn, if you're going first, just do it."

Mags looked up from her perch as I came into the main room, "Hallelujah!" she called, then went back to preening. When Decker came in, she raised her wings up and I thought she was going to squawk at him, but instead she settled back down without saying anything.

"The comm unit is back up!" Lainie sat down in front of it and spoke a command. Nothing happened. She ran her fingers over the slip. Still nothing. She tried several different things but the slip stayed clear. "Someone has changed the recognition security," she told us. "They've disabled it from the station. I can't get in."

"Intruder Alert! Intruder Alert!" Mags cried.

"It's only Decker," I said. "Are you just noticing him now?"

That didn't calm the bird down. "Intruder Alert! Intruder Alert!"

"Can't you shut that parrot up?" Decker said. "They can probably hear us all the way from shore."

"She'll stop in a minute. It's nothing, Mags." I turned back to the slip.

"Wait," Lainie held up her hand. "I think I hear something."

I felt a faint vibration of the floor. Decker started to speak but I whispered, "Be quiet."

The sound of footsteps came from the walkway and then came the sound of Ansun's voice. "As soon as they are done at the depot, bring a group out here."

"Let's go," Lainie whispered, "In case they come in here too."

"Strip the units of everything useful." Ansun's voice sounded like it was right beside us. "Bring all the food. You probably won't find any weapons. The Earthers are too foolish to think they need them."

"Not all the food." It was the voice of the raider woman. "I think I'll take up residence in one of these. I feel like being offship for a few days, and frankly, these accommodations are a bit more pleasant than yours, Ansun."

"I'm getting us some food before they take it," Decker whispered. He grabbed a storage bin and dumped the contents on the floor. "Lainie, help me." Decker ran into the kitchen, Lainie following.

I tried to decide what to take. My work area was a jumble of projects, so I just swept them all into the bin. If we were going to have to stay outside, we'd need supplies, but we didn't have anything like real Earth-style camping equipment. No one dared camp on Fosaan. I did have the small expedition pack I'd put together for exploring, but it wasn't all that impressive. I ran into my room, grabbed the pack and a couple of light coverlets. I also took the impak out of the drawer. It wasn't much of a weapon, only useful for stunning things temporarily, but it was better than nothing.

When I went back into the living room, Decker and Lainie were already there, their bins full of packs of food. "It sounds like they are only two places away," Decker said. "We need to get out now."

As the two darted back into Piper's room, I saw Mags still sitting on her perch. "Mags, come on," I whispered, though I knew the bird wouldn't know what I meant. I couldn't leave her, and the way Mira talked about food, I didn't want the Fosaanians deciding the bird might be edible. Mags didn't fly much. She couldn't, because her wings had been partly clipped by her previous owner. Occasionally, she'd venture to the peaks of the roofs, but she'd come right back if she saw any olons flying around. She couldn't find food for herself and I didn't know when we would be able to come back.

"Hurry up!" Decker said, coming back into the room.

I hesitated, and then went to get Mags from her perch. Ansun's voice was very close now. Waving at Decker to go, I took Mags into

Piper's room. Decker swung out the window and I followed with Mags, putting her on the ledge. Lainie were already in the water.

"Quinn, hurry up!" Lainie said.

"Hungry, Mags?" I whispered, ripping open a package of food. I took a bit in my hand and then climbed out the window, lowering myself in the water, so the supply bin was on my head. "Here's some food." I nearly went under, realizing it was too difficult to try to wave the bit of food with one hand, balance the bin with the other and tread water all at the same time.

The bird just stood there, so I climbed back up on the supports and set the bin down. "I'm sorry I have to do this, Mags."

Chapter 9

It all revolves around the sulfi. Who would ever guess something that meant so little to us, now is to be the means to the return of the glory of Fosaan. I must admit Ansun was very clever to understand that even though we don't value it, others should pay dearly. He was very clever to conceal how it can be collected.—Erimik, historian of the Family

I picked Mags up and flung her up in the air. Luckily, she didn't squawk, too busy trying to fly. She circled around and then disappeared over the roof line. I knew she had probably just gone to perch on another roof, but I felt better she was at least out of easy reach of anyone.

When I got back in the water, Lainie and Decker were arguing. "It's too chancy to swim back to the beach. One of them might look out a window." Lainie whispered. "I think we should stay here until they leave."

Decker swirled his hands around in the water like he was trying to part it so he could see underneath. "We can't stay in the water. We have no idea what's lurking around down there. I'd rather take a chance and swim for the beach."

"I have to say I'm with Decker," I said. I knew I'd never forget those gnashing teeth.

Lainie looked back and forth between us and then gave in. "Okay, but we'll have to be really quiet. Look, the bins float so if we push them in front of us and kick softly, we shouldn't make that much noise."

The idea was a good one, but once we started swimming, I felt like every kick and splash was loud enough to be heard all the way to the depot. It was worse when we reached the beach. Crossing the open ground to the edge of the jungle, all my muscles tensed up, just waiting for someone to spot us.

Once back inside the ruin, Decker began taking things out of his bin and lining them up in a row on the floor. "Quinn, what did you get?"

I took out the coverlets on top. They were only a little damp. I emptied out the rest of the bin, spreading out the bits of various projects. I hadn't realized in my sweep, I'd brought along the scene setter. It was so hot I was tempted to set it to snow to give the illusion of coolness.

"That's all?" The disgust in Decker's voice made me realize I should have thought a little more carefully about what might be useful.

"I did bring the impak." I took it out and laid it down.

"It's a small one," Decker said.

"I told you so. It's not like we had much that would do us any good," I said, though I was irritated at myself for not getting more. Opening my expedition pack, I held up a small canister. "I did bring an ozone generator to purify water."

"That's good, because I'm really thirsty," Lainie said. "Did you bring demineralization drops too? Purified ocean water won't do us any good unless we can get the salt and other stuff out."

"Uh, no. I was thinking of streams inland." Or at least I had when I put together the pack.

"That means going through the jungle to look for them. I'd rather go back to the living quarters to get some drops. What's that?" Decker pointed at the tip of my capture device sticking out of the top of the pack.

I pulled it out and opened it up, snapping the pieces into place. "It's something I made. I adapted an old-fashioned sport tribow so that I could use it to capture some of the bugs long enough to study them." I knew Decker would think it was stupid, but I didn't want to explain my whole strategy about getting into the reconnaissance corps training, and I had worked a long time on the device. "It shoots out modified quarrels that have a sensor on the end. I took off the sharp points. When one gets close enough to a bug, it releases a capture net." I pulled out a quarrel and put my hand in front of the tip. Immediately a small net shot out and encircled my hand.

"That's terrific," Lainie said. "I didn't know you were working on that. Why didn't you tell me?"

"I just finished it yesterday, and I haven't had a chance to really try it out. I'm not sure how well it works." I hadn't thought she'd be interested.

"Can I see it?" Decker asked. I handed it over and Decker took aim at the back wall. "What an anachronism. Give me a real weapon any day over this antique. Can I try it sometime?"

"Sure," I said.

Decker swung the tribow around and aimed it at a giant leaf above us. "Are you any good at shooting quarrels?"

I shrugged. "I've practiced some." My father had shown me how to use a whole variety of sport weapons back on Earth. Even though a military career had been disastrous for him, he'd never given up his interest in weapons and target practice of all kinds.

"It's not going to do us much good," Decker said as he put it back down beside me. "We don't need to capture Fosaanian bugs, and without real quarrel tips, we couldn't even use it to defend ourselves. Where did you get this? And did it come with tips?"

I knew I'd get Gregor into trouble if Decker found out I had convinced the man to add the tribow to a maintenance supply request list, so I just said, "My father got it for me. I still have the basic tips."

Decker scowled. "I should have guessed it was your dad. I wish I knew how to get into my father's weapons locker. We'd have all we need."

"What kind of security system does it have?" Lainie asked. "Maybe I could get in."

"No, it's a biometric lock coded to both his DNA and a

nonstress voice recognition with a code," Decker replied. "He's very obsessive about safety. Nobody but him can get in, and he's even got it set so no one could force him to open it. If they tried, his voice would indicate stress and it would stay locked. Without some sort of incredible heavy duty torch, we couldn't even cut through it."

"Oh, so that's out. I have no idea how to carve that lock," Lainie said.

Decker smiled. "Good, because your father helped mine set it up. Your father said he always tries to think of how you would attempt to carve into something. If he can outwit you, he knows something is secure."

"Ha! Someday I'll outthink him." Lainie grinned for a moment and then her face fell. "I wonder if he's okay."

"I'm sure he is," I said, though I wasn't sure. "Let's just wait until dark, and then go back to see if you can use the comm unit."

"I'm not crazy about swimming after dark, but if that's our only choice, I guess we'll have to do it." Decker said. "What a miserable place." He sat down on the other side of the room and began playing his carine softly, his eyes closed like he wanted to pretend he was somewhere else.

"What should we do until then?" Lainie yawned. "Forget I asked that. I'm going to take a nap. I didn't get enough sleep last night with everyone making noise. Quinn, your sister hums in her sleep. It would be cute if it weren't so annoying."

"I know," I picked up the tribow and polished the handle with the edge of my shirt. The silver-gray of it had a bit of a shine, and I thought it looked better without any smudges on it. "I've learned to ignore it."

"None of this looks very comfortable." Lainie circled around the room. "It's creepier in here than I remembered. I don't suppose you happened to bring along an air bed." I shook my head. "Can I use one of the coverlets as a pillow?" she asked. When I nodded, she took one and bunched it up, then lay down.

Decker got up. "I can't sit around here. I'm going out to the beach to see if I can tell what's happening at the station." He was barely out of sight before he came right back. "Quinn, your bird is out on the beach, making too much noise."

I bolted up. I couldn't believe Mags had been brave enough to fly away from the living quarters.

When I got down to the beach I saw the bird on a rock, hopping back and forth, so agitated she kept losing her balance and then flapping her wings to right herself.

"Dogs! Dogs! Dogs! Man the weapons!" She flapped her wings and flew up into a tall plant, looking down on me suspiciously.

"It's me, Mags," I said, trying to make my voice sound as normal as possible. "Calm down. No dogs here. See. It's all clear."

The bird peered around as if checking for dogs and then looked down at me. "The bird is hungry," she announced.

"I know, Mags. Come on down." I held out my arm. Mags gave one last weak 'man the weapons' and then dove down, landing on me.

She brushed my face with her beak. "Beautiful person. Mag's person," and gave an almost human sigh of relief.

"Thank you, Mags," I said. When I carried her into the ruin, Lainie stirred and opened her eyes.

"Daytime," Mags told her. "Wake up! Wake up!"

"I know Mags, but I'm sleepy." Lainie yawned for emphasis.

Mags heard the word "sleepy" and started to warble an old lullaby my mother had taught her. "Go to sleep, little person," she sang the last line and then added, "The bird is hungry."

"Here." I pulled out some of the fruit bits from the bin Lainie had brought and offered one to Mags.

"Poor bird," Lainie said. "Forced to come to a strange place with all sorts of unknowns. Why did you even bring her to Fosaan?"

I was stung by the question. "I thought she'd miss us, and she was the only one of our pets we were allowed to bring." I didn't want to think of the rest of the bunch that had been left with my grandmother, my dog Marco and Piper's cat, along with assorted fish. My grandmother had promised to care for all of them, and to keep Marco busy by having him go to work with her.

I realized I even missed Piper's cat who meowed way too much early in the morning. "I couldn't leave Mags. Marco likes my grandmother, and the cat and the fish are fine as long as someone takes care of them, but Mags thinks I belong to her."

"I guess she would miss you." Lainie yawned this time for real. After that, she seemed to fall asleep right away, judging by how her breathing slowed down and her mouth fell open. I envied Lainie's ability to sleep in all sorts of circumstances. I sat there running through events in my mind, not able to figure out how everything that happened fit together. If I could see Mira again, I knew I could get her to explain some of it. I found myself thinking of the way she had looked when I'd first seen her.

So engrossed in remembering her, it took me a while to realize it was raining. When I did, I found myself glad for it. The almost daily late afternoon shower came and went just long enough to cool things off for a little while. The rain pattered on the foliage above me, some of the droplets dripping down into the ruin, making little rivers as the water ran toward the back wall. I hadn't noticed the floor sloped down to the inner room or circle or whatever it was. I wanted to know why Mira had reacted so strongly to the markings on the wall. When things were back to normal, I'd find a way to learn more about the place.

Thinking I should try to sleep as well, I closed my eyes, but my back hurt where I had hit the ground from the shock. I still had too many images crowding my head. As long as I was doing something, I could focus on one thing, but as soon as I stopped, floods of memories overtook me. I wished Doctor Becca was around to ask how long it would last.

Restless, I gave up on sleep. I turned on my datapatch and called up the information on Fosaan. There wasn't much useful information on it, a few maps of places that didn't exist anymore, descriptions of exports that no longer occurred, and old population estimates. I had never viewed the one extensive file on the political history of Fosaan. It looked incredibly dull, but since it was all I had, I opened it up, ordering the sound off and setting it to read mode.

The history was full of names and dates, nothing that seemed important. A few images of the emperor's palace could be accessed, a not very impressive jumble of low buildings painted in vivid colors. There were pictures of the emperor and his family at various official functions. Most of them were low quality, degraded with time, the images from some antique method of recording. Only the white hair of everyone in them made it clear they were Fosaanians. Unlike modern Fosaanians, the ones in the pictures all wore very fancy colorful clothes with odd and elaborate hats. They looked nothing like the tough people Decker and I had seen in the village.

One image caught my attention and I said, "Enlarge." It depicted a group of people, including children, at some sort of outdoor party. There were food stations scattered around but all the people were watching a performance on an outdoor stage. On the edge of the image, a white cat stood on top of one of the food stations, unnoticed as it crouched eating something from a large platter.

I turned on the search function and spoke softly. "Cat." Nothing came up. I tried again. "Felal."

Words popped up. "*Fear of upsetting the ecobalance resulted in strict laws on the imports of any non-native species of plants or animals. The felal, an unknown species of the felis genus, was one of the few non-indigenous mammals allowed on the planet. The animals were brought in as pets to the royal family by an unknown source. Strict breeding rules kept the population in check.*"

The main city and the emperor's palace had been thousands of kilometers north, on another continent that had been the worst hit by the volcanoes. I wondered how a white cat ended up in small village here. "Emperor," I said. A new image appeared of an elderly man in an ornate red uniform. When I said, "Enlarge," the image zoomed in, showing the man's long thin face, his mouth pulled down in a severe expression. A small tattoo of a three-sided emblem marked his right cheek underneath his eye, the same tattoo Mira and some of the others had on their faces. More words appeared. *The last emperor had a reputation for silencing his critics. Little can be confirmed because of the closed nature of the society.*

I tried to figure out how to call up other portrait images of Fosaanians on the datapatch, trying several different words. Finally, when I said "royal family members" I got a series of images of individuals all staring solemnly at me. All of them had a facial tattoo.

Wanting to talk to someone about the images, I was about to wake up Lainie where a faint noise came from outside. I froze, hoping it was Decker. No more noises, but I had the feeling someone else was close by. Shutting off the datapatch, I got up, trying not to make a sound. A shadow moved across the wall. I grabbed the impak.

"Water person," Mags announced, not at all worried. "Beautiful water person."

"Quinn?" a soft raspy voice called. It sounded like Mira, but different in a way. Lainie stirred in her sleep.

"I'm here," I said.

Mira appeared over the top of a wall that faced the jungle. She dropped to the ground and came toward me, her arms wrapped around herself. The sight of her face made me start. It was blotchy and red, her eyes swollen like she had been crying for a long time.

"Mira, what's wrong?"

Mira saw Lainie, who was still sleeping. She came closer to me and sank down to the floor, beginning to cry without a sound. "My sister ... my sister, Cadia ... is very ill," she whispered so softly I could barely hear her.

"I'm sorry." I knelt down beside her and touched her shoulder. I wanted to take her in my arms but she flinched away from me when my hand touched her. I drew it back. "What's wrong with her?" I asked.

She lifted her head and wiped her eyes and then began to speak, not looking at me. "She was born small and she could never breathe quite right. And since the accident, she's only gotten weaker. Today she seems much worse. I know she will never become a citizen, but she should be given a chance."

Her last statement confused me. "She isn't a citizen? Everyone's a citizen of the place where they are born. Are you saying she wasn't born here?"

Now it was Mira's turn to look confused. "You mean you are all citizens of Earth as soon as you are born? Even the ones who aren't born healthy?"

"Of course, what else would we be?"

The tears ran down her face again. "Here you can only be a citizen if you are strong in all the three, mind, body and clan. If you aren't strong in one, you can't be a citizen. You are an unwanted, like Cadia. I wish I could change that." She clasped the necklace she wore, running her fingers around the cord that held the stone in place.

"Mira, what's special about the shape with the three sides?" I touched the tattoo on her cheek and she flinched away again. "Your people use it a lot. It must be important."

When she spoke, her voice was so soft, I had to lean in to hear. "It's a skele," she said. "It is to remind us of the importance of the three. Mind. Body. Clan. But it's all so stupid! I hate that I am marked with it. No one should be considered worthless if they are weak in one. Cadia can't help the way she was born! Even though she was destined to be an unwanted from the time she was born, she is *my* sister. I still want the Earth doctor to help her."

"Where are your parents? Have you talked to them about a doctor?"

"They're dead. They died of a wasting sickness a few years ago."

"I'm sorry," I said again. I didn't know what else to say.

Mira shrugged. "Many people were sick and many died. There wasn't any medicine, or at least Ansun said any medicine would cost too much currency to buy."

"Won't Ansun let Dr. Becca come down if you explain she'll help and he won't have to pay her?"

"Ansun won't do anything! He doesn't care if she dies. To him she is just a burden to the clan. I came because I was hoping to help you so you'll help me. Tasim told me what happened at the depot. What are you planning to do?"

I was embarrassed to admit we didn't really have a plan. "We're not sure. We don't really understand what's going on. Have raiders taken over the space station?"

"Be quiet!" She leaped up and took out her knife, her attention focused on something outside the wall. I didn't hear anything and Mags was busy preening again, unworried, but Mira's tension made me think there was something out there.

The girl whirled around and I was astounded to see Decker standing next to her, a stick big enough to be a club in his hand. Mira's knife lashed out, but Decker moved back, fast, out of her range. Decker looked confused, like he had expected to find someone else.

I stepped between them. "Stop you two. Decker, she's here to help us."

"Quinn, you need to stop getting in between two adversaries," Mira said. "This is the second time you've done that. It's brave but unwise." She shifted so I was no longer in front of her.

"You two aren't adversaries," I said.

"What are you doing here?" Decker demanded, glaring at Mira. "Do the other Fosaanians know about this place?" He called out to Lainie. "Lainie, wake up! We need to get out of here."

Lainie sat up and rubbed her eyes, looking confused and groggy.

"No one knows I'm here," Mira said, "but you need to leave this place."

"Decker, calm down." I tried to explain what Mira had told me. "So she's here to try to help us. Mira, you have to tell us what's going on. We can't make a plan until we have more information. Who's in charge of the space station?"

"Ansun is," Mira acted surprised we had even asked. "He sent some of our people up to take control."

"Ansun! So why are there raiders here too? What do they want with the station?"

"They want some of the new MIbots to sell, don't they?" Lainie got up.

"So it's all about currency?" Decker snarled. "You Fosaanians are the same sort of scum as the raiders."

"It's not just about currency, is it?" I said. I activated the data image and directed it so the rest could see. "Why do you and some of your relatives have the same tattoo as the last emperor of Fosaan? Look at the tattoo on his face. It's in the shape of the skele. No one else has a tattoo on their face that I saw. And why do you have a cat, a felal, when only the Emperor's family owned them?"

Chapter 10

I am weary today. I do not know if I will continue with these musings. I suspect it is my own vanity that convinced me to do this. None of the young will listen to me. They do not even come to me for advice. I know my dear Mira is somehow involved with the Earthers. Perhaps it is better she didn't come to me before taking up with them. What would I have told her to do?—Erimik, historian of the Family

Mira reached her fingers out to touch the image, but then drew it back. She didn't look at us as she spoke. "The members of my family are the direct descendants of the last crown prince. That makes my grandmother the empress and the ruler of Fosaan. Only the royal family may wear the skele tattoo on their faces."

I had suspected that, but the revelation left Lainie and Decker speechless for a moment. Lainie recovered first. "Wow! So you are some sort of princess or something?" she asked.

Decker gave a harsh bark of a laugh. "Royalty of a tiny village on a planet Earth controls, when Earth doesn't recognize anything but democracies. It's meaningless."

"I don't think it is to Ansun," I said, "or to the Fosaanians."

"It is *our* planet, not yours," Mira said, louder now. "I don't agree with most of what Ansun says, but it's true we shouldn't have to work for Earthers to survive. You should be paying us to stay here, not just giving us tiny amounts of currency for the sulfi. We had a thriving planet before the Apocalypse and we can have one again."

That silenced us all. I had never heard anyone debate whether or not Earth's arrangement with the Fosaanians was fair. From the Fosaanians' point of view, it didn't sound fair at all, but there wasn't time to think about that for the moment. "There's something I don't understand," I said. "Mira, why are the MIbots working with Ansun? How did he get control of them? They shouldn't be able to choose to work with him instead of my mother."

Mira shook her head. "I don't know."

"I don't see how Ansun thinks he's going to get away with this," Lainie said.

I agreed. Decker had been right about how the military would swoop in as soon as they knew something was wrong.

"I don't know," Mira said, "but whatever Ansun wants, he gets. You can't stay here. This place isn't good."

"What's wrong with it?" Decker asked.

She shuddered. "Can't you feel it? It's full of despair."

Mira's words surprised me. From what little I knew of her, she was a practical girl, so for her to think a building held emotion was odd. "Mira, please tell us what you know. You recognized this place, didn't you? It's the same shape as the skeles, It must be important."

A frightened expression flashed across her face. "Ansun doesn't know this place is here and I don't want him to find out. He'll use it. I've heard him say he will build a new one when he has the chance."

"So you do know what it is."

"Yes, I'd heard of these places but never seen one. The location of this one was lost. It's a testing ground, a passage." Mira clasped her hands together so tightly, every muscle stood out.

"Testing for what?" Lainie asked.

"It's an ancient place they used to use to see if a person was strong enough to be a full-fledged citizen."

"I don't understand. How do these rooms test you?" I didn't think I'd want to live in the place, but I didn't see it as frightening. The feeling came more from it being abandoned than the place itself.

"I don't know exactly. It's not the outer rooms anyway. There's something in the center room that tests you. If you aren't strong in all three, you fail."

"I don't really care about Fosaanian history," Decker said. "Once I'm away from here, I never want to think about this place again. We've got to get back to one of the units so Lainie can try to override the security."

"I've been thinking about that," Lainie said. "I doubt if I'll be able to. If they are using my father's security systems, I can't carve them. He's way better than me and he won't share his secrets. He says if I'm smart enough I'll eventually figure them out, but we don't have time for that. The only thing I can think of it to sneak into the depot and wait until someone isn't using a connected unit. I could even send a message to Quinn's father's ship from one of those. It will have to go through the station, but if it's a short message, I think it would go through before anyone realizes what it is and blocks it."

"That's very chancy." I tried to walk through her plan in my head. "We'd have to assume you could get into the depot without anyone noticing you, hide without being caught, and then find a unit you could access. Any one of those would be hard to accomplish, much less all three."

"That's the only idea I've got." Lainie said.

"I know where there is another communications unit," Mira said hesitantly. "But it's very primitive compared to yours. It's very old, from before the Apocalypse."

Somehow I wasn't surprised to learn the Fosaanians had communication equipment. If they had been in league with raiders for any length of time, they could have all kinds of equipment we didn't know about.

"How are we going to get to it? We can't just walk into the village." I said.

"It's not there. I'll take you to it and you can see for yourself. It's too hard to explain."

"Why would you do that for us?" Decker asked. "How do we know you aren't leading us into a trap?"

I jumped in to explain about Mira's sister. I could tell from Mira's face she was angry at Decker's question, but I understood why Decker would be suspicious.

When I finished talking, Decker said, "I guess that's believable." He sighed. "I suppose that means another trip through the jungle."

"Yes, and we should go now," Mira said. "There are fewer predators out in the daytime."

"If that's our only option," Lainie said, "We should do it."

At least everyone agreed. I tried to figure out what to do about Mags. There was no way she could come with us and no way I could get her to stay here if she didn't want to. I took the empty bins and stacked them on top of each other, turning the top one so that the opening faced me. I took another pack of fruit and put the bits inside. "Mags, beautiful cage," I said, pointing at the bin. The parrot stared at me. "Beautiful cage," I repeated as I held out my arm for her. She stepped on it and I carried her over to the stack. Tilting her head from side to side, she examined the place, then hopped in and started to eat.

"You don't have a door," Lainie pointed out.

"I know, but I don't want to shut her in anyway. At home, she likes to be in her cage with the door open, like it's her room. I'm hoping she'll stay here until we get back. Hey, Decker, at least Mags didn't call you an intruder this time when you snuck in. She must have heard you even if we didn't. Maybe you're growing on her. Do you like Decker now, Mags?"

Mags stopped eating long enough to look at Decker. "Dog

person," she stated, and then went back to her fruit. Lainie burst out laughing.

"I'm about ready to feed that bird to some hungry sea creature," Decker pretended he was going to grab her, but Mags just ignored him. "I don't know why she doesn't like me. I've never done anything to her."

"You have to admit it's kind of funny you draw such an intense reaction from a bird," Lainie said. "Oh, don't look so hurt! Other people like you. I like you, at least sometimes."

Decker smiled at that. "I think Quinn taught her that. She probably really does like me."

"I'll let you believe that if it makes you feel better," I said. It was funny Decker actually cared about how Mags felt about him.

"I didn't even hear you approaching," Mira said to Decker. "I didn't know Earthers could move so quietly." I thought I could detect a hint of admiration in her voice, though it was hard to imagine she could actually admire Decker.

"I practice," he said. "Once I get to the academy I want to be selected for advanced training. You're very quick with that knife. You almost got me." There definitely was admiration in Decker's voice.

"Can we just go?" Lainie said. She sounded as irritated as I felt.

"I agree," I knew the longer we waited, the closer my father was getting to the station. As the rest of them climbed over the wall, I went over to Mags. "Bye, bird," I said. "We'll be back."

Mags took a step forward and I feared she was going to protest me leaving. She rubbed her beak on the side of the bin instead, and said, "Send word when you find work. Beautiful cage."

"Yes it is," I said. Mags tucked her head under her wing and I went over the wall.

As soon as I caught up, Mira said, "There's no path, so watch your footing. And if I give you an order, you need to do what I say without questioning it. Agreed?" She spoke to all of us, but she was looking at Decker.

"Yes," Decker said. "Let's just get this over with."

Even without a path, Mira was able to find her way through areas that were passable, leading us between patches of the dense growth that looked impenetrable. I had a strange sense that I was recording everything around me. I noticed every detail of every plant and every twist we took and remembered it all. It was as if an exact map was forming in my head. I'd always had a really good memory for some things, but never like this. If this was also a result of the shock, I didn't want it to wear off, as long as I could get the other jumble of images out of my head.

When Mira and Lainie drew a little ahead of us. Decker motioned to me to hang back. "Are you sure we can trust her? She might be leading us right to Ansun."

"She wouldn't do that. She hasn't said it outright, but I think she hates him." After letting her parents die from lack of medicine, it would be surprising if Mira didn't hate him.

"I hope you're right." Decker brushed at his arms and legs like there was something on them. I noticed he was sweating heavily.

The humidity clung to us as always, but it wasn't all that hot. I asked, "Are you feeling okay, Decker? You don't look so great."

"I hate this place," Decker said, picking up his pace. "And I especially hate the bugs here. I didn't like spiders on Earth, but these are ten times worse. I can't stop thinking they are crawling on me." He slapped at the back of his neck. "As soon as we get this problem solved, I'm going to tell my father I want to go to the military academy early. I don't want to stay here one day longer than necessary."

"Watch out for that plant. Don't brush up against it." Mira stopped to point at a plant that had large oval leaves.

"It's not carnivorous, is it?" Lainie asked. "Those plants are just too bizarre."

"No, the ligitin has a substance in it that will make you very sick if the leaf is broken. Humans won't die from it, but you might wish to." Mira smiled, though it didn't sound all that funny to me.

I drew closer to examine it. "Lots of plants on Earth have medicinal value if you use just the right amount of them. Dr. Becca would be interested in this."

"I don't know how it would help anyone," Mira said. "The children play a game with it. They use it on the tips of the spears they make to see who can hunt and kill the most anguists."

"Sounds like a game any parent would approve of." I couldn't even imagine my mother's reaction to such an idea.

Mira didn't recognize the sarcasm. "It is," she said. "It teaches useful skills and it's enjoyable. I haven't played it for years, but I did like it. On my best day, I killed four, though the record is six."

"Nice," I said. The more I learned about the Fosaanians, the more I realized I couldn't assume anything about them.

"It looks like every other plant out here," Decker said.

"Not quite," I brought my finger close to one, but didn't touch it. "The veins in it are purple."

"Yes," Mira said approvingly.

"Well if I'm being chased by something through the jungle, I'm not going to have time to stop and check out plant veins," Decker grumbled. "Can we just keep going? I don't want to stand around talking about plants all day."

We moved on. It was odd that the jungle seemed so empty of life compared to our trip to the village. I almost wished for strange sounds. The emptiness was kind of eerie.

Lainie dropped back and began talking to Decker so I stayed with Mira. After a few minutes of silence, Mira said, "What is this academy Decker spoke of? Is it a school? My grandfather told me of such places."

"It is a school. Decker is talking about one of the military academies. All Earthers have to spend at least two years doing some sort of military or civil training. Decker is slated for the officer program."

"And what about you? Will you do officer training?"

"Not if I can help it," I said. "I'll do something else. I'm better at figuring things out, not giving orders." I didn't add it all depended on standing up to my grandfather. I wondered if anyone had ever successfully stood up to him. My own father hadn't managed, but instead had just flamed out on the career my grandfather had chosen for him.

She looked like she was going to ask more questions, but instead stopped and held up her hand for quiet. I didn't hear anything, and apparently whatever Mira heard wasn't a problem, because she motioned us forward again, taking up where we had left off. "I'd like to go to a school of any kind. I'd like to learn how to do something," she said. "I don't know how to do anything special. My grandfather told me Fosaan used to have scientists and engineers and architects and teachers. No one knows how to do anything now except survive."

"What would you like to do?" I asked.

"I want to learn to build buildings," she said, "buildings that stay warm or cool when you tell them to change the temperature. Buildings that don't let in rain, and buildings that are more than just a place to sleep. Beautiful buildings." She sounded shy all of the sudden. "Do you think that's strange?"

"No, of course not," I said. "I've never met anyone who wants to be an architect, but that's a good profession."

Mira smiled at that and then began quizzing me on different buildings I had seen. I tried to remember details, though I struggled to find ways to describe them beyond the basics. The details weren't that interesting to me, but I liked seeing the excitement on her face when I described things like some of the linked spiral towers on Earth.

"You should be able to go to school," I said. "People from all planets can attend schools on Earth."

Her face brightened just for an instant, and then fell. "No, I wouldn't be allowed to do that."

"Your family can't control your whole life," I said.

"It's not just my family. I have responsibilities to my clan."

"What kind of responsibilities?"

She didn't answer. We had reached a rocky area. "Pay attention now," she called to Decker and Lainie. "We're almost there, but we have to go downhill through a treacherous area, and some of the terrain isn't all that stable. Test where you put your feet, because you don't want to slip."

Mira hadn't been exaggerating about the instability. We made so much noise going down that I was sure every predator in the area knew exactly where we were.

"Through here." Mira said when we reached the bottom. She led us around a jumble of boulders and into a narrow passageway formed by two rock walls on either side. Mira and Lainie got through easily, but it was so constricted both Decker and I had to squeeze through more slowly. The girls disappeared around a curve and I heard Lainie say, "Amazing!"

Decker was stopped at the most constricted spot and I wished I wasn't behind him. "What is it?" I called to Lainie.

"Come see for yourself," she answered.

"I think I'm stuck," Decker admitted to me.

"I'll push," I said. "Breathe in." I shoved Decker as hard as I could and got him through.

"Ow!" Decker protested. "I think I don't have any skin left on my chest."

"Hurry up, you two!" Lainie called.

"You'll heal," I said. "Come on, I want to see what they found."

When I came around the corner and out into a clearing, I couldn't believe what I saw in front of me. Decker opened his mouth and then closed it again. Mira motioned for us to come closer. A spaceship loomed above us, a dull black giant, three curved arms coming off the center, just like the shape of the skele.

"How did a spaceship get here?" Lainie asked.

"It looked like it crashed here a long time ago." I said. Discoloration marred the outer surface and one side of one of the three sections was collapsed inward. "But it doesn't look like it crashed during a battle." I could see the arrays of weapons turrets, but there were no blast burn holes anywhere on the outer armor plates. The collapsed side looked more like a huge dent than anything else.

"It crashed from mechanical problems, probably caused by sabotage." Mira walked around one side. "The Crown Prince and his retinue were trying to leave Fosaan when the supervolcano erupted, and his ship came down. We've been here ever since, for four generations."

"Four generations! That's about ... I tried to add up a number of years in my head and then realized I didn't have to. "One hundred and twenty years. The supervolcano erupted one hundred and twenty years ago. The ship doesn't look like it crashed that long ago," I said, trying to figure out why I had that impression. As I went closer, I realized what it was. Someone had kept the jungle at bay. The clearing was maintained like a landing pad. There were no vines or larger plants anywhere near the ship. If the area had been left alone, some sort of plant growth would have engulfed the ship years ago.

"We don't have much time to discuss old relics." Decker pointed to another path on the other side of the clearing. "I'm guessing that leads straight to the Fosaanian village. What if someone decides to come up here? Lainie needs to get in there and send that message."

"Here." Mira showed us how to pull down a ramp.

"I hope it has some power," Lainie said, "because I can't work a comm unit with just my mind."

"It does." Mira led the way up and into it. "It doesn't have enough power to lift off but there is a small amount that can run some of the systems."

Inside, I felt the air change. It was drier and stale, without an odor of sulfur. I didn't realize how accustomed I'd become to the smell of sulfur until it wasn't there. The bridge was still in good condition, so clean it looked as if the crew had just stepped away for a moment. I walked around examining the old-fashioned consoles with their switches and levers. "It's like being in a museum."

Mira laughed but there was no happiness to the sound. "Just like my people. We exist like we are trapped in a museum, a museum of past lives that aren't ours." She went over to a wall panel and pushed a mark. A few lights came on and some of the consoles lit up.

Lainie had already found what I assumed was the comm unit, though I wouldn't have recognized it as such on my own. "There's no voice activation on this unit," I said when I went over to her. "It must be too old."

"It doesn't matter. I can code faster with my fingers than with voice recognition. Quinn, what's the ident on your father's ship?" I told her and she worked steadily at the slip, her fingers flying so fast I couldn't tell what she was doing.

"How close is this ship to being operational?" Decker asked Mira.

"I don't know," Mira said. "Ansun has been in negotiations with the raiders to get what is needed to repair it, but I don't know if they've come to an agreement."

I felt someone's presence behind me, but before I could react, could even move, Tasim was there pulling Lainie up and away from the slip. She cried out but the Fosaanian twisted her around and held her tightly against him. "Don't struggle," he ordered, "I don't want to hurt you."

Decker lunged toward them, his fist ready. "Let go of her!"

Tasim dragged Lainie backward, still holding her with one hand. A knife appeared in the other. "Stay back!"

Mira came up beside Decker. "Tasim, please, they're trying to help me to get help for Cadia."

"I don't care what they are doing," Tasim said. "What did you send?" he said to Lainie.

"Nothing. I couldn't get it to work." Lainie's face had gone white.

"I saw it working!"

"You stopped me before I could complete the message." I hoped Lainie was lying. She sounded convincing enough.

I moved slowly around to the side and slightly behind Tasim, thinking if I rushed at him, it might give Lainie a chance to get away. Before I could move, Lainie sagged down like she was fainting. When Tasim shifted his weight to keep hold of her, Lainie leaned backward, making him lose his balance. His grip loosened and Lainie slipped away, doing three handsprings across the bridge, landing too far away for him to catch her again.

Tasim went into a fighting stance next to the comm unit. "No one gets close to this," he warned.

"How did you know we would be here?" Mira asked.

"I'm not stupid. I knew you'd be helping the Earthers and I also knew this was the only communications unit you could get to." He looked at Decker and me, an expression of disgust on his face

"What did Ansun say?" Mira asked.

"He hasn't noticed you're gone. He's too busy making plans. If you come with me now, he'll never know."

I was surprised by that. It showed that while Tasim wasn't willing to stand up to Ansun, he was still willing to try to protect Mira from the man.

"No!" Mira said. "I won't go back until we can get the Earth doctor here. Cadia needs her."

"Ansun won't allow it. You know that." Even though Tasim's face was angry, I could hear the pity in his voice.

"You Fosaanians are never going to get away with this. We were ready to crush you in the last war and we can do it again if we have to," Decker said.

"You Earthers have only yourselves to blame for what is going to happen to you." Tasim stood up straight as if he was no longer worried about Decker, but didn't put his knife away. "Mira, you need to come with me."

"We're to blame! You're the ones working with the filthy raiders." Decker said.

"This is our planet and we are taking it back." Tasim pointed the knife at Decker. "For Mira's sake, I won't tell anyone you have been here, but you need to leave. You need to accept that Ansun can't be stopped. He will reclaim the glory of our world and he won't let anyone stand in his way."

"He wants the power back, too, doesn't he?" I asked. "For your family?"

Tasim didn't answer. Decker said, "He may want power but he's crazy to think he will succeed. He'll never get away with it. How many Fosaanians are there all together? Less than a thousand? He's the assistant leader of a tiny village. That hardly makes him a crown prince. Besides, Fosaan lost the war."

"The war didn't end," Tasim said angrily. "You Earthers triggered the Apocalypse before there was ever a treaty. Our war never ended.

We were still fighting for our rights."

"What?" I was stunned. "We didn't trigger the supervolcano. It was a natural disaster."

"That's what you have been taught," Mira said. "It's not true."

"It is true!" Decker shouted. "You go ahead and have your delusions. The supervolcano just happened. And don't make it sound like you were some freedom fighters. You wanted to take over another planet! That's why Earth had to stop you."

"If that's what you believe, why should the Earthers be allowed to come take over this planet? They've taken over too many planets. This one is ours." Tasim swept his arms around the spaceship like he was claiming it all.

"He has a point," Lainie said. "Maybe if Ansun talked to someone and explained who he was, they'd acknowledge him as the ruler of Fosaan. It is their planet after all."

"No," I said. "Earth doesn't recognize governments ruled by families who try to pass on the rule to their descendants. They have to have some form of democracy."

Tasim sneered. "Earth will have to change that or face war. There are many leaders of other planets who are dissatisfied with Earth's rules. Not everyone wants to live like you. Why do you think you can come in and impose your system of government and the way you live on other people?"

"This doesn't seem like a good time to have this discussion," I said. I looked out one of the viewports. There was no sign of the night mists yet, but once night fell it would be harder to find our way back. "It will be dark soon."

"Don't you understand, Tasim?" Mira said. "Ansun's plan will never work and I don't want to be part of it."

"You don't get to decide. You are a Fosaanian and a descendent of emperors."

She crossed her arms in front of her. "I'm staying with the Earthers."

"No you aren't. You're coming with me."

"Ansun doesn't care about me!"

"No, but Cadia does." As soon as Tasim mentioned Mira's sister, I knew there was going to be a problem. "If she gets any weaker," he continued, "Ansun will just order her care to stop. Without you there to stand up for her, how long do you think she would survive?"

"He wouldn't … " Mira's voice trailed off, and the words lacked any certainty. She closed her eyes, her body swaying back and forth.

"He would," Tasim said. "You know him. It's been done many times before."

"It's wrong, Tasim! Why do you follow him?" Mira's whole body was shaking back and forth, like something was literally trying to pull her apart.

"What choice do I have? With power comes control. Without it, nothing. You of all people should know that. Cadia has been asking for you."

Mira gave a strangled cry. "I'm sorry," she said to me. "I have to go back to my sister."

"It's okay. We'll figure out a way to get Dr. Becca to her." I reached out and touched her cheek. Tasim made a hissing noise at my action and I dropped my hand.

"You won't tell anyone the Earthers were here, will you, Tasim? Please." Mira begged.

Tasim looked at Decker, frowning. "Just get out of here," he ordered, using the knife to point at the entry. "Don't come back. From now on you won't find it empty anyway. We need to leave here too," he said to Mira, "before anyone returns."

"Go while you can," Mira said to us and then walked over to Tasim.

"If you're smart," Decker said, "you'll convince your people Ansun's plan will never work." He motioned to Lainie and me and then headed off the spaceship. As I followed Decker down the ramp, I looked behind me, wondering if I would ever see Mira again.

When we got to the narrow opening between the boulders, Lainie asked, "Who knows the way back?"

Voices came from the pathway that led to the Fosaanian village.

"Get out of sight!" Decker hissed, pushing Lainie ahead of him through the opening. Since I was behind both of them I didn't wait for Decker to ask for help getting through the opening. I shoved him as hard as I could.

Chapter 11

There will be no entry today. My granddaughter is quite ill and I shall tell stories to soothe her.—Erimik, historian of the Family

He didn't complain, though I could tell it was painful. As soon as we were all through, we took off running to put some distance between us and the Fosaanians. We hadn't gone too far when I realized we were going the wrong way.

"Stop," I said.

"We need to go this way." Decker pointed to the right.

"No," I said. "We need to keep going straight until we come to three rocks piled on top of each other."

"I'm sure it was this way." Decker said. "I have a good sense of direction."

"No, I remember the path exactly."

"Quinn, we know you can remember really weird facts that

don't matter, but I think Decker is right. I vote we go Decker's way," Lainie said.

"No, I'm telling you all the sudden I can remember everything, better than before. Details and conversations and … everything. It's been like that since the bot shocked me. Something strange happened in my brain."

"You're expecting us to believe you've suddenly developed a super memory from a bot shock?" Decker scoffed. "I'm going this way. If you really want to go the other way, go ahead. Lainie?"

Lainie scuffed her feet on the ground, and then said sheepishly. "Sorry, Quinn. I'm going with Decker."

I knew I couldn't let them go off alone, even though it would serve Decker right to get lost in the jungle. But Lainie shouldn't suffer because of Decker's arrogance. "All right," I said, "though I get to say I told you so when you realize we're going the wrong way."

It didn't take long for us to become completely lost. Decker pushed through a mat of vines and when I followed, I saw we were in another clearing, this one much smaller, surrounded by tall plants with long pale leaves that spiraled around the stems. Olons perched everywhere.

"Wow! I've never seen so many olons in one place." Lainie exclaimed.

"It must be there nesting area," I said, fascinated. The nests were almost like miniature hammocks, made of some sort of shredded plant material, attached on one side to the edge of the leave and on the other side to the stem. They were occupied by the ugliest little creatures I had ever seen. The eyes and the heads were enormous, stuck on tiny stick bodies covered with dull black scales.

"Are those really olons?" Lainie asked, getting up close to one of the nests. The creature in it made a startled whistling noise and some of the adult olons hooted in response.

"I don't think the adult olons would care for some other species," I said, though I couldn't see any resemblance between the young and the adults.

All at once the olons ceased both sounds and movement and the jungle around us fell silent.

"Am I imagining it, or did everything just stop?" Lainie asked.

"That's a bad sign," I said.

"Listen." Lainie pointed to her right. "There's a hissing noise from that direction."

The hissing noise following by a clicking sound reminded me of something. "That's a really bad sign," I said, remembering the lizard puppet and the noises it made in the show. "I think it's a tachesum."

Decker gave a start and moved to the other side of the clearing. "We have to get out of here!"

"Do I want to know what a tachesum is?" Lainie asked.

"No," I said. "Let's just say it's not cute and fuzzy. Come on!"

As we reached the other side of the clearing, a giant creature crashed into the middle of the nesting area and starting swiping the baby olons from the nests. I froze, a stupid thought flashing through my brain that they hadn't quite gotten the color right on the tachesum puppet. The actual skin was more the color of dried blood.

"This way!" Decker yelled as he tried to push through the foliage. It was too thick. Wirevines wound around and through the spiral plants like a fence. The tachesum noticed the movement and swung its head in our direction.

Another baby fell out of a nest and the tachesum reached for it.

I finally realized I shouldn't just stand there. "Over here," I said. I found a spot between two clumps of plants next to a split pod tree and motioned for Decker and Lainie. We crowded into the small space.

"Maybe it won't notice us," Lainie whispered. The smell of something burnt filled the clearing and I realized it was the odor of the tachesum.

The adult olons were going crazy, diving at the giant creature, driving their beaks into its leathery skin. Some of the other adults tried to pick up the babies with their beaks and fly away, but there weren't enough of them. The babies all whistled frantically. A group of olons landed on the ground just in front of the tachesum and began wobbling around, dragging their wings as if they were injured.

When the tachesum saw them, it bent down and scooped one up, swallowing it in one gulp. The others continued, acting as if they were trying to get away from it, but kept just a few meters away from it. I thought I saw the olon with the single marking in the group.

"What are they doing? It's going to catch them for sure!" Lainie said.

"They're trying to distract it away from the nesting ground. There are Earth birds that do the same thing." I shifted, trying to see better and nearly fell when my foot came down on a fallen split pod. The tachesum lowered its head and reached for another of the olons on the ground. I leaned down and picked up the split pod. "We can help with the distraction."

I tossed the pod at it right as Decker yelled, "No!"

The pod nicked the creature's shoulder but didn't explode. The tachesum roared and turned its head in our direction, looking right at us. It had huge freaky yellow eyes. The pupils were like black Xs that kept pulsing from almost nothing to nearly covering the entire eye. The creature moved its head back and forth as if it were trying to either see us or scent us.

"Not a brilliant move, Quinn," Decker said. "Now who's going to distract it from us? Let's get out of here. Try to crawl underneath those vines. There, Lainie, go first." He pointed at a space underneath the thickest part of the vines and Lainie dropped to the ground, belly crawling as fast as she could. The tachesum still couldn't seem to find us, and when another olon dove at it, it raised its front limb, trying to swat the attacker from the sky.

"Go!" Decker said, pushing at me. I followed after Lainie, hearing Decker gasping for breath right behind me. I could see an opening in front of me and Lainie standing there, her feet and legs visible. I shimmied faster, not liking the fact I couldn't see what was happening behind me. Once I was through, I got to my feet and then turned around to help Lainie pull Decker all the way out. The vines above Decker snapped with sharp cracking sounds as he tried to stand too soon.

A hiss came from too close and then the thing crashed toward us, going right over the plants, trampling them beneath it. The three of us didn't need to speak. We all took off running, pushing through the dense growth as plants whipped at our faces. I got tangled in a vine, but Decker and Lainie were already ahead of me. I didn't want to call for help because I thought the creature was tracking us more by sound than motion. The tachesum stopped, and I could see through the foliage that it was swinging its head back and forth again.

I thought about just waiting it out until the thing gave up and moved away, but then it started to move around in increasing circles. If it kept going, it would eventually step right onto me. Timing myself for when it was turned away from me, I finally managed to get free, and took off again, this time trying not to make noise. I came around a clump of splitpod trees to find Lainie and Decker backed up against a mass of giant boulders, too tall and too smooth to climb.

I listened, hoping I would not hear anything. No such luck. More hissing, and it was coming closer.

"I'll boost you up," Decker said to Lainie. "Quinn, help me."

"No time," Lainie said, "This way." She darted off to the side and I saw she was making for some of the boulders that weren't quite as huge. She climbed up on one. "Hurry! Maybe that thing is too big to climb after us."

When I made it to the top of the closest one, I saw that not all the boulders were packed closely together. There were some narrow spaces between them. From the crashing noises, I knew the tachesum was almost on us. I feared the thing might be able to either climb up or jump up and grab one of us.

"Down here," I said, sliding down behind one until I reached the ground.

Decker and Lainie followed. "Let's hope it can't climb up and reach down in here," Decker said.

"It can't. Its forearms are too short for such a big body. It doesn't look like it would be able to climb. I think it tracks by sound, so we need to be quiet." We all held still, straining to hear if it was going to try to climb after us. I hoped the thing wasn't a good jumper, though with its huge back legs, it was possible. Then its arms wouldn't matter.

The burnt smell came from above us and a small rock dislodged, sliding down and hitting Lainie on her shoulder. She muffled a startled cry. There was silence, and then the sound of crashing moving away from us. The smell disappeared.

"Maybe it's given up." Lainie whispered.

"I hope so. I hope it's not just waiting for us to come up." I said.

"It can't be that smart," Decker said. "Let's go." More cracking noises came from the jungle, the sound of breaking trunks and ripping foliage.

"Maybe we made it mad and it's stomping away. I hope we can climb out here," Lainie said as she tried to find a foothold.

I went to give her a lift when the burnt smell overpowered me again. A broken tree trunk came straight down, the jagged point of the end hitting the ground centimeters from my foot. I fell back, knocking Lainie and Decker down.

"It's throwing trees at us!" Lainie yelled, trying to squeeze into a smaller space.

The trunk lifted up as if it were being taken away and then came down in a different spot.

"It's not throwing it!" I said "It's trying to skewer us! Move, move! Squeeze in there." I pushed them to another space.

"I thought you said the thing wasn't very smart," Lainie said.

"I guess I was wrong." Decker barely managed to move to the side as the trunk came down again.

The creature kept after us until we were all out of breath and soaking with sweat. After another narrow miss, I said, "We can't keep this up. It's going to get us eventually." I took a deep gulp of air so I could keep talking. "I've got an idea, but I need to get to a splitpod tree. I saw some in that direction. You'll have to distract the tachesum to give me time to get to them. When I throw you some splitpods, crack them and get the pulp all over you."

"Why would we do that?" Lainie said. "Are we adding sauce to ourselves to make us taste better?"

I would have laughed at that if I hadn't been afraid she might be right. "Mira told me nothing except bugs will eat splitpod pulp, because it's the same color as a really poisonous creature called an anguist. Maybe the tachesum will leave us alone if it thinks we are poisonous."

"That's a big maybe," Decker said. "Go that way!" He pushed us back the other way as the tree came down again. The creature roared louder.

"Unless you have a better idea, I'm going with this one," I said. "Are you going to distract it or not?"

"Okay, but I hope you can get up that tree fast enough," Decker said. "I'll yell and then move that way and yell again. Lainie, we'd better separate to give us more room to maneuver. Ready?" I nodded. Decker yelled, "Hey you, leather skin! This way!"

When the creature brought down the trunk where Decker had been, I scrambled up the boulder and bolted to the tree, climbing as fast as I could, ignoring the stinging of the bark against my hands. At the top, I nearly lost my balance and a frond snapped loudly. The tachesum lumbered over toward me, hissing furiously. It grabbed hold of the trunk and shook it, biting at me. The burnt odor nearly gagged me. I pulled at the pods as fast as I could, tossing them in the direction of the rocks, hoping at least a few of them would get there. I could feel the tree swaying as the creature continued to pull on it. Taking one of the pods, I hit it as hard as I could against another one until it split open.

I smeared the pulp all over me, and then reached for another and split that one open too. The tree swayed far to one side and I nearly lost my hold. I wiped at my face trying to keep the stuff away from my eyes and my nose.

The creature gave one tremendous roar and the tree was lifted out of the ground. I grabbed at the top clump of fronds, hoping they wouldn't break on me. I clung to the tree, not knowing what to do. The tachesum roared again, and then brought the tree thumping down on the ground. I fell, hitting a thick mass of wire vines. I rolled off them, the breath almost knocked out of me. When I opened my eyes, I saw the creature's head bend down, nearly touching my face. I went rigid, trying to hold as still as possible. The creature sniffed at the one leg I hadn't managed to cover. I shifted so that my other leg covered it up, tiny bits of pulp flying up and hitting the tachesum in the face. The creature reared back and then moved away, back to the boulders.

Decker came up from behind one and threw a pod that hit the tachesum right in the head. The pod split and the pulp spattered all over it. The creature frantically scraped at the pulp, thrashing around in a circle as it tried to get it off. I got to my feet and when the tachesum saw the motion, it took one look at me and then headed off in the opposite direction.

"Are you okay, Quinn?" Lainie appeared next to Decker. She slid off the boulder and ran over to me.

I moved my arms around, feeling pain in the shoulder that had hit the ground. The dizziness was back too. "I'm okay. Let's get out of here." I was afraid it would come back. "We need to go back toward the spaceship and start over so I can find some landmarks."

We were all so shaken, no one spoke on the way back. It was

slow going. Decker had done something to one of his ankles and limped along. When we were almost at the spaceship, I spotted a familiar patch of plants. "I recognize this place," I said. "We go this way."

The going was slow as I led them back to the ruin. When we reached it, we climbed over the wall. I collapsed on the floor, thinking I didn't want to move for a long time. Mags peered at us. "Hallelujah," she said, hopping out of her cage and swooping down. She landed on me and then raised one foot, examining the bits of pulp stuck to it. With a squawk, she flew back to her cage and began cleaning her talons. "Bath? Bath?" she said.

"In a minute, Mags." It would feel good to wash the pulp off, but I didn't know if I had the energy to drag myself out to the water. I couldn't believe we had come so close to disaster.

"You weren't joking about remembering things," Lainie said. "You led us straight back here. How did you do that?"

"I told you the shock did something to my brain." Now that I was resting, all the images came back in a rush, too many to untangle.

"That's a good side effect to have," Decker said. "I wish I could remember everything. Enjoy it until it wears off. I have to get this pulp off me. It's going to attract bugs." He slapped at his arm as he got up.

"I'm coming with you." Lainie said, opening up a pack of nut candy and popping some in her mouth.

"Water person? Beautiful water person?" Mags asked.

"She had to go home," I said, wondering how Mira's sister was doing. Even though I wished Mira hadn't gone with Tasim, I would have done the same had it been Piper who needed me.

"Why does Mags call Mira a water person?" Lainie got up and went over to the food supplies.

"When Mags first saw her, Mira was all wet. She swam out to our unit to ... to look around. I guess that's where the 'water person' comes from."

"Getting all wet sounds perfect right now. I want to be a water person too," Lainie said. "Let's go."

I forced myself to get up, even though I could easily have closed my eyes and fallen asleep. Decker went first, creeping forward to make sure no Fosaanians were on the walkway or anywhere on the beach where we might be spotted.

The water felt great and revived me enough to go back to the ruin and eat something. As I sat down and pulled out a food packet, I said, "We've been going about it all wrong. We've been so focused on contacting the outside world and just assuming once we do, someone else will come up with an idea. We need to come up with our own ideas. Ansun has some sort of complicated plan and I'm sure he's not going to be caught by surprise."

"It would be excellent if you came up with an idea," Lainie said. "I'm all out."

"I'm trying. It all hinges on the MIbots. The raiders are only here because of the bots, and without them to sell, Ansun won't have enough currency to do anything. We don't have much time though. I know my mother said the bots are programmed to assemble other bots just like them. Once there are enough of them to do that, Ansun won't need the researchers anymore."

"What can we do about it?" Decker asked. "I'm sure you mother and the other researchers would have already done something if they could."

"I don't know yet. Lainie, you got that one bot to do what you wanted by talking to it. Even though they are hyperintelligent, they should still value logic. Can you think of a way to convince the MIbots not to help Ansun?" My arm began to tremble again and I folded both arms together so it wouldn't be noticeable. The aftereffects of the bot attack were getting annoying. I really needed Doctor Becca.

"Wow, that's a tough one" She yawned. "I'm not sure why they are helping him in the first place. Maybe, but I'll have to think about it. And I need to sleep on it. I've never been so exhausted. Being chased by a giant lizard is not something I want to repeat."

Lainie's yawn made me yawn. It felt like it had been weeks since I had slept, but I couldn't quiet my brain down. I was still bothered by something Mira had said. "Do you really think Earth caused the supervolcano?" I asked.

"No!" Decker scoffed. He was up roamed around examining the floor. I knew he was checking for bugs. "They must tell themselves that as a way to find someone else to blame. I've never heard of anyone having the technology to do that. Earthquakes yes, but not volcanic eruptions."

He was right. If it had been possible a hundred and twenty years ago when the Apocalypse happened, no one could have kept that technology hidden for so long. "I need some sleep too. How about a holo campfire?" I asked, taking the scene setter from my pack. I needed a distraction, a way to stop thinking about all the events of the day.

"Good idea," Decker said. "Maybe the bugs will think it's real and stay away."

I turned it to "fire-single-small" and added in "scent-woodburning." I'd have to keep it low or else Mags would get agitated and start making siren noises. The campfire setting wasn't one of her favorites. I took the impak out and laid it beside me, though I hoped I wouldn't need it.

"Decker, can you play us some music?" Lainie asked. "Please?"

Decker looked like he was going to refuse, but then he sat down and took off the strap from his neck that held his carine. Lainie moved closer to Decker. He smiled at her, and continued to play.

I had never felt quite so unwanted. I moved so I couldn't see them and watched the fire as I listened to the music, thinking of Mira.

Chapter 12

It has begun, but I do not have the strength to record it.—
Erimik, Historian of the Family

During the night, I dreamed of a volcano exploding and of me trying to escape from the ash and the lava. I woke suddenly, aware of a sharp stinging smell and a feeling I was crowded into a small space. I opened my eyes. Ansun stood over me, surrounded by Fosaanians who filled the room. All of them were completely silent, their faces lit by the torches topped with skele shapes which burned and sparked with a red fire. The odor of sulfur permeated the place so that I wanted to gag. I leaped to my feet but then sank back against the wall, my knees nearly collapsing on me. A Fosaanian had Lainie in his grasp, her arms pulled behind her, a red mark on her face like someone had hit her. There was no sign of Decker or Mags.

Ansun's eyes glittered as he pointed at me. "This Earther is contaminating one of our ancient places. The Earthers come where they do not belong, take what is not theirs to take, and expect all to follow their way and only their way."

A Fosaanian dragged me upright, and another one bound my hands behind my back with something that felt like coarse rope. As my vision adjusted to the gloom, I was shocked to see Mira behind Ansun. I couldn't believe she had betrayed us. Her face was completely expressionless. She acted as if she had never even seen me before. I felt sick. How could I have trusted her? Had it all been an act?

Ansun made a slight motion of his head and the man holding me dragged me to the back wall of the room, the Fosaanians clearing a path for us. The one holding Lainie came after us. Ansun followed.

When we reached the wall, the men turned us around so we faced the crowd. I tried to catch Lainie's eyes but she didn't look at me. I wondered if she was in shock. In the flickering torchlight, I could see the older people stood around the perimeter, still and serious, but the younger ones gathered in the middle looked excited as if they were anticipating something. They were murmuring to each other and moving about like they couldn't stay still. I recognized all the ones I had seen at the village. Mira's grandmother and her grandfather were not there.

"The time had come," Ansun said and then stopped. He waited until everyone was listening and then pitched his voice louder.

"The time had come to bring back the old ways. The way of the Mind, the Body, the Clan." Ansun stopped again and I could feel the tension in the crowd, as if they couldn't wait to hear what he said next.

Ansun's voice grew even louder. "It is what brought Fosaan to greatness, and it will bring us to greatness again." His voice reverberated through the chamber. It had a power to it I had never heard before and when Ansun raised his arms and shouted, "Greatness!" the crowd took up a chant of its own.

"Mind, Body, Clan! Mind, Body, Clan!" I could see the exhilaration on the faces. The ones holding the torches raised and lowered them in time with the chanting, sending sparks flying around the room.

Ansun let them chant for a few minutes and then held up his hand for silence. "It is what will make us strong again. We will not let the tragedy of the past beat us down nor will we allow others to control us." He raised his fist in the air and yelled, "Fosaan will rise again!" The chanting turned into a roar and the people began stomping their feet, the noise echoing off the walls.

When it had gone on for what seemed like a long time, Ansun again raised his hand and motioned to Mira with the other. The man beside her took her arm and led her into the open area next to me. It was Sato, the sentry.

Ansun's voice dropped and he spoke directly to Mira. "The people will expect you to take the test, but it's not the right time. Just act the way I told you." He moved a step toward the back wall and then faced the crowd again. "The Passage shows us who are true Fosaanians, but it is also a warning for those who oppose us. Go against us and this is what awaits." Ansun laid his hand on one part of the inner wall and an opening appeared.

The chanting started again, "Mind, Body, Clan, Mind, Body, Clan."

I could see nothing but darkness inside. Ansun motioned to us and when we didn't move, two Fosaanians came and got us, picking us up and bringing us to the entrance.

Ansun turned to the soldiers. "Throw them in."

In my mind, I knew that struggling was futile, but my body reacted to the soldiers by fighting against them as we were dragged to the entrance.

"It is not tradition for outsiders to face the test." I recognized the voice. It was Mira's grandfather. He was here after all. The old man stepped forward and the chanting stopped. I could hear a few mumbled voices. I had a surge of hope, but then Ansun said, "Enough! This is a new day for the clan and it has been agreed. You had your voice earlier."

"At least unbind them," the older man said. "Or are you afraid Earther children can pass the test?"

"They would never be a strong as a Fosaanian!" Ansun snarled. "Unbind them and then put them in. Now," he said to the soldiers. Mira didn't say anything.

I felt the prick of a knife on my wrist and then the rope fell away. The soldiers pushed me closer to the opening, and I felt, rather than saw Lainie next to me. A dark opening loomed in front of us. I could see nothing but blackness inside. A dank smell flowed from it, like something old and decaying was in there. I couldn't believe this was happening to us. I had a crazy thought that Ansun wasn't serious. He was just trying to scare us.

At the last second I wanted to yell, but before I could there was a shove and I fell forward, putting out my hands to stop myself from hitting whatever was below me. I was under water struggling for breath before I even realized I'd hit water. It filled my mouth and nose, so foul I instinctively coughed it out and clamped my mouth shut, fighting to get to the surface. I could hear sounds of splashing from Lainie but couldn't see her. I coughed again and reached for something to grab onto. There was nothing. The walls of the room were perfectly smooth. I fought to keep panic under control, moving my hand along the wall as far as I could, but it was all the same, slick and flat. Treading water, I managed to yell, "Lainie!"

I felt the movement of water close to me and then her voice came through the gloom, "I'm here."

It was so dark I couldn't see her even though I could feel her breath warm on my face. "Are you okay?" I asked, trying to breathe slowly enough to calm my heartbeat down.

"I don't know." She gave a strangled little gurgle. "As well as can be expected after being thrown in a dark pit of disgusting water. I don't even know what happened exactly. I just woke up to find some Fosaanian pulling me up and then all that bizarre chanting and then this. I can't believe Mira gave us away."

"I can't either," I said, relieved Lainie sounded almost like her normal self. "We're going to have to figure out something. Check the walls in your direction," I said. "See if there is something we can grab hold of."

I doubted we'd find anything. That would be just too easy. The room was small and in no time I met Lainie on the other side. It was a shock to actually be able to see the outline of her head and shoulders. "I can kind of see you. Is there light coming in?"

"Look up," she said, and when I did I could see the roof had some tiny holes in it, like stars in the night sky. "It's not much, but it's better than nothing."

"Wait, I'm such an idiot." I reached one arm up to my opposite shoulder and pushed the flashmark on it. The room brightened. The relief I felt disappeared fast as I examined our surroundings. There was nothing but smooth walls. I could see the outline of the door far above the water line. There was no way we could reach it, and I suspected even if we could, there was no way to open it. And opening it meant coming face to face with a bunch of Fosaanians.

"Mine isn't working," Lainie said, pushing at a mark on her own shirt. "I think some of the holes I cut messed up the circuitry."

"At least we have some light." I tried to clear my mind and concentrate on the problem at hand. "I don't suppose the test is to just make us tread water until they decide to get us out," I said. To keep the panic under control, I tried a feeble joke, "I don't think this is going to be a popular tourist attraction."

"No," There was a waver in Lainie's voice.

"Look, if Fosaanians could make it out of this, so can we," I said. My anger at Ansun and at Mira was giving me some energy. "It wouldn't do them any good to build something that half their population couldn't survive." At least I hoped they wanted more than half their population to live.

"That's true." Lainie's voice strengthened. "And we know our choices. We either go up, go down or find something in the sides to go through. Did you feel anything that might be an opening in the wall?"

"No," I said, "but we should look again now that we have light."

"Let's stick together, so we can make sure one of us doesn't miss anything."

As we moved, I realized there was absolute silence. The room let in no sound from the outside world. The walls were an even matte black, no dents, no discolorations, no lines to show a carefully concealed opening. We swam, trying to press against the wall with one hand while using the other to keep afloat.

We went around once more until Lainie stopped. "There's nothing here."

I hated to admit it, but she was right. "We have to think of something else then. We can't tread water forever." I could already feel my leg muscles tiring.

"I just don't get it," Lainie said. "How is anyone supposed to figure out what to do?"

I couldn't stop thinking about Mira and her face when everyone else was chanting *Mind, body, clan.* Mira had said it too when she had told me about Cadia. Maybe that's what had made her betray us; the clan was more important than outsiders. "Mira told me Fosaanian citizens had to be strong in mind, body and clan," I said, an idea forming in my head. "If this is normally a test to become a citizen, maybe we have to use a combination of those three things."

Lainie turned to float on her back. "I didn't think of that," she said. "I get the body part. You have to be strong enough to stay above water while you figure it out. And the mind part must be because you have to think of a solution. So what's the clan part? Does that mean someone outside, someone from your family has to help you? If that's the case, we're done for."

"I don't know." I didn't voice it, but I had a suspicion that in the old days someone from the clan who had already been though the test was supposed to help those enduing it. We had no one. Did Ansun even know what the test involved? And what kind of strange civilization would think this up? It was barbaric.

I hadn't realized my treading had slowed until the water touched my chin. It spurred me to move my legs and arms faster. Eyeing the ceiling, I said, "There's no way we can go up, nobody could, so that just leaves down. Maybe there's an opening in the bottom. We don't know how this water got here."

"If we can actually reach the bottom. I suspect it's really deep. I dread to think of what may be down there."

I did too. "I'll try first," I said, because I wanted to stop treading. My leg muscles were aching with the repetitive motion.

"If we take turns, we can save a little bit of energy." I took a breath of air and held it, then dove down, one hand out in front of me. The light from the flashmark only lit up a small area in the murky water. Beneath me was utter darkness. I kicked as hard as I could, making myself go down, my ears popping. My lungs protested, and I desperately wanted to take a breath. There was no bottom that I could see. Turning toward the surface, I kicked hard, knowing if I didn't reach it soon, I would take a breath of water. I broke the surface and gasped for air.

"Anything?" Lainie asked.

I could only shake my head.

"Let me try," she said.

"Wait," I took a few more breaths and then managed to say, "Take my shirt so you have light." I pulled it over my head, going under as I did so. When I came back up, I handed it to Lainie and supported her while she tied it around one arm, She pushed off from the wall with her feet as she dived down and I saw that gave her a little extra push of speed. I watched the light grow dim as she moved away from me. It seemed as if she was underwater forever. I strained to see but could only make out the wavering light.

She came back up, sputtering. "I touched the bottom! There's something there, pieces of stone sticking up all over the floor, like handles. They have to be important. I tried one but then I ran out of air."

"Maybe they are levers to open up the bottom so the water will drain out. We'll go down together," I said, feeling a small amount of hope. This time I made sure I took in as deep a breath as possible. We both pushed off from the wall, Lainie gliding ahead of me. When I reached the bottom, I spotted the handles. There were almost imperceptible, even with the light, the same color as the floor. I grasped one and pulled, but nothing happened. Lainie touched me on the arm and shook her head, pointing up.

It felt like it took longer to get to the surface. I didn't know how many more times I'd have the strength to dive down. I couldn't believe just a day without enough food or sleep had worn me out so much.

Back on the surface, when I had enough air in my lungs, I said, "We have to figure out the mind part, which means use our brains. This is a test of how smart we are. I wonder what Fosaanians learn?" I tried to figure out some sort of mathematical thing that might be related to where the handles were placed, but all the math I ever knew seemed to have deserted me. I flipped around so I could float on my back for a while, wondering how long I could keep this up.

The light coming in from the tiny openings in the ceiling made me wish I was back in my own living unit, the scene setter surrounding me with a night sky. Something in the pattern of lights caught his attention. The brightest ones were in the shape of the three-sided skele. *Mind, body, clan.*

"Did you see any pieces of stone in the shape of the skele?" I said, turning around to face Lainie again.

"No, but the flashmark only lights up a small area."

I realized the flashmark had dimmed. It was supposed to be

waterproof, though whatever caused the murkiness of the water might be causing it to malfunction. I couldn't imagine swimming in almost total darkness, trying to figure a way out. But the Fosaanians in the old days might not have had lights. If there was something on the bottom in the shape of skele, the person undergoing the test would have had to have found it by touch alone.

"I'll look again," Lainie said. I let her go by herself, trying to save my strength in case she found something. My arm was shaking again, more than it had before. I suspected the cold water was making it worse.

"It's there," she said when she surfaced. "There is one stone shaped like a skele, but nothing happened when I pulled on it."

"We're still forgetting the clan part," I said. "It has to fit in somehow. What's important about a clan?"

"Well, I suppose everyone in a clan works together like a family."

"So maybe they had more than one person take the test at time?"

"Maybe it takes two of us."

We went down and pulled together. Nothing happened. I signaled up and we swam back to the surface. This time, I had to take several gulps of air to get my breath.

"We're still missing something."

"I want to go back down," Lainie said.

I couldn't believe she had the endurance for another dive, but she was under before I could stop her. All that running around with Saunder made her stronger than I had realized.

She resurfaced. "There are two more, arranged in three points the same distance from each other."

"Of course! I should have realized there would be three in total. I know what it means. There would have been three in here at once, three to help each other. How far apart are they? If they are some sort of lever to open up a drain, we probably have to pull on them at the same time."

"I can't reach between them," she said. "They're too far apart."

"Let's try again." We didn't have an alternative. "You concentrate on one, and I'll see if I can reach between the two. Can you point down and show me about where they are?"

She swam to three different spots in the water, stopping at each one. I realized the spots made the shape of a triangle, and they were about five feet apart. I knew I couldn't reach two of them at once, but if I pulled on one, then moved quickly to the other, it might be enough.

When we reached the bottom, an idea came to me. I hooked my foot under one and struggled to move my upper body down enough to reach the other, stretching between them, hoping I still had enough strength in my legs. When I grabbed hold of the remaining one, I pulled as hard as I could, using my feet to pull on the other. I thought both moved a fraction, but I couldn't tell. My lungs were screaming for me to take a breath. I couldn't stay under any longer.

Letting go, I tried to push off from the bottom but my legs

were too tired. Lainie was already swimming above me, the light illuminating her as she rose. Using my arms, I tried to swim upward, focusing on the light. The surface seemed too far away. I had to take a breath. Without being able to stop myself, I opened my mouth and let the water flow in. As my mouth filled, I felt Lainie grab my hair and yank me up. When I broke the surface, I coughed and gagged, Lainie struggling to hold my head above water. My flailing around took us both back under a few more times, until I finally managed to breathe without coughing.

"I'm sorry," I gasped. I almost wished she hadn't pulled me up. I knew I would sink back under the water as soon as my legs refused to move anymore and Lainie would eventually wear out too. "I don't know what else to do."

Lainie pointed behind me. In the wall just at the water level, a circular opening had appeared. At first I couldn't believe what I was seeing, afraid it was just some sort of illusion from the shadows cast by the flashmark.

"That's it!" Lainie said. "The skele handles below opened this." She reached the opening first, but when she tried to pull herself up into it, her arms were trembling so much, she fell back in the water. "I can't do it," she said.

"If I can get up, maybe I can pull you in. My arms aren't as tired as my legs." It took two tries and only the overwhelming desire to get out of the water gave me the will to pull myself up. Once out, I wanted to just lie there, but forced myself to get up to help Lainie.

"Lift your arms up," I said, kneeling on the damp floor of the tunnel. It was a good thing she was light, because I could barely manage to pull at all. Between the two of us it was enough. Once she was up, we both just sat huddled on the floor.

Lainie crawled a few meters away from the opening. "It's a tunnel," she said. "I can see it curving up and away."

I put my shirt back on, even though it did nothing to stop me from shivering. Right now I'd welcome the scalding heat of the beach.

I managed to stand, finding the tunnel just slightly taller than my head. It was made of the same dull black material as the inner room. It twisted around and up and I couldn't see an end. I also realized something strange about my left eye. There was a black spot in the center of my vision. I couldn't see whatever was right in the middle of my view. Rubbing it didn't help. The black spot remained. I suspected it was an aftereffect of the shock I'd received.

"Are you all right, Quinn?" Lainie asked. "You're just standing there."

"I was thinking that I hope this doesn't take us right to Ansun's door." I wasn't going to tell Lainie about the eye.

"We'll be careful," she said, "when we get to the end."

We hadn't gone far when the black walls of the tunnel turned into red stone walls. "I can't believe it," I said, examining the perfectly formed tunnel in front of us. "The builders tied their tunnel into an existing lava tube."

"Interesting, I suppose," Lainie said, "but I'm really too worn out to care right now. Let's just get out of here."

We moved forward and at times even though I had to duck my head, I couldn't get over the size of the tunnel.

"Do you know what happened to Decker?" Lainie asked. "I slept so soundly I didn't hear anything." Her voice broke a little and she didn't look at me

"I didn't either. I thought I heard him moving around in the night, but I might have been dreaming. He must still be free, or they would have thrown him in too."

"If he is still free, he'll be close to the beach. There's nowhere else to go."

I thought she was probably right. Given the way Decker hated the jungle, I couldn't imagine him being anywhere else.

The tunnel ended in a dense tangle of vines in the jungle, and I saw why none of the Fosaanians knew it was there. The entrance was completely covered. We were in a part of the jungle I didn't recognize, but I could tell from the sun which way we needed to go to get to the beach.

"I'm really tired, Quinn," Lainie said. "I may have to stop for a rest."

"You did good, diving all those times. No wonder you're worn out. I wouldn't have made it without you." I put my arm around her and felt her shaking. "We need to keep moving though. Once we get to the beach we can rest." She nodded her head and took a step, so I kept up with her, catching her when she stumbled. Luckily, we didn't run into anything dangerous or too dense to pass through, and soon enough I could smell the ocean.

At the edge of the jungle, I said, "Wait, let me figure out where we are before we go out in the open. I don't want to just walk right out in view of the station." I pushed aside some of the foliage to get a better view of the beach. It took me some time to orient myself, until I finally realized we were north of the living quarters, further up the beach than I usually ventured. At least that was a good thing. If Decker had gotten away, he would have to head north as well. South was the station, the cliffs and then the Fosaanian village. Hoping we wouldn't run right into a Fosaanian, I stepped out onto the sand.

Chapter 13

E ven with the knowledge Decker would go north, we wouldn't have found him at all if Mags hadn't heard us approaching. The bird swooped down from a tree and landed on my shoulder, brushing my face with her beak. "Hallelujah! Hallelujah!" she squawked. "Mag's person. Beautiful person."

"Hi Mags," I said, so done in I could barely make my voice loud enough to be heard.

"Lainie!" Decker appeared from behind an outcropping of the rocks and ran over to us, grabbing Lainie away from me and hugging her.

"How did you get away?" I asked him.

"I was on the beach when I heard the Fosaanians coming and I tried to get in to warn you, there wasn't any time," Decker said. "I've been searching the jungle ever since the Fosaanians left without you. What happened?" Lainie shook her head, like she wasn't able to talk.

"It's a long story." I told him. I didn't have the energy to explain about the Passage. I didn't even want to think about it, ever again. "We need to sit down. Lainie's really tired and I'm starving," I said. "I don't suppose we have any food?"

Decker motioned up the beach. "I collected some solger from the nets this morning before the Fosaanians showed up."

It figured that would be the only food. "Okay, I'm that starving. Where is it?"

He led us to a small flat rock and picked up a slimy handful. "I've been trying to dry it out, but it's still sort of wet."

"Great." I took what Decker held out to me and sat down, Mags still clinging to my shoulder. I managed to swallow a few bites without gagging.

"I saw Mira with the rest of the Fosaanians," Decker said. I tensed, waiting for Decker to make some remark about how stupid I had been for trusting her, but instead he just added, "I think she was forced to tell them where we were. I bet Tasim made her do it."

"Maybe," I mumbled, not convinced. Decker hadn't seen her complete nonreaction to Ansun throwing us to our expected death.

"I've been trying to come up with a plan," Decker said, "and now that there are three of us, it will be a lot easier to carry it out. I think we should steal the shuttle, take it up and out close to the shipping lane. We can wait until your father's supply ship comes along and hail it."

I tried to concentrate on what Decker was saying, but the exhaustion was hard to fight off. Finally, I said, "Except I don't think Ansun and the raiders are going to let us hang around in space waiting for help." Ansun wasn't going to let us get away with anything. "Once they realize we have the shuttle, the raider ship will come looking for us, and just blast us to bits. There are no weapons on the shuttle at all."

"If we time it just right, we can meet up with your father's ship before they can do that." Decker sounded so convinced his idea would work, I was almost convinced too, until I thought about how we'd carry it out.

"And if we don't time it right?" I asked. "They'll blast both us and my father. His ship doesn't have much more fighting capability than the shuttle."

"Do you have a better idea?"

I shook my head and took another bite of solger, forcing it down. I ran through all sorts of plans in my head, all of which were too impossible to carry out. If only we could disable the bots, we'd be better able to deal with the Fosaanians. There was something on the edge of my mind, an idea that I couldn't quite form. It came from something Mira had said, but I couldn't pick out which of her statements linked up to the idea.

Trying to form a plan was tough without knowing how many Fosaanians were up on the station. The station was huge, even though it took only a few people to keep it operational. It must seem like a strange world to the Fosaanians, given the simple way they lived. I remembered how even one small piece of Earth technology like the scene setter has seemed unimaginable to Mira.

"I still can't believe Ansun thinks he's going to get away with this," Decker said. "No matter how much he's trained the Fosaanians, they've never had any military experience and they know nothing about modern technology. My father always says you have to train for everything because soldiers aren't good at reacting to the unknown."

Mags hopped around next to me. "Beautiful cage? Beautiful cage?" she said.

"I'm sorry, Mags." I held out a bit of the solger to her but the bird refused it. "We'll get you a new beautiful cage soon." I paused, thinking about Mags and Decker's last statement. A cage. I snapped my fingers. "Mags just gave me an idea," I said, picturing the layout of the station in my head. "Lainie, how familiar are you with the control room on the station? Can you work the systems there, like the lights and the door seals and the feeds to the information slips?"

"Sure, it's not that complicated," she said. "I've been in there watching the operators. It's so easy, even Piper could do it."

"If we can get up there and get you in the control room, can you do something to lock the entrance to the room so no one else can get in? Like putting yourself in a cage?" I asked.

Lainie examined the ground like she was envisioning the control room. "I don't know. My father never showed me, but a room lock should be fairly obviously. There will probably be a Fosaanian or a bot in there though. It's manned all the time. Do I lock myself in with one of them?"

"I have an idea about that too," I said, "but I'll need some supplies from the living quarters. You and Decker both have scene setters in your places, don't you?"

"What good are they going to do?" Decker asked.

"Hold on. I'll explain it all. First I need to know what Lainie can manage to do. Once you're in and can see all the security slips showing the whole station, can you lock down certain rooms and trap the Fosaanians in them?"

"Fosaanians are hard to trap," Mira said as she walked out of the jungle, her knife pointed at us. All of us leaped to our feet, and Decker grabbed the same stick he had been carrying around since the night before. I strained to see if there were other Fosaanians behind the girl, but nothing moved in the foliage.

"Water person!" Mags squawked.

Mira looked as exhausted as I felt. She had dark circles under her eyes, vivid against the paleness of her skin. A purple bruise on her jaw marred the lower part of her face. "I don't suppose you will believe me when I tell you how happy I am you are alive," she said, looking right at me.

I was astounded to see tears running down her face. "I don't believe you," I said. "You led Ansun right to us and let him try to kill us."

"And you just stood there!" Lainie shouted. "You just stood there."

Mira dropped her knife. "You may not believe me, but I didn't lead Ansun to you. It was Sato. He was spying on me." She touched the bruise on her face. "He's the one who told Ansun."

"I don't care who told Ansun," Decker said. "You aren't going to stand in our way."

"I don't want to stand in your way. I'll help you if I can." She held her hands out as if to show us she wasn't a danger.

"Don't try to tell us you came here just because you thought Quinn and I might have survived," Lainie said. "We're not that stupid."

"I didn't think that. I've been sick with sorrow ever since I knew what Ansun was planning. I came because I wanted to find Decker. I thought you were the only one left," she said to him. "And I wanted to show you a safer place to hide. I knew it wouldn't make up for the loss of your friends, but I had to do something." Her lips were trembling. I really wanted to believe her.

"You said you would help us. Why now when you didn't before?" I asked, trying to ignore the blind spot in my eye. I thought it might be getting bigger. At least the shaking in my arm had stopped for the moment, though I suspected it would return.

"Ansun forced me to go along with him by threatening Cadia. He said he would order her be put out in the jungle if I didn't act like I supported him in front of the clan. I had to choose between my sister and you. Can't you understand what I did?" Her voice was pleading now.

"So what's changed?" Decker said. "As soon as he finds out you are helping us, he'll just threaten her again."

"He won't find out, or at least when he does, I hope it will be too late." she said. "He thinks Lainie and Quinn are dead and he's busy with his plans. My grandfather has said he would look out for Cadia. He's starting to doubt Ansun." Her voice got less shaky. "I don't know if he can stand up to Ansun, but now with you, there might be a chance to stop all this, not only for my sister's sake, but for the rest of the clan. You were right," she said to Decker. "Ansun will never manage to succeed, but the more quickly he is stopped, the less damage to the clan. If we go to war with Earth, I don't think I can keep my sister alive no matter what I do. If the noncombatants of the clan are forced to move and go into hiding, as Ansun plans, she is not strong enough to survive that."

"Look, I believe Mira," I said to the others. I didn't know if my own feelings for her were making me gullible, but she did sound like she was telling the truth. "And if she's going to help us, she won't have a chance to tell anyone anyway. I think we should get on with the plans." I was afraid if we didn't do something soon, I'd completely lose the sight in my eye. I didn't know how much use I'd be then.

"Quinn's right," Lainie sank back down on the ground. "Let's just figure out what we need to do and do it. None of us will survive otherwise. Now, how are we going to get the Fosaanians into different rooms? Some will probably be walking around in the corridors."

"I'm still working on that," I sat down as well, acting as if it was all decided. Mira didn't move any closer to us, but when Decker joined me on the rocks, she found herself a place a little distance away from us, close enough to hear.

"I think it will be my job to get them into rooms," I said, "and I'll get some of the researchers to help. There can't be that many Fosaanians up there. Decker's going to need to stay close to the shuttle, because if things go wrong, we'll have to use it to get away. I can show you the schematics of the whole station on my datapatch and we can go over the plan."

"How did you get the schematics?" Decker asked, frowning. "It's supposed to be a big secret, remember? The government doesn't just hand out the plans."

"I copied them from Gregor's data," I said. "It was such a boring trip from Earth to Fosaan and he was studying the schematics all the time, so I wanted to take a look at the data too."

"Did he just let you have all that information?" Decker snapped. "He'd lose his clearance if anyone found out. And he'd be demoted, though I don't know how much lower than janitor you can go."

"He's a maintenance specialist, not a janitor. And he knows every part of the station, which is good for us. It doesn't matter how I got it." I was annoyed that Decker was still thinking about rules. I powered up the datapatch and commanded it to project the layout of the space station. "Lainie, we just have to get you from the landing bay through this corridor and then around here to the control room. That part's the easy part. There are still some others I don't know how to manage though."

Decker and Lainie began to throw out ideas and between the three of us, we came up with a plan, though none of us seemed very confident it would work.

"It's a really crazy idea," Decker said, "but maybe that's an advantage. It will take them by surprise."

"I wish I had my pack," I said. "It would have been useful, but it's back in the ruin, or if a Fosaanian found it, it could be anywhere."

"I have your pack," Decker said, pointing to the spot where he had been hiding. "I took it because I wanted to practice with your tribow, and I was making too much noise trying to get it out while you were sleeping. The impak is gone though."

I went over to pick up the pack, relieved to have it, though I wasn't quite sure what we could use.

"You've left out an important detail," Lainie said. "How are we going to get to the space station? Are we stealing the shuttle?"

I looked at all of them, one by one. "We're going to let ourselves be captured."

Chapter 14

"You're joking, right?" Decker stood up and moved away from me like my idea was contagious. "There's no way I'm putting myself in the hands of the Fosaanians."

I tried to keep my temper in check. I should have known Decker would immediately reject any idea that wasn't his own. Tempting as it was to just go ahead without him, I knew for the plan to work, I needed Decker. Taking a deep breath, I tried to speak in a reasonable tone. "It's the best way. They think Earthers are weak, and they especially don't think much of us, though they are going to be a little shocked when Lainie and I appear. It's the best way to get on the station and really take them by surprise. Besides, if it all works out, we won't be in the hands of the Fosaanians for long."

Decker didn't say anything, but I could tell he was at least considering the scheme.

"How are we going to get Mira on the shuttle?" Lainie said. "They won't let her just go with us."

I looked over at Mira. She hadn't said anything for a long time. "Mira is going to have to stay here. It wouldn't be safe for her to go with us. I know you want to help us," I said to her, "but I don't know how you can."

"No!" Mira leaped up. "I can't stay here. I need to go with you. There's something else I didn't tell you." She moved in so close to me, I found myself wanting to reach out and touch her. I was so distracted, I didn't focus on what she was saying until I heard the words "marry Tasim."

"What?" I asked.

"Ansun thinks he can make me to marry Tasim tonight. I was going to go ahead with it when I didn't know you were alive, but now I won't."

Mira's statements stunned me. I didn't know anything about when Fosaanians got married, but surely Mira was too young. I'd thought she was my age or a little younger. She also said she'd decided not to go through with it because of me. At least that's what I thought she meant.

"Wait, Tasim is your cousin. Cousins don't marry each other," Lainie said.

"Why not?" Mira sounded baffled.

"They just don't, at least not on Earth," Lainie replied. "It's an old cultural taboo, from when genetic disorders couldn't be repaired."

"That's Earth. It's not like Fosaanians have many partners to choose from," Mira said. "But it doesn't matter, because I'm not going to, at least not today."

"You mean you might marry him on a different day?" I asked. I didn't like the thought of that at all.

She shrugged. "I don't know. It's not important now. You have to take me with you. I'm good in a fight. You may need me on the station. It will be hard to make this plan work the way you say. I think there will be fighting."

To my surprise, Decker said, "She's right. It's probably not going to go so easily. She's quick and knows how to use a knife if we need it. Do you still have the bracelets with those stones in them?" he asked her. "Those are extra weapons we need."

Mira nodded and pointed to the pouch attached to her belt.

I thought for a moment, trying to figure out how we could manage to get Mira aboard the shuttle without anyone knowing. While I was thinking, I picked up another piece of solger and almost took a bite, but the thought of it made me feel sick. It also gave me a new idea. "Mira, what exactly what does the ligitin plant do to people?"

"It gives people severe pains and makes them feel like they are going to throw up."

"And how fast does it act?"

"Right away, if you get enough on you."

It all came together. "Perfect. I need your help to find some. Decker, do you know how to override the auto pilot on the shuttle?"

"Yes, I sit up with the pilots all the time. It's just a touch mark."

"I don't suppose you've ever actually flown it, have you?"

"No, but it can't be that hard."

I wasn't so sure about that, but we didn't have much choice. I'd have to trust in Decker's confidence.

"Okay, here's what we need from the living quarters." I went over the list. Teeny, Piper's bot, was at the top.

When I finished, Decker said, "You realize you're the one most likely both to get caught and to make the Fosaanians angry enough to just to go ahead and blast you."

"That's true," I said, "but I know my way around the station better than you do, and I can't run the control room as well as Lainie, so I'll just have to take that chance. We need to get going to get everything together as soon as we can." I looked up at the sky and the Fosaanian sun to judge the time. "My father's ship will be arriving soon. We can't wait."

It took us nearly an hour to collect everything. Decker and Lainie went back to the living quarters, which turned out to be empty, making the job much quicker. While I was working on my part, using the leaves Mira and I had collected, the girls disappeared down the beach. Decker fastened the scene setters to the inside back of his shirt, trying to make them unnoticeable. "I'm going to take a look at the station and see who's there," he said. "If there are too many Fosaanians, we should wait until later."

I didn't intend to wait, but since I wasn't ready, I didn't argue with him. I was so intent on my job that when Lainie reappeared and asked, "What do you think?" I looked up and nearly fell over.

A strange girl stood next to Lainie, wearing long pants, a long-sleeved shirt and a hat. The girl pulled off the hat and the Mira's curls sprang free. Lainie laughed. "You should see your face. She doesn't look exactly like an Earther, but we thought a little disguise wouldn't hurt in case someone spots her on the station. I used some of my mom's skin finishing lotion."

"It fooled me," I said. "At least at first glance." I didn't like the change but I was smart enough not to say so. I wanted Mira to look like Mira, not some stranger.

"Where's Decker?" Lainie asked.

I explained and then said, "I'm done. We can go as soon as he gets back."

"I hope he hurries up," Lainie said. "I hate waiting around." She headed down the beach. "I'm going to go find him."

I was getting impatient too, but it was nice to have a few minutes alone with Mira. She sat down beside me. "You didn't know me for a moment, did you?" she asked.

"No," I admitted. "But only for a moment. Even with the lotion covering up the skele on your cheek and your hair under a hat, I'd know your face."

Mira touched her cheek. "I wish I could get rid of the skele forever." She took off her necklace. "My sister made this for me. She's very good with her hands."

"It's great," I said, paying more attention to Mira's face than the necklace. I didn't know why we were talking about jewelry unless she was going to tell me the necklace was also a weapon.

"Look at how all the threads around the stone are intertwined." She smiled and held the necklace up right in front of me so I had to look at it. "This should be our symbol, not the skele. We all are part of the clan and our lives are intertwined. Each thread strengthens the whole, and not every thread needs to be able to stand alone."

I could tell this meant a lot to her so I tried to concentrate on her words. "That's a better philosophy than the whole mind, body, clan idea," I said.

Her smile grew wider. "Yes it is," she said. "You understand."

"Are you sure you want to do this?" I asked. "Ansun will find out you've helped us."

"I know. But he has to be stopped. It's time. We have an old saying that to survive, one shouldn't go beyond the known. That no longer is true. We have to take chances. I have to take a chance. It's time to go beyond the known."

"Are you ready?" Decker's voice boomed so close to my ear, I started. I hadn't heard them come back.

Mira put the necklace back on. I stood up, trying to remember what we were supposed to be doing.

"I'm ready," I said as I pulled on the extra shirt Decker had brought back from the living quarters. It covered my tribow, which I'd placed flat against my back. I handed Teeny to Lainie. That motion made my shoulder ache. Between my shoulder, my eye and the way my muscles trembled, I hoped I could manage to carry out the plan.

"Ready, Mira?" I asked. "Are you sure you know the spot we described? We'll give you a few minutes head start." She nodded her head, pulling at the hat like she had never worn one before.

We watched her disappear into the jungle. If the plan worked and we made it up to the station, I wasn't sure I'd ever want to see Fosaan again.

"Quinn, you look like you are asleep standing up," Lainie said, startling me. "We've given her enough time. We should go."

"Okay." I rubbed my face, trying to stay alert. "Play really young and stupid," I said as we headed down the beach. I didn't think we needed to worry about the Fosaanians underestimating us. As a group, the three of us weren't very impressive. Except for my extra shirt, the rest of our clothes were ripped and filthy, and all three of us sported cuts and bruises. I suspected I looked as worn down as Lainie and Decker. Only Mags seemed happy to be going somewhere. She sat on my shoulder, peering around as if she was interested in the scenery.

"Do we really have to take the bird?" Decker asked. "She'll be a distraction."

Mags muttered, "Dog person," and then turned her head away from his direction.

"Okay, dog bird," Decker shot back. "I've had it. I tried to be nice, but if that's the way you want it, that's the way we'll play it."

Lainie giggled, linking her arm with Decker's. "Do you realize you're talking to the bird just like Quinn does?"

Decker looked embarrassed. "She sounds too much like a human."

"We're not leaving her," I said. We came into view of the depot and I was relieved to see the shuttle was there and not up at the station. Only a few Fosaanians were standing outside, looking bored. No sign of Ansun. I supposed someone planning a planetary takeover had more important things to do than to hang around the depot.

"I'll do the talking," Lainie said. "I don't think either of you could be very convincing."

When they saw us, the two men straightened up, taking out their weapons. I recognized both of them. One, who had his hair cropped very short, had been holding one of the torches in the ruin. I remembered how the man's face had been slick with sweat and how his eyes had fixed on Ansun the whole time. The other was Sato. The memory of the whole scene in the ruin made my heart pound faster. I hoped my ability to remember so well would disappear soon. There were too many things I didn't want to remember in great detail.

"We're really hungry," Lainie called out, adding in a limp as we came up to the men. "And we miss our parents. We've decided we want to be sent up to the space station to be with them. Can you tell someone in charge?"

It took a few moments for the Fosaanians' astonishment to wear off. The cropped-haired one seemed particularly startled by Mags. He couldn't stop looking at her.

Sato said, "Don't move. I'll tell someone you are here." He went into the depot and we waited in an awkward silence.

"How did you survive the Passage?" the remaining one blurted out to me.

I took a step closer to him and said in a low voice, "I'll tell you how to survive if you pass the word along," I said. I didn't want anyone else to have to go through that, and I was sure Ansun was going to force everyone to be tested. It would serve Ansun right if everyone knew the trick before they had to go in. As I told the story, I could see the amazement growing on the man's face. Before I could get to the part about the lava tunnel, Sato came out of the depot, looking angry.

"They are to be sent up," he barked, not even meeting our eyes.

The sentry said, "Do we let them take that creature?"

Sato examined Mags and I held my breath, hoping the bird wouldn't speak. I didn't want a Fosaanian to decide they needed their own talking bird.

"What is this creature?" Sato asked.

"It's a parrot," I said. "From Earth. I wasn't supposed to bring her here. It's against your old rules, but I did it anyway. I think Fosaan needs birds. We were going to let her go when we left."

"No," Sato said. "Take it with you. We don't need Earth creatures contaminating the planet." He motioned to Teeny. "What is that thing?"

"It's just his sister's toy," Lainie said. "I know she is crying herself to sleep without it."

The Fosaanian took it and examined it. Teeny was looking more ridiculous than usual. I had added as many ribbons as I could find, and had attached the furry cutout ears Piper used when she was pretending it was a pet. I hoped Sato wouldn't accidentally trigger the ball release.

When Sato handed it back to me, he said to the other Fosaanian, "Ansun is right. The Earthers are nothing like us. Get on board," he ordered us.

I walked as quickly as I could up the ramp, tense now, hoping the plan would work. It appeared we would be sent up alone. I turned to say something to Lainie and then saw not one, but both Fosaanians following her. I nearly groaned out loud. The plan would work with one, but we hadn't even considered the Fosaanians would send two guards for just the three of us.

I didn't know what to do, and I could see from the expressions on Decker and Lainie's faces that they were thinking the same thing. I sat down, desperately trying to come up with another plan. Sato went to the control panel and spoke into it. "We're ready. Lift off." He sat down across from me. My eyes met Lainie's. I nodded my head to encourage her to go ahead.

She repositioned Teeny in her lap and ran her hand over some of the sensors.

"What are you doing?" Sato asked sharply.

"I just wanted to make sure it wasn't broken. His sister will be really upset if it is." Lainie leaned toward the man and held out the bot as if intending to show him something. "See, this part here sticks all the time." She pushed the markon that controlled the manual ball release and a ball shot out.

Sato put up his hands up as if to ward it off. The ball hit the palm of the right one, bouncing off and rolling under the seat. He rose, his face furious.

Lainie sat back, pretending to cower in her seat. "I'm so sorry, I didn't know it was going to do that." I hoped I had put enough ligitin on the ball. There was more ligitin on the quarrels of my tribow, but I didn't think I'd be able to load one and shoot before the Fosaanians would take me down.

The other man rose as well, just as Sato sat back down with an odd expression on his face. Sato clutched at his stomach and doubled over.

"What's wrong?" the second man asked.

Lainie rose too. "He looks like he's going to be sick. Do something!" She took hold of the man's arm and continued to talk. I motioned for Decker to get up, then pointed to the storage hatch on the floor and raised my hand slightly to indicate Decker should open it. Luckily, Decker understood. He got up and then knelt down, raising the panel of the hatch. Sato was moaning now, trying to speak, trying to point at Decker, but not able to get words out.

I jumped up and took hold of him. "You should sit down before you fall down. You look terrible." I glanced back at Decker. Decker had the hatch open. He nodded and I said to Lainie, "It's a little crowded in here. We need more room."

Lainie pretended to stumble, pulling the man backwards, taking him off balance. I whipped out a quarrel and jabbed the man in the thigh. Before the man could react, Decker was on the other side of him. Decker kicked him in the back of the knee and the man crumpled. Between Lainie and Decker, it didn't take them long to get him into the storage bin and shut the lid. We could hear him yelling what sounded like curses. He pounded on the hatch a few times, then began groaning.

Sato collapsed on the floor. He looked like he was unconscious, but I kept my eyes on the man's face as I knelt down to take the walthaser off Sato's belt. As soon as I had it in my hand, I jumped back just in case Sato came to.

"We've got to move fast before the shuttle accelerates to get us out of the atmosphere," Decker said. "Lainie, get on the comm unit. You do the talking." Decker pushed past me and sat down at the controls, switching off the auto setting and adjusting the course.

Immediately a voice came over the unit. "Shuttle, why is the auto control off? You are not on course."

"Something's wrong!" Lainie said, sounding all panicky. "We're going to crash!"

"Who is speaking? Put one of the escorts on," the man commanded.

"There's only one and he's sick! He can't talk! Do something!"

Decker already had the shuttle descending over the small open area in front of the boulder field where we had been the day before. I could see Mira standing next to the uprooted tree waving at us. "Turn off the audio on the comm unit," I said to Lainie.

Lainie spoke into it first, stuttering, "I ... can't ... hear ... something ... wrong ... oh no!" She shut it off and smiled. "Good imitation of a failing comm unit, right?"

"That area is smaller than I remembered and the tree is taking up too much room. I don't think I can land there," Decker admitted. "I can hover, but you will have to help her aboard."

Lainie and I went to the ramp as Decker lowered it. We each took a side, holding on to the edge of the shuttle as it came down. "I can't get any lower," Decker called back.

Motioning to the boulder closest to us, I yelled, "Mira, you're going to have to jump. Up there!"

Mira scrambled up it. I was concentrating so hard on her and the shuttle was making so much noise, we didn't have a warning. A tachesum crashed out the jungle. I yelled but it was drowned out in the creature's roar. Mira moved fast, but the tachesum was faster. It grabbed her leg, making her fall flat on the boulder. It began to drag her toward it.

"Hold on!" Decker yelled and swung the shuttle around, bringing the nose of it down practically on the tachesum's head. The creature sprung backwards, snarling and batting at the shuttle, letting go of Mira. Mira was already up on her hands and knees trying to get to the ramp.

"Quinn, hold onto my legs!" Lainie shouted as she laid down on the ramp and reached her hands out for Mira. I knelt down and grabbed hold, hoping Decker wouldn't tip the shuttle too far in the other direction. I didn't know if I could hold on to Lainie if she started to slide out. The tachesum was still batting at the shuttle. It hit the side and the vehicle rocked, shifting us to one side. Mira stood up and leaped toward us, catching hold of Lainie's hands. The sudden extra weight caused both Lainie and I to slide toward the opening. I hooked my leg around one of the seats. I knew I'd never be able to pull both girls in.

"Decker, get higher and then put it back on auto so you can help!" I shouted. My hands were so sweaty, I lost my grip on one of Lainie's ankles.

"Quinn!" she yelled. "Don't you dare let us fall!"

I used my free hand to tighten my grip on the one ankle I still held, but I knew I couldn't hold on much longer. My arm began to shake and I lost strength in it.

Lainie begin to slide away from me and then Decker was there. He grabbed at Lainie and yelled at me, "Pull!"

I did what I could, but it was Decker who saved them. When both girls were up on the floor of the shuttle, I closed my eyes in relief trying to quell the tremors that were running up and down my arm.

Decker returned to the controls and switched the shuttle back to automatic. It immediately began to ascend. "Get clear of the ramp," he said, ordering it to shut.

Mira smiled at us. "That could have been bad," she said.

I managed to choke out a weak, "Yes," still a little stunned by it all.

"I'd better tell them we aren't going to crash after all." Lainie turned the audio back on.

"Respond, shuttle, respond immediately!" A different voice came through the speaker.

"Everything is fine now," Lainie said. "Just fine. We almost crashed but the shuttle starting working again. I'm so relieved! We're fine."

I thought she was pushing it a bit far and made a cutting motion with my hand.

"Earther, what is the status of the escort?" came a MIbot's voice.

"He's very sick," Lainie said. Sato had regained consciousness but was curled up in a ball on the floor, groaning. "He can't talk now."

"There's another one in the storage compartment," I whispered to Mira. "The ligitin doesn't seem to be strong enough to knock them out and Sato here saw us put the other one in. As soon as he can talk, he's going to tell."

Mira reached around to her back and pulled out her knife. I saw she still wore her belt under Lainie's shirt. She shifted the knife to her other hand and went over to the man.

"Hello, Sato. Who's the burden now?" she asked as she brought the knife in front of his face.

Sato opened his eyes.

Chapter 15

"**M**ira!" Lainie cried. "What are you going to do?"

With a quick motion, Mira pricked the man's arm with her knife. He let out a strangled moan, then closed his eyes and went limp. "I had to kill an anguist while I was waiting," Mira said. "I left a drop of blood on the knife. It's not as lethal as the poison from the skin. Sato should just be paralyzed for a few days."

I glanced at Lainie, whose mouth had dropped open. "Okay ... " I said. "I take it you really don't like the man."

Mira sneered at the figure on the floor. "No, Sato went to Ansun last year and told him he'd be willing to make a great sacrifice and marry me, even though as he put it, I'm burdened with Cadia and come from weak parents. As if I'd ever want to marry him! Sato didn't like it when I told him I'd rather let an anguist poison me than marry him." She eyed her knife like she was tempted to give the man another dose.

"Remind me not to make you really mad," Decker said over his shoulder.

"There's probably not enough to work on the other man." Mira examined the knife tip. "We'll have to gag him, but I'll need your help." She ripped off a strip from the bottom of her shirt and handed it to me.

I couldn't believe how calm the girl was. She acted as if she did this sort of thing every day. I was impressed and glad we hadn't left her behind.

"Are you going open the compartment?" Mira asked Lainie.

"Um ... okay," Lainie said. She opened it slowly but the man didn't have the strength to even protest when Mira leaned in, took his walthaser, setting it aside, and then lifted his head. "Tie the gag tightly," she said to me. I knelt down and wrapped the fabric around the man's mouth. When it was knotted, I moved back and watched as Lainie lowered the lid.

Mira picked up the weapon. "I've never been allowed to use one of these," she said. "How do they work?"

"They're simple." I examined the one I had taken off Sato. "You slip this part over the top of your hand for stability, touch the safety release with your thumb and then push here." I pointed to the different parts of the weapon. "But these are ancient. These pieces shouldn't be fused together. It's like someone did a bad repair job on it. I'm not sure it's operational. Let's see the other one." I examined that too, then set it down. "I don't know. I wouldn't trust these. They might blow up in your hand. Have you ever seen people actually use these?"

"No," Mira said. "They practice away from the village, or at least they go somewhere and say they've been practicing."

"I don't think we can risk using these," I said, regretting their loss. We had so little in the way of weapons.

"We're almost there," Decker called. The heat fog surrounding the shuttle cleared as we ascended out of the upper reaches of the Fosaanian atmosphere.

"I see the space station," Lainie said. We continued our ascent as the three stacked rings of the station grew larger in the viewport.

I watched it, struck as always by how serene it seemed as it slowly rotated in its orbit, hiding whatever was going on inside it. We'd know soon enough.

Lainie gasped and then leaned in closer to the viewport. "Something is wrong with it," she said. "Look. There are parts of the station missing."

She was right. The rings were no longer continuous. At three different points, sections were gone, as if they had been sliced off.

"I don't understand," Mira said.

I took in the various markings on the outside of the station to orient myself. When I realized what I was seeing, I couldn't speak for a moment. Finally, I said, "Some of the main labs are missing. Dr. Pelletier's lab was located there between B40 and B42."

"Are you sure?" Decker asked.

"I'm sure. That other section that's missing was Dr. Mehta's lab and that one there is where Marshall and Khoury work."

"How could some of it just be gone?" Mira asked. "How do they keep air in the station if parts of it are missing?"

"It was put together in sections," I explained, trying to envision what had happened. "Each of the numbers on the outside is a separate section they connected together. I guess someone just reversed the process and disconnected them, sealing up the sections on either side so it stays airtight." I pointed to a small vehicle attached to the side of the station. "That's odd. There's one of Gregor's repair pods. I don't know what it is doing outside. They are usually in his maintenance bay."

"It doesn't look like it's doing anything," Lainie said.

"We can't worry about it now. We're coming in," Decker said. The airlock field shimmered as the shuttle slid through it. As we had hoped, the landing bay was almost deserted.

"I see two Fosaanians and a MIbot," Decker said.

"I was hoping we'd only have to deal with Fosaanians. Mags, you're on your own for a bit." I said, feeling terrible I was putting the bird through all of this. Mags had withdrawn in all the excitement and had retreated to an empty seat, her head tucked under her wing. I hoped she'd be all right when this was all done. "Everybody ready?" I asked.

Decker pulled the scene setters from beneath his shirt and handed gave us to me. "This had better work."

"Just give us long enough to get Lainie and Mira to the control room." I set the scene for 'fire-multiple-large' and made sure to add in the scent of burning wood. Handing it to Lainie, I said, "I'm going to say something about the shuttle still acting strange, and distract them a bit. Turn it on when I give the signal."

The shuttle settled to the ground and I saw both Fosaanians and the bot move toward it. The ramp came down and I sprinted out, talking fast and excitedly. "This piece of junk is worthless. Something is leaking! I don't know what's wrong!" Immediately the shuttle began lifting up and down, bumping the ramp up and down on the floor. "I think there's something burning."

Lainie jumped out and turned on the scene setter at the same time. Holographic fires sprang up everywhere and the smell of smoke filled the air. Screaming "Fire!" Lainie ran for the door. I was about to follow when Mags swooped off. The bird spotted the fires and began making siren noises, landing and then taking off again, flying so low the Fosaanians kept ducking as they backed away from the shuttle like they feared it would go up in flames too.

The bot stayed in place so I dashed back to it, trying to put some urgency in my voice, "The fire suppression gas should be on by now. There must be a problem. Can you operate it manually?"

The bot didn't respond but maneuvered over to a control panel on a wall and flashed some lights at the slip. The room immediately began to fill with a cloudy blue gas. Mira saw her chance and slipped off the ramp, bending down and creeping through the gas. The Fosaanians weren't even paying attention. They were over yelling into a comm unit.

"Now," I said, and the three of us sprinted for the door. I took a look back over my shoulder to see Mags landing on a partly disassembled bot. She was squawking something but I couldn't tell what it was. I'd have to get her back on board before we left. Decker was out of the shuttle and running to a tool storage compartment we'd identified on the schematic as a good place to hide.

There was no one in the corridor connecting the landing bay to the main space station, but as soon as the three of us went through the door into the circular passageway of level two, we nearly ran into two more Fosaanians who were coming out of one of the snack stations.

"There's fire in the docking bay and it's getting out of control. Communications are down!" I yelled. "Get yourselves some protective gear from room A72, upper level. If it reaches B17, the atmospheric controls could go down. Hurry!" I broke into a run and headed for the ramp to the upper level. When I was sure everyone was following, I pretended to stumble and fell against the wall. "Ow, my ankle!" I yelled. Mira and Lainie stopped and the two Fosaanians did as well. "Go on without me," I said. "I'll catch up."

The Fosaanians started off again, Mira and Lainie jogging behind them. The two men went up the ramp and around a corner. Lainie and Mira veered off, I followed them.

"They'll come after us as soon as they can't find any protective gear," Lainie said.

"It may take them awhile," I said. "There's no room A72. Where is everyone?" I had expected to see a few researchers out in the passageways, but the whole place was strangely quiet and empty. Deciding there wasn't time to worry about it, I said, "We need to slow down because we're getting close to the control room."

"It's really hot in here," Lainie said. "That's strange."

I hadn't noticed before Lainie spoke, but she was right. "Maybe the Fosaanians have the heat system set higher so it's more like the planet. They wouldn't be used to the normal cold. Jog in front of me so the security eyes can't see what I'm doing." I used my head to make a slight motion at one of the black dots set in the ceiling. "We don't know if they're watching this corridor." I took the other scene setter out of my pocket and switched it to 'fog-thick'. When we were almost at the control room entry, I turned it on. The corridor clouded so I could barely see the girls next to me.

"This way," I whispered. "The mechanical compartment is here. Mira, feel your way along the wall until you are past us and past the door of the control. There's a small opening in the wall where you can wait." I said, remembering it from the schematics. I pushed on the door so it slid open and put the scene setter on a shelf. "Let's do this before someone else comes along." The vision in my left eye was almost gone now, so I used my right eye to read the controls, setting it to "stream-fast," but not turning it on.

"Go!" I said to Lainie as I turned off the fog setting. The corridor lit up again and I turned on the setter. Immediately, holographic water began gushing out the compartment, running down the corridor.

Lainie ran over and pounded on the control room door, "Help!

There's a flood out here! Something broke in the wall and water is everywhere. Help!" The door slid open and a Fosaanian peered out. "It's coming from over here!" Lainie pointed.

I joined in, trying to make my voice sound as panicky as Lainie's, "There's a valve but it's stuck!" The man took a step out into the passageway. "It's getting worse!" I turned the control up to make it look like more of the area was flooding. I hoped the man would have the same reaction Mira had when she first saw the scene setter. I also hoped the man wouldn't notice that even though I was standing right underneath what looked like water, I was perfectly dry.

Lainie darted into the control room. "No, that's not the right mark. It's here," I heard her say. If the Fosaanians were too surprised to react, so much the better. I knew she was probably making her hands fly over the slip. "Uh oh," she said, "It's malfunctioning. I can't shut down the water flow on this level. There's a malfunction in the docking bay too and a fire. What's happening out there?" she called.

The Fosaanian in the passageway took a step back toward the control room. "It's getting worse!" I yelled. "Help!"

Lainie said, "You'd better go help too! I'll see what I can do in here." The other man came out and both men moved toward me. Mira slipped in behind them. The control room door slid shut and the men didn't even notice.

The first man was already at the compartment. "I don't see anything to shut off," he said.

"Keep at it," I said, backing away. "I'll go find more help."

The second Fosaanian stuck his hand in the stream of water,

and then brought it out again to examine it. "This isn't wet," he said, puzzled.

"Are you sure?" I didn't wait for the man to respond. I turned and ran. A few seconds later I heard the men pounding after me. I thought I'd be able to outrun them, but I hadn't taken into account how tired I was from the past two days. They were gaining on me. I spotted a room I knew had an access ladder concealed in one of the wall panels. Dodging in it, I opened it and headed up, wishing I'd been close enough to a room with a ladder going down instead of up. I knew the other two Fosaanians were probably still on the upper deck looking for A72. When I got to the top of the ladder, I stuck my head out, hoping not to see them.

When I was sure the corridor was clear, I dashed into one of the rooms, a small lab supply room, and punched the markon on the information slip to do a voice connect with the control room. "Lainie, tell me you've managed to lock some people up!"

She turned on the view slip and her face appeared. "We've locked up some." She looked frightened.

Something must have gone wrong. "What is it?" I asked, fearing the answer.

"I don't know where all the Earthers are … " she said. "My father's not here. Saunder's not here. I need to keep looking. I can't talk now."

I wasn't sure I had understood her. "What do you mean, they aren't here?"

"There aren't any Earthers on board. They're all gone."

Chapter 16

"I can't talk now," Lainie said, turning away.

Her voice was calm, but I knew she must be as shocked as I was. I tried to focus on what I needed to do. I made the door slide open a fraction. No one. I went back to the slip. "Lainie, I can't just stay here. I need to know where the Fosaanians are."

I waited. There was no response. "Lainie?"

Finally, she said, "We've caught two of them and I've put up a message on all the room information slips that the station is having mechanical problems. But the two who were in the control room are right outside the door now. They're really angry we tricked them and I don't think they are going anywhere soon. Quinn, the security scans show the space station is almost empty. Except for us, there are only seven other life forms on board."

"Is there someplace not covered by the scans or the sensors that read life forms?" I couldn't imagine where everyone had gone. "Could they be locked up somewhere?"

"I don't know. I don't think so. They just aren't here. They aren't anywhere."

"If Ansun didn't need them … " It was Mira's voice, and she didn't have to finish her thought for me to understand.

"I don't believe it," I said. "Even Ansun wouldn't just jettison them out into space. He needs them. They're here somewhere. Tell me a clear path to the control room and we'll figure out a way to find them."

"There are the two Fosaanians on the upper deck but it looks like they will be there for a while," Lainie said. "I think they are still trying to find A72. I've sealed off the ramp to the middeck so they can't get down unless they know about the access ladders. Where are you? I don't see you on any of the middeck sensors."

"I'm on the upper deck. I didn't think about you sealing off the deck levels. I'll have to take the ladder again, but I need to know if any Fosaanians are on the middeck. If they go into a room, make sure you lock them up, okay?"

A faint sound caught my attention, a sound like a panel opening. I froze, fearing a Fosaanian had found me. A hand clamped down on my arm. I looked down at it. It was covered in dried blood. I twisted around and shoved at the person holding onto me, freeing myself but falling over a bench in doing so. The pain in my shoulder made me cry out when I hit the floor. My vision in both eyes completely blacked out for a moment but when it came back, it took me a moment to recognize the battered figure before me.

"Gregor, I nearly knocked you out," I said, relief rushing through me.

Gregor stared at me like he didn't know who I was. The maintenance man looked terrible. He had a bandage on one side of his head, blood seeping through it. His skin was grayish and his face was bruised.

"Quinn?" Gregor mumbled.

"Yes, it's me," I replied. "What happened to you?"

"You have to get off the station," Gregor said. He put a hand to the bandage and winced.

"We're trying to. Where is everyone else?"

"I don't know. They took them away." The man swayed and then leaned back against the wall. "You have to listen. You have to get off. The whole station is going to blow up as soon as they finish taking the parts they want." He looked around suspiciously. "Did you hear something?"

I listened. There was only silence. "I don't hear anything. Why would they blow up the station?" I wondered if Gregor's injury was affecting his reason.

"I don't know. They've set charges on the outside. They tried to make me tell them the exact spots where they should place them but I didn't. That was very military of me, right?" Gregor grinned, a crazy twist to his mouth that did not resemble an expression of humor.

"Did one of them do that to you?" I pointed at the bandage. I wasn't sure I wanted to know what was under it.

Gregor brought his hand up to the bandage again but didn't touch it. "The Fosaanians have really sharp knives," he said, "For a primitive society. When they were done, they thought I was dead. I thought I was dead. Maybe I am." He squinted at me. "Are you real?"

I tried to sound calm. "I'm real. If you didn't tell them where to set the explosives, how do you know the station will blow up?"

Gregor lost his confused look, and spoke in a normal voice. "Even if they just blow part of it, the rest won't stay in orbit if it destabilizes enough. It will be pulled down into the atmosphere. Who all is on board?"

I told him.

"That's bad," Gregor said. "They never told me when I signed up that this sort of thing might happen. It wasn't covered in any of the drills. And to think *I* get written up for poor planning. Ha! I should write up the commander for this mess." The crazy grin crossed his face again. "I guess since no one else is here that makes me senior officer aboard." He paused and looked around as if expecting someone to appear and disagree with him. "What do you think about that?" Holding up his hand, he stared at the dried blood on it. "I don't like blood." His knees sagged and I was afraid he was going to pass out.

Taking him by the arm, I said, "Why don't you sit down for a little while?" Gregor nodded and I lowered him to the floor. I didn't know what to do with him. He needed a doctor but he was in no shape to go anywhere.

I heard Mira's voice. "Lainie, what does this shape on the slip mean?" she asked. I went back to the slip.

"Oh that's really not good," Lainie said. Her face appeared, but she was looking at something out of my view.

"What's not good?" I asked.

"Another ship just landed in the docking bay, a raider ship. Wait, oh, that's really not good."

I pounded my hand on the wall next to the slip, "Tell me what's really not good!"

"Ansun and Bald Woman just got off."

I gulped, realizing my mouth was very dry. "I'd say that's more than not got good, it's really bad. Can you see corridor A, section sixteen?" I asked.

"Wait, I need to switch to a different view. We've only got ten corridor slips working for some reason. Yes, I see it."

"Do you see any Fosaanians?"

"No!" Lainie yelled so loud I jumped.

I didn't think the 'no' was in answer to my question. "Lainie, did you hear me?" I said.

She didn't answer. I wanted to shake the slip to get her to talk. "What's happening?" I yelled.

"They've found Decker! The bot went right to the compartment after Ansun said something to it. It must have sensed him. And they've found the Fosaanian in the storage compartment."

"Find me a clear way to the control room!"

"No! A Fosaanian just hit Decker! His nose is bleeding, Decker's, not the Fosaanian. Ansun is walking up to him." She stopped speaking.

"Lainie, you have to keep talking to me."

"Just listen. I'll switch you in," Lainie said. "He's talking to the MI."

Ansun's voice came through. "Set the oxygen to turn off in thirty minutes. That will give us enough time and will get rid of any stray Earthers on board."

Lainie's face reappeared. "Did you hear that? What are we going to do?"

"Can the MI turn off the oxygen from there?" I asked, trying to stay calm.

"I don't know. Ansun thinks it can."

"What's Ansun doing now?" I asked. "What's he saying?"

"He's moving to the door of the docking bay. He's ordered the Fosaanian and one of the others to stay there and guard Decker. The rest of them are following Ansun."

"He can't get out of the bay, right? You've got it locked down and you changed the code right?"

"Yes ... wait, the MIbot is doing something. It's directing energy bolts at different spots around the door frame. I think it's trying to disable the locks." She went quiet again. "That's what it was doing. It worked. The door is opening and they are going through. Quinn, I know they are coming here. What do we do? We can't leave. The other two Fosaanians are right outside."

"Just hold on," I said. I turned around to get Gregor, but the man was already partway out the door.

"Where are you going?" I asked. "We need to get to the control room."

Gregor stopped and stood up very straight. "No, I've decided no one is going to blow up my station. I'm going to take the explosives off it." He turned and walked down the passageway.

I ran after him. "How are you going to do that?"

Gregor looked at me like I should know the answer. "In an Auxpod of course. I've got one off A12."

"I'm not sure you are in any shape to do that," I said. Gregor's skin had gone even more grey.

Gregor examined his hand again, rubbing at the blood. "There's no one else who can do it. Get your friends off the station in case I can't manage."

I didn't have time to argue with him. I needed to get to Mira and Lainie. "Once you get the explosives off," I told Gregor, "get as far away from the station as you can. We'll pick you up from the auxpod with the shuttle." I hoped Decker could handle a maneuver like that.

Gregor gave a salute, probably the only time he'd done such a thing since his training and headed off down the passageway.

I sprinted for the access ladder and slid down it, pausing for moment to catch my breath, rubbing my shoulder. It didn't help. I crept out into the passageway and moved down it to the control room. As I got closer, I heard Ansun say, "Open this door."

"This security door is operated by a nonstandard mechanism," the MIbot said. "It won't be disrupted by typical methods. If it is not opened from the inside or by the proper code, it will not open unless the controls are overridden in the inner core of the mechanics."

"How long will that take?

"Approximately twenty-seven minutes, forty-two seconds," the bot stated.

"Earth girl," Ansun said. "I know you are listening. I've heard what you have done and while you have been clever up to this point, it's over now. Open the door and I will see to it that you get back to your parents. You're the one with the brother, correct? I wasn't happy your brother tricked us. It will go easier for him if you open this door. You do understand my meaning, don't you?"

I went cold. If anything could get Lainie to open the door, it would be a threat to Saunder. I waited, watching Ansun watch the door and hoping Lainie would resist the man's threats. There was silence. The door didn't open.

Ansun turned to the MIbot. "Get the door open, and once it is, take back command of the control room by whatever means necessary. If she opens the door after we're gone, make sure she ceases to function, as you say." He spoke to the raider woman. "We'll take the Earth boy in the docking bay with us. His father has been very resistant to persuasion, and with a little added incentive, he might give us some of the military codes we need. The other researchers have been very agreeable to working with us in exchange for letting them keep their children with them."

"We're not leaving yet." the raider woman voice was soft, but held a menace even I could hear. "Given the fact that a few young Earthers have been able to disrupt your control, I'm not quite as confident in your abilities as I was before. I want the backup helicos with the MI specifications. Just in case, you understand. I feel the need to protect my investment."

"Your investment is safe." Ansun's voice was very angry. I wondered if anyone had ever questioned him before. "And I doubt you can break the encryption on the helicos," the Fosaanian continued. "I have the man who developed it, along with the other researchers. You can't make MIs on your own."

"I can do anything with enough currency." The raider woman's voice hardened. "Now I want those helicos. Or the deal is off."

"I am very displeased that you are adding in new conditions."

"I don't care about your level of pleasure or displeasure. You're not the emperor, nor will you be."

"Don't be so sure of that," Ansun said. "Death has changed the succession before."

The woman sneered. "That's your issue for the future. I deal in the here and now. I don't care if you are displeased or not. The helicos, or nothing."

Ansun opened a section of his belt and took out the helicos. He handed them to her without a word.

She took them. "That was an intelligent decision. Now, before we leave, I want to see the commander's office. Who knows what we might find there?" She strode off but Ansun didn't follow her immediately. I was surprised to see the anger on Ansun's face change to a look of satisfaction that even included a faint smile. Ansun waved at the Fosaanians to follow him and headed in the same direction as the raider.

I didn't understand Ansun's reaction but didn't have time to worry about it. Once they were out of sight, I focused back on the MI. It already had the panel off the door unit and was sending tiny streams of light in it.

I had to disable that bot before it got through the door but I couldn't think of a way to do it. My tribow would have no effect on it. I wiped some sweat off my face, as more dripped onto my hand. Staring at the drops, an idea formed in my head and I ran into the next room to the info slip there. Punching the voice control, I yelled, "Lainie, turn up the heat!"

"What?"

"Just do it, turn up the heat as hot as it will get in this corridor. Cook the place." I hoped the heat control went very high.

"Okay, I'm doing it. Why am I doing this?"

"The MI. The sulfur iridium isn't stable at a high temperature. Right, Mira? You told me the puppeteers heated the sulfur iridium to make the fireworks, and my mom told me she was worried about the heat on Fosaan affecting the MIs. But we've seen the MIs work on Fosaan, so that means we'll have to make it hotter than the planet. It might make them malfunction."

"I've got it set as high as it can go," Lainie said, "but I don't know if that's high enough."

I could feel the heat rise, and I began to sweat more, so I pulled off the extra shirt, letting it drop to the ground. When I put my head out into the corridor to check on the MI, a section of the bot lit up when it sensed me, but it continued to work. I realized it wouldn't do anything to me as long as I didn't try to stop it. It hadn't been given any orders about me.

The bot sent another flash of light and the control room door slid open a fraction. I moved closer, trying to think of what to do if the bot got the door open before the temperature went high enough. "Can you hear me, Lainie?" I called.

"Yes," Lainie said. The door opened another few centimeters.

"Is there an indicator showing the temperature is still rising?" I was drenched in sweat now.

"Yes, but it's creeping up very slowly." The door slid open almost enough for the bot to get through.

I moved over to the bot. "Halt," I ordered. "I have another task for you."

"Do not interfere," the voice from it said calmly. The temperature in the corridor was now so hot it was hard for me to breathe. The door opened all the way and the bot moved forward. A chair came flying out of the control room and then another, slamming into the bot. "Pick up that one," Lainie yelled and a third flew out. The bot continued forward, unaffected and I ran at it intending to grab it, though I knew that wouldn't do more than give us a few more seconds.

As I reached it, it lit up all over. I was sure it was about ready to jolt Mira and Lainie with all the energy it could produce, but instead it fell to the floor. The red coating started to spark, until the whole sensor was throwing out tiny fireworks. They sparked until they fizzled out and the bot went motionless.

"Is it dead?" Mira asked as she and Lainie edged out of the control room.

"Yes," I said. "Good riddance." I kicked it and it rolled down the hall. "Come on. We have to get to the hanger bay before they take Decker." There wasn't any time to waste. I took off running.

Chapter 17

"How are we going to stop him?" Lainie asked as she and Mira followed me.

"I don't know," I said, hoping we'd think of something.

When we reached the bay, we stopped a few meters short of the door. I didn't want to run right into Ansun. He wouldn't stay in the commander's office for long unless he countermanded the order to turn off the oxygen. We crept up to the door and looked in. One Fosaanian stood by Decker, who was looking down at the floor. The other was roaming around examining some of the equipment. I didn't see Mags at all.

"You can use the tribow, can't you?" Mira asked. "Shoot at the one furthest away while Lainie and I are walking to the shuttle," she said. "Our movements will make Decker's guard look at us and not the other guard."

I didn't think I could actually hit someone from so far away with just one good eye. "Wait," I started to say, but Lainie and Mira were already moving in the direction of the guard. I took aim as best I could and let loose the quarrel. It passed right by the Fosaanian, who spotted me and raised his own weapon, shouting something.

I heard Ansun's voice in the distance. I forced myself to stay still, concentrating on my aim as the Fosaanian ran toward me. I let loose another quarrel. This time the man had brought himself close enough that the quarrel grazed the Fosaanian's arm as he took a shot at me. The shot went wide and I ducked behind a stack of supply cartons. I waited, hoped the ligitin on the tip of the quarrel would be strong enough to affect the man before he could get off another shot. He continued to advance and I thought he hadn't gotten a big enough dose.

Mira pulled her knife on Decker's guard. She lunged at the man, but he dodged out of her way and took aim with his walthaser. Decker came at the man from the side, kicking him hard in the knee. The man went down. Mira knelt and hit him with the back of her bracelet. He lost his grip on the weapon and she kicked it across the floor.

"Come on!" Decker yelled as the three of them ran for the shuttle ramp. I dashed out aiming my tribow and yelling at the Fosaanian aiming at me. My action startled the man enough so that he hesitated. Just before he could get off a shot, the ligitin took effect and the Fosaanian's knees buckled. He went down. I ran past him, making it up and inside the shuttle as Ansun and the raider woman came into view.

Decker took the controls, making the shuttle swerve back and forth as he headed it toward the airlock. When the shuttle moved clear, Decker punched the power to full, and the shuttle flashed away.

I sank back into my seat, relieved to see Mags had flown back inside at some point. Looking up at the bird, I realized my left eye had gone completely blind.

No one else noticed anything was wrong. Mira was huddled in a seat opposite me, her eyes closed. Decker and Lainie began to discuss what to do next. "Let's land this shuttle in some clear spot until we can get in contact with Quinn's father," Lainie suggested. "Ansun can't search the whole planet for us."

"Wait," I said. I couldn't believe I'd forgotten about Gregor and his claim about the explosives. I tried to explain.

"He couldn't be there. There weren't any Earthers on the station," Lainie said.

"He was there," I insisted. "I don't know if it's true about the explosives, but he was convinced the place was rigged to blow up."

"I don't believe it," Decker said. "And even if there were explosives, Gregor is fairly hopeless at some really basic tasks. Do we really think he's going to manage to remove them without blowing the station and himself up? Plus, if we go back, a raider ship will spot us. They're probably already after us."

"We can't leave Gregor behind," I argued. "You of all people should believe that. Military code, you know, no man left behind. Besides, he's my friend."

Decker looked out the viewport for what seemed a long time and then sighed. "You're right. Let's hope the shuttle is too small for the raiders to pick up on whatever defense system they have, or if they do pick us up, they've decided we aren't worth bothering about." He reversed the shuttle's direction.

It didn't take long for the station to come back into view, but it wasn't the only thing filling the viewport.

"That is the strangest ship I've ever seen," Lainie said.

We crowded around to look. The giant vessel that was closing in on the station appeared to be half a dozen junked ships seamed together into one lumbering monstrosity.

"It's a salvage ship," I said. "I've seen a few at space docks. They all look cobbled together. This one is the biggest one I've ever seen though."

We watched as the ship eased in very close to the space station. When it was only meters away, two giant arms unfolded and fastened on to a section on the middle ring of the station. Through the clear tubes in the arms I could see people approach the station.

"A13." I paused. "That is my mother's lab. They're taking it off the station just like they did with the other lab sections."

The people inside the tubes set to work with cutting tools.

"Look what's up on that flat part on the right side of the ship." Decker pointed and I saw the raider woman's vessel perched on a makeshift mooring platform.

"So if it's there, we know that means Ansun and the raider woman have decided not to try to find us, at least not at the moment," I said.

"I don't see Gregor," Lainie said.

"He was in bad shape when he left me." I feared Gregor hadn't even been strong enough to make it to the repair pod. And if he hadn't, the oxygen in the station was due to be shut off any time now. "We should go back to the station and see if we can find him."

"There he is!" Lainie cried. She pointed to the bottom ring of the station and I spotted the tiny repair pod creeping along.

"I don't see anything on the station that looks like an explosive pack," Decker said. "But they could be small enough to miss on such a massive structure."

I recalled all the various images of the station I had seen in the past and compared them with the view in front of me. I found the difference. "It's those silver cylinders. I haven't seen those before." I pointed out three cylinders attached at odd angles to the bottom ring.

"Those are so small, it might just be part of the station you've never noticed." Decker argued.

I knew they hadn't been there before. "Watch, Gregor is heading right toward the one outside C16."

We watched him try and fail to get the pod's arms to unlatch the cylinder from the side of the ship. He tried again, and again, he failed.

"He was shaky when I saw him. I don't know if he's going to

be able to do this." I said. It was painful to watch Gregor's clumsy maneuvering.

"I can get a closer view of him from one of the console slips," Lainie said. She selected n and made the view on the slip zoom in on the pod. "He looks like he's going to pass out," she said. Gregor's face was slick with sweat and the bandage over his ear was covered in fresh blood.

"What happened to his head?" Decker asked.

"Ansun," Mira whispered.

Just when it seemed like another attempt had failed, one arm freed the cylinder from the station and the other grabbed it. "He got it!" Lainie pounded Decker on the back like Decker had done it himself. Gregor reversed the pod away from the station and then had the arm release the cylinder with a push, sending it off tumbling away into space.

Lainie gave of whoop of excitement, but I caught a movement on one of the other slips. "Move in on the raider woman's ship."

Decker brought it into view. "There's someone in the weapons bay."

"They see Gregor!" Lainie cried.

"Can we warn him?" Mira asked.

"I don't know how to hail the pod," Decker told her. "He's not wearing an earpiece and I bet the pod only connects with the comm on the station."

"He sees them," I said quietly. Everyone fell silence. We watched Gregor move the pod to the next cylinder.

An energy blast from the raider ship shot by the pod, just missing it.

"He's got to get out of there!" Lainie yelled. "Why doesn't he just forget the pack and go!"

I felt someone touch my hand. I looked over to find Mira right next to me. I took her hand in mine as we watched.

Gregor got hold of the other cylinder more quickly this time. As he moved away and sent it into space after the first, another brilliant flash of light came right out at pod. The whole display lit up. Where the light disappeared, tiny bits of debris floated where Gregor's pod had been.

No one said anything. I stumbled back, letting go of Mira. A sharp wave of hatred for Ansun filled me. Lainie let out a sob and put her head down on the console.

Decker was the only one who stayed in place. I watched as he maneuvered the shuttle underneath the bottom ring, out of sight of the raider ship and then dropped the shuttle back toward Fosaan.

Forcing myself to speak, I said, "Good move. They might have come after us next. I want us to be around long enough to tell someone what Gregor did. He should be awarded some sort of medal for that."

"I wish he'd blown up Ansun," Lainie said, "instead of just wasting those explosives. And I wish I knew where Saunder was so we could get to them before Ansun hurts anyone else."

"We need to focus on that. The question is where could Ansun take everyone?" Decker asked. "It's not like he has another planet or access to many ships. At least not yet."

"Good point," I managed to say, trying to concentrate on the missing Earthers instead of Gregor. "They can't be far away. What do you think, Mira?"

She just shook her head and sat down. I realized she didn't look good. Her fingers clasped the edge of the seat like she was barely holding herself upright. I could see she was breathing very, very fast and she was shaking all over. When I touched her arm, it was ice cold, so I went over to the shuttle's emergency kit and took out a warming blanket. When I had it activated, I sat down next to her and wrapped it around her. She didn't look up. "Mira," I said, "Put your head down. It will help you feel better." She laid her head on my lap. I brushed the hair away from her face, feeling her shiver.

Lainie knelt down in front of her. "It's all right," she said. "That was intense."

"I'm sorry," Mira whispered. "I didn't even know your friend. I should be more in control of myself. I should have done something about Ansun a long time ago. It's all my fault. I had a responsibility to the clan and I did nothing. Ansun is right. I am weak."

"You're not weak at all." I began to realize what a drastic action Mira had taken, cutting herself off from everything she had known. "You've taken a stand against Ansun when no one else in your clan would. We wouldn't have managed without you."

Lainie nodded her head in agreement. "I don't understand something," she said to Mira. "Back on the station, the raider woman said something strange to Ansun. She said he'd never be the emperor. Why would she say that?"

Mira took so long to answer, I was almost convinced she wasn't going to speak at all. Finally, she sat up, taking the warming blanket off. "Ansun has always wanted to be rid of me, but he just couldn't find a reason before, or a way to do it without the clan revolting. My mother was Ansun's older sister, and the heir to the Empire after my grandmother. After my mother died, I became the heir, though we don't exactly have an empire."

"I don't understand," Lainie said.

"I do," I said. "After Mira's grandmother, Mira is the next ruler of Fosaan. Ansun wants to be named Emperor, but he couldn't claim the title with her still around."

Mira raised her chin. "Quinn is correct. I will be the next Empress."

"Wow," Lainie said. "So you'll be in charge of a whole planet?"

Mira shrugged. "A mostly empty planet. And it doesn't matter now. Ansun has everything he needs to stay in control. I can't go back and take over from him."

Decker started to say something but a beeping noise from one of the display panels made him stop. He moved over to it. "I'm picking up a signal from the planet. It's not from the station. In fact, it's not coming from anywhere near the station."

"What are the coordinates?" I asked.

Decker entered them. "That's the middle of the ocean."

"Maybe it's an atmospheric anomaly." I said.

"Some of it sounds like an actual signal." Decker tapped a

markon. "I'll replay it. The first part matches a military distress signal, but the rest is just noise or really strange music. Listen."

Bizarre music filled the shuttle. "That just sounds like random notes to me," I said. "There's no melody or rhythm. Definitely an anomaly."

"It's a signal all right." Lainie smiled. "Turn down the sound and turn on the visual so I can see the sound waves."

She leaned over Decker's shoulder, watched the pattern of waves move across the display for a moment and then said, "Let me sit there."

They changed places. "It's a code," she announced, breaking into a smile. "The wave patterns are the message. See, each note stands for a letter. My dad and I came up with the idea, though we never tried it."

"That's a terrific way to hide a message, but it doesn't do us much good if we can't read it," I said. "Is that standard enough to run through a translator?"

"We don't need to. I can read it. That's my dad's signature. This bit here. See the repetition." She pointed at the display. "It starts here, ends there and then repeats. I need to slow it way down to read the rest of the message."

"Why would he use that sort of code?" Decker's voice was skeptical. "How would anyone know it's a code?"

"Experienced comm people would," Lainie said patiently. "Either he doesn't have access to anything fancy or he doesn't want it picked up by the wrong people. I guessing Baldy and Ansun are the wrong people. Now be quiet and let me concentrate."

It seemed to take no time at all for Lainie to read it. She leaned back in the chair. "They're on an island somewhere. He doesn't know where. They were put there and told the Fosaanians would be back to move them somewhere else."

"Where would Ansun have them moved? Mira, do you have any ideas?"

Mira shook her head. I tried to remember everything I knew about the geography of Fosaan. Unfortunately, Ansun would know far more than any Earther.

"I suspect the raiders have a base somewhere and they'll take them there," Decker said. "Ansun doesn't have the capability to provide what they need."

"Don't underestimate him," Mira said.

"We've got to do something before they are moved again." Lainie got up, acting too agitated to sit still. "My dad may not be able to contact us from a different place."

"What can we do? Only a few people would fit on here even if we could get to them first," Decker said. "I say we wait for Quinn's father to show up. He can communicate from his ship with military command. They may be able to rescue the scientists and stop Ansun."

"They won't be able to stop Ansun," Lainie said. "Even if they do rescue the scientists, what if he gets away? He's got all the technology now, and he's smart enough to have secured it somewhere. He doesn't even really need the scientists. With the raiders backing him, he can hire other scientists and make as many bots made as he wants. It may take him a little longer than it would with the current scientists, but it won't set him back for long. Who knows what he'll do then?"

"He doesn't have everything. And I don't think we can wait for my father," I said, thinking of the look on Ansun's face after he'd given the raider woman the helicos. It had been nagging at me. "Take me back to the station."

"What are you going to do there?" Decker asked. "Because if you don't have a good reason, I'm not going back."

"The current MIs are still flawed. Ansun gave the raider woman the technical specs but he looked like he knew something she didn't. I think he knows the fix for the bots is in a piece of equipment in my mom's lab." I explained about Gregor's adaptation of the machine my mother had told me about the last time I had seen her. It seemed ages ago, even though it had only been a few days. "We can't let Ansun have it. I'm going back to the station. I'll get rid of it before they can finish taking off the lab."

"That's crazy, Quinn," Lainie said. "It's too risky. You're just basing this on a look on Ansun's face. And even if it's true, you don't know if the equipment worked the way your mother thought it would."

For once, Decker surprised me by not immediately objecting. "I would like to stop that scum," Decker said. "But, Quinn, I don't think you are going to be able to carry it off. You don't look like you are in great shape either."

I knew I wasn't, but that wasn't going to stop me. "We don't have any other options except just hanging around hoping my father gets here soon. I don't want to do that."

Lainie finally nodded. "You're right. We have to do something."

I looked at Mira. She said, "I want Ansun stopped too. I'm sorry you all have to be a part of this."

Decker sighed. "All right. Let's do this then," he said, going back to the controls. As we came closer to the station, I was relieved to see the salvage ship still at work. I'd been afraid my mother's lab would already be gone.

When Decker landed the shuttle in the bay, we could hear a voice from the station's audio system. "The station's oxygen content has fallen below the safety range. Use supplemental oxygen." It repeated itself over and over.

I grabbed an oxygen pack out of one of the storage units, trying not to think about what would have happened to us if we hadn't been able to get off the station.

"Quinn, wait," Mira said, moving over to me until she stood just inches away. She took off her necklace, reached up and put it around my neck. "We'll see you soon." Then she kissed me.

I kissed her back, forgetting everything.

It was only Decker's voice that made me stop. "Um, while you may be enjoying yourself," he said, "we can't just hang around here. If you are going to do this, you should go."

I broke away from Mira, wishing she and I were anywhere but here. "Later," I whispered to her. I put the oxygen pack around my neck.

"Wear an earpiece too," Lainie urged.

"Why?" I asked, trying to clear my head. I told myself I'd have time to think about Mira later.

"What if you can't get to the lab?" Lainie said. "All those sections are still sealed off. I can direct you if I can remember which ones I sealed."

She was right. I didn't have time to wander around the station. I found an earpiece and attached it, "Okay. I'm ready." Decker lowered the ramp and I went out into the bay.

The station was eerily quiet. I jogged through the corridors trying to make my way to the lab, but I had to keep doubling back every time I came to a sealed door. Lainie tried to direct me, but obviously didn't remember what she had shut off. I nearly knocked myself out running into a panel she swore was open.

"This isn't working," I said. "Let me figure it out. I think I know how to get to an access ladder."

When I was nearly at the panel that concealed the ladder, I ran around a corner right into a cleaning bot and fell over it. My head hit the wall and then the rest of me hit the floor. For a moment, the vision in other eye disappeared too. I lay there knowing if I had gone blind, I'd never be able to find my way back to the shuttle.

"Quinn, are you there?" Lainie asked.

I blinked and the sight came back in my right eye. "It's nothing," I said. I got up carefully, fearing the movement would make the vision go away again. The audio warning about the oxygen content continued. I decided I'd better move faster and hope for the best.

I reached the access ladder and climbed up. "I'm almost there," I said. "I'm at A18." I took off again but after a few meters, a horrible screeching sound made me clap my hands over my ears.

The audio system's voice said, "Breach detected. Initiating sealing. Ten countdown." The floor shook beneath me. I turned to find clear panels sliding shut on the corridor behind me and the voice counting down from ten. "Ten, nine, eight ... "

"Quinn, what's happening?" Lainie screamed.

"Seven, six, five ... "

I didn't have time to answer. I dived for the opening and made it through just as it sealed shut. Trying to catch my breath, I lay on the floor, shaken at the close call.

"Quinn, are you there?" It was Mira's voice.

I rolled over on my side and propped myself up with one arm. "I'm here." I got to my feet and went over to a view port. Outside, I could see the salvage ship had my mother's lab fastened between the two arms as it drew them back from the station.

"I was too late," I said, almost to myself.

"Good try," Decker said. "Come on back. I'd like to get out of here."

I took a couple of steps in the right direction, so angry I stopped to take a punch at the wall. When my hand connected with it, I recoiled in pain. "Ow!"

"What's wrong now?" Lainie sounded panicky.

"Nothing. I was just acting like Decker."

"What?" Decker asked.

"Nothing." On my way to the hanger bay, I stopped by a sign that read, *Until we can get the parts we were supposed to get thirty fissing standard days ago or until I come up with a brilliant new idea, this water supply station is closed until further notice.* It was signed, "Your friendly maintenance officer, Gregor."

"Oh, Gregor," I said, images of the man filling his head. I stood for a moment thinking, and then reversed direction. "I'm going to try something else," I announced. "Decker, get the shuttle away from the station right now. I'm not finished with Ansun yet."

"What are you going to do?"

"I'm taking another one of Gregor's pods out to get that other cylinder. No one is getting away with that lab. Pick me up when I'm done."

I heard Mira's voice. "What does that mean?"

"I'm going to blow up that ship," I said.

"No, Quinn. The raider ship is still moored on the salvage ship," Lainie said. "They'll spot you just like they spotted Gregor. You won't be able to do it."

"Yes I will. The maintenance bay is on the other side of the station, and the last cylinder is down there too. With any luck I can get it and get to them before they see me."

"Not a good idea," Decker said, his voice calm. "Do you even know how to operate a repair pod? You saw what trouble Gregor had."

"I know how," I said. I didn't tell them I hadn't actually operated it. The time Gregor had shown it to me, it had been in the docking bay and we hadn't powered it up. I'd just have to figure it out. "I'll check back in once I'm there."

I ignored their voices trying to argue me out of it, adjusting the volume so I couldn't hear them. Luckily, I managed to find a clear short route to Gregor's maintenance area. I stopped when I walked in, struck by how Gregor's presence permeated the space. He had broken regulations by filling his workshop with weird souvenirs from out of the way places, which hung from the ceiling like giant mobiles. I didn't know if they were tools or artwork or musical instruments, or all three of those things. I wished I had taken the time to ask him about them.

I turned away but when I reached over to open the repair pod airlock I caught sight of an image propped on Gregor's desk. It was of a girl with wild purple hair and blue swirls decorating her face. I didn't recognize her. Gregor had never mentioned a girlfriend. Picking it up, I slipped it inside my shirt, thinking I'd try to find out the girl's identity when this was all over. I'd tell her what Gregor had done.

I entered the airlock, powered up the pod and opened the outer doors. As I maneuvered the tiny craft out and along the edge of the station, I tried to get a feel for how to increase and decrease its speed but couldn't do anything very smoothly.

I turned the earpiece back on. "Okay, I'm out of the station," I said, making the craft move along the bottom ring in the direction of the salvage ship and the last remaining cylinder.

The repair pod had an assortment of arms that could be

extended with various tools on the ends of them. Closing my eyes, I pictured Gregor pointing out the function of each one of them. Gregor had spent a lot of time explaining them, because he loved using the pod even when there was nothing to repair.

"So far, so good," I muttered to myself.

"Can you hear us?" Lainie's voice came over the earpiece.

"Yes," I said, "but I can't see you. Stay out of sight of the salvage ship."

It felt like it took forever to get to the cylinder and once I was there, I couldn't get ahold of it. I tried three times, failing each time.

"Quinn, the salvage ship is moving further away," Lainie said. "Even if you get the cylinder, you're not going to be able to get to the ship once it picks up speed."

"You are supposed to be out of sight of it. How do you know it's moving away?" Leave it to Decker to ignore my order. I redoubled my efforts.

"I got it!" I shouted when I finally had the cylinder secured in one of the pod's grasper arms.

"You'd better hurry if you are going to do something with it," Decker said.

It was frustrating the pod didn't have much speed, but then neither did the salvage ship. I pushed the acceleration on the pod as hard as I could, though it felt like it was barely moving.

Yet another warning came from the same voice that gave the warnings in the station. "You have exceeded recommended velocity for this model. Shutdown may occur."

"Not yet, it won't," I said.

I dipped the pod under the station and made my way along the lowest ring until I could see the salvage ship above me.

I brought the pod up along the bottom part of it to something that looked like part of an old sightseeing vessel. There were people inside seated at tables. One of them saw me and pointed. I grinned and waved at them, wondering if my grin looked as crazy as Gregor's had.

"Just get rid of that explosive and get out of there!" Lainie shouted.

"I have to put it in the right place," I said. "Too low and it may only take out part of the ship."

"Quinn, they see you! Someone is back in the weapons bay! Get out of there!"

Midway up the salvage ship I spotted the perfect site. I set the cylinder down on a piece of wing that had belonged to an early liger model. I maneuvered the arm to set the timer on the explosive, thinking I had to set it for a short enough time to blow before someone could remove it, yet give me enough time to get away. I chose twenty seconds and then armed it, setting a timer in the pod as well. The countdown began.

Reversing the pod, I backed away from the salvage ship.

"Quinn ... " Lainie said.

A booming noise cut her off and I felt myself spinning out of control.

Chapter 18

Mira's voice came through the darkness. I felt something tickle my face and when I opened my eyes, she was leaning over me, her hair touching my face.

"You blacked out," she said. "Decker got you back."

From somewhere close by I heard Mags warbling her lullaby. I looked beyond Mira to see Decker and Lainie standing there. They wore such serious expressions, I said, "Don't look so grim. From the sounds of it, I didn't die, right?"

Lainie managed a smile. "Right," she said. "But you nearly scared all of us to death. And you don't look so good. Your one eye is kind of murky looking."

"I'll be fine once I see a doctor," I said.

"That was crazy," Decker said, 'but nice job."

"So I guess it worked?" I asked as I struggled upright. I looked out the viewport. Large pieces of debris were everywhere.

"You blew up the salvage ship and the lab," Lainie said. "But you nearly blew yourself up too."

"The explosive went off too soon. I guess the timer was faulty. What about the raider ship?"

Lainie's mouth turned down. "It got away. With luck, Ansun wasn't on it. I hope he was still on the salvage ship."

"I hope so too," I said. "Though we shouldn't count on it." I sat back down, my legs unsteady. "I feel like a tachesum has been stomping all over me."

That only brought a weak smile to Lainie and nothing from Mira. Decker went over to the control console. "We could go back to Fosaan and wait it out until your father gets here, Quinn. Or we could go back to the station and get the oxygen turned back on."

I was too wiped out to care what we did. With Mira beside me, I leaned my head back and closed my eyes while Decker and Lainie debated.

I reopened them when Lainie said, "Whoa, something huge has just entered the system."

I forced myself to get up again, worried that the raiders had some other crazy ship, though once I got to the viewport, I knew it wasn't a raider vehicle. A giant gleaming vessel filled the display, the word EVEREST emblazoned across the top of the command deck. "That's a Military Command and Control Ship. I can't believe it. Those monsters don't just hop around the galaxy." I sighed. "Not good. It's under my grandfather's command. He's probably aboard."

"Why isn't that good and why would it be all the way out here?" Lainie asked.

"I don't care why they are here," Decker said. "As long as they are, no raider ship is going to come after us."

"They are probably hailing the station," I said. "Can you get into that frequency to let them know we are here?"

"No, it will be scrambled," Decker leaned back in his chair. "There's nothing that sophisticated on this shuttle. But it doesn't matter. They have to know we're here. They'll be hailing us soon enough."

He was right. Seconds later a voice said, "Shuttle pilot, state your ident." A young woman in a lieutenant's uniform appeared on the display.

"No one aboard has a military ident," Decker told her. "There's been an emergency on the space station. It was taken over by raiders. There are no authorized personnel there anymore."

The woman paused for just a fraction of time at the news, but then asked, "Where are the military personnel?"

"We're not quite sure. We think they've been taken to an island on the planet." Decker gave the coordinates. "There may be raiders on the way there to get them."

"You have to get there first," I called out to her. "You have to send someone to pick them up."

"And who are you?" The woman frowned as she stared at Decker through the display.

"My name is Decker Rigan. My father is Commander Leif Rigan."

"What is the source of the debris around the space station?"

"A raider ship blew up," Decker said.

I could tell from the woman's expression she didn't believe Decker. Ships didn't just blow up on their own, and the station had no offensive weapon capability.

"Who blew it up?" the woman asked.

Decker looked back at me. I moved forward so I was in view, "Um … I did."

The lieutenant's eyes widened. There was a moment of silence and then, "Remain on your current heading. Any deviation will be assumed to be a hostile action." The visual slip blinked out.

"Great, now they're going to be really on edge," Decker said. "Could you have said that a different way? They'll probably just blast us in case we're raiders too. If I were them, I wouldn't let us on board."

"What was I supposed to say? Let me sit there. I want to try something." I hated to use my grandfather's name as leverage, but if any moment seemed to be good time to do it, it was this one. "Hello. Hello. Please respond with visual."

The woman's face reappeared.

I leaned in so she could see me. "This is Quinn Neen, Admiral Neen's grandson. If he is aboard, he will recognize me. Or just check the records of the space station personnel and their families. My name and image will be on there."

For just a moment, the lieutenant's mouth dropped open and then she snapped it shut. "Just a moment please," she stuttered, disappearing from view.

It took longer than a moment for her to reappear. "You are cleared for landing. Is someone aboard capable of piloting the ship into the docking bay or should we send a pilot to rendezvous with you?"

Decker snorted. "I can do it."

The woman launched into a series of headings and instructions. I stepped back, deciding I wouldn't distract Decker. It wouldn't be good if Decker nicked part of the command ship coming in.

"Your grandfather is an admiral?" Mira asked.

"He's not just an admiral," Lainie said. "He's the head of the Konsilan, which means he's basically in charge of the entire military."

Mira's mouth turned down and I felt her pull back a little.

"It doesn't matter who he is," I said, thinking she probably assumed my grandfather was like Ansun. "I barely ever see him."

It didn't seem to reassure her. She took hold of one of my hands and pleaded, "Don't tell him about me. Don't tell him who I am. Please."

"Why?" I asked, not understanding the desperation in her tone.

"What would they do with me?" Mira let go of me and moved away. "Before the Apocalypse, Earth wanted the Fosaanian royal family to abdicate and leave the planet. I don't want to be forced to go somewhere else that I don't choose."

"I don't think they would do that. Not now."

"How do you know?"

I had to admit I didn't know. "All right. I won't say anything. None of us will. Right, Lainie, Decker?"

Lainie nodded her head in agreement. Decker was too busy piloting to answer, but he did nod his head. "You don't seem happy your grandfather might be on that ship," Lainie said to me.

I went back to look out at the giant ship. "It takes a major issue to get a command and control this far out in the galaxy. I wonder how they found out about Ansun so quickly."

"We'll know soon enough," Decker said. He managed to get the shuttle into the hanger bay without incident, but when he brought it to a stop, we just stood there looking out, all of us awed at the sight of the place. It was at least three times as large as the station's hanger.

An array of people in uniform stood waiting for us. I didn't see my grandfather.

Mira held back, looking more frightened than I had ever seen her. I was surprised at her reaction. I said, "It's okay, really."

"There are so many Earthers out there. I've never seen so many at once."

"No one out there is as tough as Ansun, and you can face him down, so there is nothing to worry about." I took off the necklace she had given me and handed it back to her. "I think you need this more than I do right now."

Mira clasped her hand around the stone like she was happy to have it again. "I gave it to you as a gift," she said. "I shouldn't take it back."

"We can call it mine, but it looks better on you than me," I said. She smiled and put it on. I took her hand. We walked down the ramp. I hadn't realized the mere sight of Mira would cause a reaction. A man in a major's uniform walked toward us and then stopped when he saw Mira. Many people in the group began to talk and I heard the word "Fosaanian" several times. The major recovered himself and continued toward us. There was no welcome in his expression.

"Mr. Neen," he said to me, "I'm Commander Escarr. Does any of your group need medical attention?"

"No," I said, thinking I'd ask for a doctor later. I wanted to find out what was being done to rescue the scientists first.

"We didn't realize you had a Fosaanian with you," the major said, frowning at Mira.

"This is Mira." I realized I didn't know her last name, or even if she had a last name. Mira didn't volunteer one.

The major didn't acknowledge her. "I'm to show you and your companions to a conference room," he said to me. A woman in civilian clothes, a purple robe and a colorful headband holding back her hair, stepped forward and spoke to the officer, so quietly I couldn't hear what she was saying. She looked over and caught my eye, smiling at me. She appeared friendly enough, reminding me a bit of Dr. Becca. Both were about the same age and with an easy manner that radiated confidence.

"Stay here please," the major said to us before walking to the back of the room with the woman.

We just stood there awkwardly until the two came back. She smiled at all of us again and held out her hand to me. "I'm Raisa Nakano, Mr. Neen. I'm the new teacher, but I'm also a cultural anthropologist and I'm very interested in Fosaanian culture. Mira, I'm so delighted you are aboard. I thought since your friends need to be debriefed, I could show you around and we could talk."

Mira moved closer to me. "I don't know the word 'debriefed.'"

"They just want to find out what happened," I told her. I knew if it had been decided Mira would go with the woman, it was no use arguing she should stay with us instead. I'd been around military people enough to know now we were aboard the ship, it was all about following orders.

"I thought my father was bringing you," I said to the woman. "Where is he?"

"Your father is on board. When your grandfather decided to make this trip, he arranged for your father's ship to be picked up. It's in another hanger bay."

I wondered why he wasn't here to meet us, but didn't think it would be a good time to ask.

"Admiral Neen is waiting," the major reminded us, shifting around like he was impatient to get us where we were supposed to go.

"We'll see you again in a little while," I said to Mira. I let go of her hand, missing the warmth of it as soon as I did. Raisa led her away, but before the major could escort us out, I turned to the two cadets who were positioned at the entrance to the shuttle. I hadn't noticed anyone ordering them to guard it, but that was clearly what they were doing.

"You aren't going aboard the shuttle, are you?" I asked them. "My parrot is on board." I knew Mags wouldn't take well to strangers. The men stared at me like I was speaking an unknown language, so I repeated myself a few times. "The bird will get upset if strangers come on board."

Finally, one of the men threw up his hands. "We don't have any orders at this time to board. We just follow orders."

"Right," I said. "If your orders change, tell someone about the bird."

The major led us to a room which had one large table in the center and chairs all around the walls. It was crowded with people who all turned to stare at us when we walked in. It grew more crowded as the group following us found places. I saw my grandfather seated at the head of the table beckoning me forward.

The crowd moved aside as I walked over, trying to act like I wasn't about to fall down. An older woman in a uniform with nearly as many decorations as my grandfather stood next to the table. "Let me introduce you to my grandson," my grandfather said, not even looking at me. "Quinn, this is Commodore Oshiro. She's in charge of the academy at Wellton."

The woman shook my hand. "I'm very pleased to meet you. From what little I've heard of your exploits in the last few hours, you'll make a fine addition to the officer trainee corps." I just nodded at that, knowing this was not the time to go into detail about my other plans.

My grandfather said to the group, "I'll speak to my grandson alone for a moment before we start." The room cleared out just as quickly as it had filled up. My grandfather motioned me to a seat near him.

"Is there any news about the scientists?" I asked as I sat down. "Have they found them?"

"There has been contact. We've sent a crew to pick them up." He tapped his fingers on the table, but didn't say anything. It made me uncomfortable. My grandfather was never at a loss for words. I hoped nothing was wrong with my mother or Piper. I started to speak but my grandfather held up his hand for silence. I shut my mouth.

"I'll wait to hear your story when everyone else is back in the room," the man said, "so you won't have to repeat it. I wanted to speak to you about another matter. I was watching your arrival. Who is that Fosaanian girl and how did she end up with you?"

I hadn't thought this would be about Mira. I tried to explain who she was and why she was helping us, though my grandfather's steady gaze made me fumble over some of it. I feared I wasn't telling the story very clearly. As Mira had requested, I left off the part about her place in Fosaanian society.

Grandfather asked a few questions and when I was finished, he said, "Why were you holding her hand? It was extremely inappropriate. You made a spectacle of yourself."

I couldn't believe holding Mira's hand would be an issue, certainly not something my grandfather should care about at a time when there were far more serious things happening. I didn't understand it at all. "We're friends," I said, knowing I sounded defensive. "She was scared. She's never been off Fosaan before."

"Do your parents know about you and this girl?"

"There's nothing to know."

He kept his gaze fixed on me like he didn't believe me. I stared back at him, determined not to let him know I wasn't quite telling the truth. Finally, he said, "I'm relieved to hear that. As long as you realize it means nothing, we'll let it go. Your next years are going to be taken up with far more important things. Just be aware every single thing you do will be under scrutiny, not only because of our family's name, but because there are some out there who would like to see you fail because of me. I paid a high price for your father's bad judgment. I can't have anything else happen that would reflect badly on me. Especially not now."

My anger flared. I didn't want to be the one to make up for the actions of my father. I didn't even know exactly what he had done that was so terrible, and my grandfather's concern over his own reputation seemed petty and meaningless. At that moment I wished for nothing more than to go back to Fosaan and forget I was even part of the Neen family.

Grandfather apparently thought the conversation finished. "We need to get through this debriefing," he said.

"What's going to happen with the remaining Fosaanians?" I asked. "They don't have enough food and there are some that need medical care."

"You don't need to concern yourself with the Fosaanians. We'll send people to evaluate the situation. Because of the uprising, we'll put a military presence down on the planet."

"How did you know there was an uprising? It's only been a few days and they took control of the communications."

"I can't tell you. It's classified." He pushed a markon on a table panel and spoke into it. "Get everyone back in."

"Did Earth trigger the supervolcano that caused the Fosaanian apocalypse?" I blurted. Tasim's claim had been nagging at me.

My grandfather went still. He looked at me, his eyes unreadable. "Don't ask that question again," he said. "It's a preposterous idea. Go sit over there." He motioned to the opposite side of the table.

I did as I was told. Decker and Lainie joined me. The next few hours were exhausting. It felt to me as soon as one of us would tell a part about what happened, someone new would come in the room and want to hear it all again. The same questions were asked over and over. I found myself becoming more and more aware of just how terrible I felt. As the tremors in my arms increased, I let Decker and Lainie do most of the talking, trying to concentrate on just staying upright.

After what seemed a long time, the admiral held up his hand for silence, tapping his earpiece. After a moment he said, "I'm happy to report the station scientists and their families have been recovered without incidence. They are on their way here."

Clapping broke out, but the admiral quickly silenced it, as if it were just another daily maintenance task. The questions continued. I was frustrated that no one seemed to realize just how dangerous Ansun could be, if he was still alive, and I thought he probably was. From the remarks people made, they saw him as a minor figure who could easily be captured and punished.

The dizziness increased. My stomach did an odd little twist that brought on a wave of nausea. I thought if I just closed my eyes, everything would be fine. I didn't realize until later I passed out then, effectively bringing the debriefing to a close.

I came to in a bed in the ship's sick bay, my parents standing over me. I was happy to see them, but couldn't work up the energy to tell them that.

"You've had quite a time of it, I hear," my father said. "The doctors gave you some meds and some fluids. They said you passed out because you were suffering from exhaustion and dehydration, though they do want to do some more extensive testing once you've rested up."

I flexed my fingers. I didn't feel any tremors and my head did feel much clearer.

"Saunder told us how you got the shock," his mother said, her lips were trembling. "I don't know how that happened with the bot. No one should have been able to reprogram it that way."

"I'm good now. I feel much better." I didn't want my mother thinking any of it was her fault. As I lay there trying to figure out what else I could say to reassure my mom, I became aware I had to turn my head to see my father. Reaching my hand to my face, I realized there was a patch over my eye.

"What's up with this?" I asked, dreading to hear the answer.

"The doctors want to give that eye time to recover," my father said. "It may take some additional surgery."

"But it will be all right, won't it?"

My father just looked at me for a moment. "Probably, but you know doctors. They don't want to commit themselves."

The words sunk in. If it came to an artificial eye, I knew they never worked as well as real ones. My parents stood there, as if waiting to see my reaction. I didn't know what I felt, so to change the subject, I asked, "Where's Piper? Is she okay?"

"She's fine. She's with some of the other children in the exercise area," my mother said, sounding relieved I didn't say any more about the eye. "You'll see her later. And before you ask, Mags is fine too. She's in our quarters after causing quite a commotion when we took her off the shuttle. She took an instant dislike to the poor guards there. When did she start calling people 'dogboys?'"

I managed to smile at that. "Blame Decker for that." I sat up, realizing I was still very sore.

As if he had heard his name, Decker walked into the room. "You look better," he said to me. "I was afraid you were going to throw up all over me in the conference room."

"I almost did," I said, relieved Decker didn't mention the eye patch. I wanted everyone to ignore it so I could too. I took in

Decker's outfit, all in black in a basic cadet's uniform. "So why are you dressed like that? Did you instantly join up? I guess you were serious about getting offplanet."

Decker shook his head. "They found us some uniforms that don't have any rank attached to them yet. Our clothes were in such bad shape, they got rid of them. There's one for you too. So are you well enough to go?"

"Go where?"

"There's a celebration starting in a little while," Decker replied. "The entertainment officer thought the scientists' rescue would be a good reason for a party. I think they just want to keep the little kids occupied so they don't run all over the ship."

"The doc says you can get up when you want to," my father said.

"Yes," my mother added. "But I think you should rest instead."

I didn't want to go anywhere. As far as I could tell, there wasn't much to celebrate. "Have you seen Mira?" I asked Decker.

"No, but Lainie said we'd see her at the celebration."

That made me reconsider. I swung my legs over the edge of the bed and stood up, realizing I felt far steadier than I had just a few minutes before. Even if I didn't feel completely back to normal, I was well enough to go see Mira.

After my mother saw I was determined to go, she stopped arguing, and my parents left me to dress. By the time Decker and I got to the entertainment clubroom, the party was already in progress. When the two of us entered the room, we were swarmed by the space station scientists and the younger children.

I didn't see my sister at first, but then I heard Piper's voice. "Quinn! Quinn!" She ran up to me and threw her arms around my waist. "Do you like the eye patch I chose for you? They had them in all different colors but I thought you'd like the silver."

"Thank you," I said. "I do." I was glad she wasn't weirded out about the idea of me wearing an eye patch. I looked over her head to see Lainie and Saunder approaching, their arms linked. Piper tugged on my arm. "They have some great food here. Want to come get some?"

"In a minute. You go ahead." She danced off. I shook my head. "Well, I guess there's someone who is totally back to normal."

"She's a good kid," Decker said.

Lainie and Saunder were all smiles when they reached us. "I wasn't sure I'd ever see any of you again," Saunder said. "Lainie's told me a little about what happened. Unbelievable. I want to hear more."

"Later," I said, thinking maybe never, though I knew I'd not forget everything that happened. I was happy Saunder looked okay. I'd feared Saunder would have suffered some of the same injuries as Gregor had, but besides dark circles under his eyes, Saunder seemed fine.

Lainie had on a basic uniform similar to the one Decker and I wore, one that didn't fit her well. She pulled at the collar of the jacket. "This uniform-thing is driving me crazy. I'm glad military carvers don't follow strict dress codes. I couldn't stand to wear this sort of thing every day."

"You're going to have to wear a uniform during training, and that's coming soon. Did you hear?" Decker asked me.

"Hear what?"

"They've lowered the age for training. Unrest in various places is straining the force. We're all in just as soon as they can process us." Decker smiled when he said it, but I felt like someone had punched me in the chest. I didn't know what that meant for me, especially with the eye injury. I didn't think the reconnaissance patrol would take me if I was blind in one eye. My grandfather probably couldn't make the officer training program take me either, though I had never thought of alternatives. What if I was unfit for anything? And what did it mean for Mira and me?

A couple of girls walked by who smiled in our direction, cadets by look of the emblem on their uniforms. I looked around behind me to see who they were smiling at. There was nothing there but a wall.

Lainie nudged my arm. "They were smiling at you, in case you can't figure that out. I've already had some other cadets ask me about you." She rolled her eyes. "You'd think they'd never seen a couple of scruffy hero-type boys before."

To hide my embarrassment, I asked, "Where's Mira?"

"She'll be along soon," Lainie said. "That woman Raisa brought along some replicas of pre-Apocalypse Fosaanian dresses and when I left, Mira was trying them on."

I was confused. "Why would Raisa bring those?"

Lainie shrugged. "She said it was research. She wants to know how much Fosaanian culture has changed since the Apocalypse."

"She'll be in for some big surprises," I said.

The sudden quiet in the crowd made me turn around. Mira had entered the room, my grandfather next to her. She was dressed like the Fosaanians I had seen in the old images, in a long flowing colorful dress. Her hair was piled on her head and decorated with some sort of gleaming little ornaments. She looked nothing like the girl I'd first seen, dripping wet and wary in my quarters. When she realized everyone was staring at her, she stopped and ducked her head.

I walked over and took her hand, not caring that my grandfather was watching. Out of the corner of my good eye, I saw my grandfather frown, but then someone came up and spoke to the man, drawing his attention away from us. I took the opportunity to lead Mira away from the crowd over to the large viewing port.

"Your eye?" Mira said, reaching a hand up to my face but not touching me.

"The eye is fine," I lied. "It just needs some time to recover. You look amazing."

She turned her head away from me as if she hadn't heard, but I saw a smile appear on her face. We stood side by side watching as Fosaan spun slowly below us. "It's beautiful," Mira said. "I never realized just how beautiful. So green."

"It is an amazing place," I said. "Even with its giant lizard creatures and sulfur smell. I was kind of getting attached to it. How are you? No one has been treating you badly, have they?"

"I'm fine. They seem to think I'm just an ignorant native girl who knows nothing. At least for now, that's the way I want them to think, until I know more about what's going to happen to the rest of the clan."

"You know I'll help in any way I can. Just tell me if you want me to talk to my grandfather or you want me to be with you when you do."

"I know," she said. "But for a few hours, I don't want to think about it. Tomorrow, and the days after that will be time to decide what to do. Tonight I want to see how the Earthers live and I want to taste all the wonderful food and I want to dance."

I didn't want to think about tomorrow either. Not with a girl like Mira standing right in next to me. "What is this about dancing?" I asked.

"Raisa said there would be dancing. She's given me what she calls a 'rush course' in Earther dances so we could dance."

"I need a rush course too."

"You don't know how?"

"Not very well." The music started. "But let's see how we do," I said as we went out to join the dancers.

ACKNOWLEDGEMENTS

Thanks are due to all who helped me build the world in this story. First, as always, thanks to Dean, who is my idea sounding board, my science advisor, and much more. Thanks to Garret for always being willing to read bits, talk through plot problems and come up with solutions. Thanks to Hope for casting a keen eye on details.

Major thanks to two of my readers, Jacob Meazle and Riley Foster. I wouldn't be confident to go forward with the story without input from readers like them. Thanks to Amanda Avutu and Lori Foster, who helped this story in its earliest days.

And last, thanks to my brother Kim Garretson, who first introduced science fiction to me. All those amazing books that shaped the genre are my inspiration.

DEE GARRETSON

Dee Garretson writes for many different age groups, from chapter books to middle grade to young adult to adult fiction. She lives in Ohio with her family, and in true writer fashion, has cat companions who oversee her daily word count. When she's not writing, she loves to travel, watch old movies, and attempt various kinds of drawing, painting and other artistic pursuits.

OTHER MONTH9BOOKS TITLES YOU MIGHT LIKE

SACRIFICE

NAMELESS

THERE ONCE WERE STARS

PROJECT EMERGENCE

Find more books like this at http://www.Month9Books.com

Connect with Month9Books online:

Facebook: www.Facebook.com/Month9Books

Twitter: https://twitter.com/Month9Books

You Tube: www.youtube.com/user/Month9Books

Tumblr: http://month9books.tumblr.com/

SACRIFICE

"Serpentine's world oozes with lush details and rich
lore, and the characters crackle with life. This is one
story that you'll want to lose yourself in."
— Marie Lu, author of PRODIGY

"A brilliant second act."
— *Kirkus Reviews*,
STARRED REVIEW

CINDY PON

NAMELESS

JENNIFER JENKINS

"Jenkins brings edge-of-your-seat adventure to this intriguing new world. I can't wait to read more!"
- Jessica Day George
New York Times bestselling author of
SILVER IN THE BLOOD

THERE ONCE
WERE *Stars*

She never questioned what she was
told until the impossible became real.

MELANIE McFARLANE

A Promised Future. A Traitor on Board.
The Fight of Their Lives.

PROJECT
EMERGENCE

■   ■   ■   ■   ■   ■   ■   ■

EMERGENCE

JAMIE ZAKIAN